WALKING AMONG THE SHADOWS

Awakening

NAVÍ ROBINS

Walking Among the Shadows: Awakening
© 2014 by Navi' Robins
NorthShore Publishing House, Inc.
ISBN: **9780692297742**

Book cover design by: Navi' Robins www.navirobins.net
Interior design by: Navi' Robins www.navirobins.net

TO KAI AND ROSEMARY
Gone but never forgotten. We miss you.

Death can be Complicated

CHAPTER ONE
LET IT RAIN

I was drenched in blood, my body dragging with exhaustion as I stumbled toward what used to be the front door. It hung crooked on its hinges, split down the middle, barely clinging to the frame after the violence that had erupted within. The air inside was thick with the stench of burnt flesh and death, a miasma that clawed at my throat. I needed to escape it; I needed to breathe something other than decay and despair—before the darkness inside consumed me entirely.

Forcing the door open took more strength than I had left, the scraping sound echoing hollowly through the empty house. Cool air rushed in as I pried it open, but it did little to sweep away the horrors that clung to the walls. The estate was soaked in blood and misery, and it would take far more than the night air to cleanse it.

Outside, the storm greeted me with a thunderous applause, the downpour crashing over the earth as if it too was trying to wash away the sins of the night. I could almost imagine myself on a stage, the spotlight burning down on me, my hands stained red, the eyes of the world fixed on my every move.

Take a bow, you sick bastard. You've outdone yourself tonight.

I knew my brother Manny was on his way, and when he arrived, I would submit myself to the rain, let it wash away the filth that clung to my skin and soul. The blood would rinse off, but the memories of what I'd done would never fade. I dropped onto the front steps, staring out into the darkness, waiting. It had been over an hour since I called Manny, and yet, no one had shown up.

Where the hell were they? With everything that had happened, how could they take so long? Maybe the Navy had decided to lower its standards for promoting leaders. Manny had always been too impulsive, too incompetent to lead anyone, but then again, what did I know? I was just the kid brother who had once believed in heroes. Tonight, though, had shattered any illusions I might have had left.

The weight of the night bore down on me, the blood on my hands like a brand I couldn't wash away. I'd promised myself I was done killing, but when revenge called, I answered with a brutality I hadn't known I was capable of. By the time the smoke cleared, I'd sent seven souls to the afterlife, one more brutal than the last; until my rage was finally satisfied.

After another thirty minutes, the low rumble of military vehicles broke through the storm. The estate lit up as soldiers fanned out, securing the area, shouting "Clear!" after each sweep. I chuckled darkly. They were securing the scene, yet I was the reason for all the death that surrounded us. How could they feel safe when I still drew breath?

And here comes Manny now. This should be good.

"Aiden, what the hell happened here?" Manny's voice cut through the rain, sharp and demanding.

I wanted to answer, but why should I? He was the one who left our family with a security team so clueless they couldn't stop a kitten with a tank. The mighty, highly decorated eldest son, he should have been here, protecting us. Instead, he handed that responsibility off to others, and when death came knocking, they let me in. And now, he's concerned?

"Aiden, I'm talking to you! Where is everyone? Where's Mom, Sarah, and our grandparents?"

"They're inside," I replied, rolling my eyes.

"Are they okay? Are they alive?"

"Go inside and see for yourself."

Manny shot a glance at the two men flanking him, nodding for them to move inside. Then he knelt in front of me, searching my eyes for answers he wouldn't find.

"Aiden, how many are dead? How many bodies are inside?"

His question was like a dagger twisting in my chest. I began to count the lives snuffed out by my hands that night, the faces of the dead flashing through my mind.

"Seven," I said, my voice cold and distant. "Including a young boy."

"Who was he? Why was he here?"

"Jason's son. His only son."

"What was his name?"

"He was dying before I could ask," I muttered, my gaze drifting to the stormy sky above.

Manny's frustration grew, but he knew he wouldn't get more out of me. Without another word, he stood and followed the others inside, leaving me alone in the rain.

At seventeen, I had already killed before, but never like this. Seven people lay dead in our grandparents' home that night—one of them a boy whose father I had once loved as my own. The weight of what I'd done settled over me, suffocating, and I couldn't help but think back over the lives I'd taken, wondering how I had ended up here. What had driven me to such lengths? As grotesque as it was, the answer was simple: love. A love that had twisted into something monstrous, something that had turned me into a killer.

I was lost, adrift in a sea of violence and self-loathing. What I wanted seemed forever out of reach, and with every life I took, the person I used to be was torn away, leaving behind nothing but a hollow shell. The old Aiden had died that night, along with those I'd killed, and all I wanted was to wash away the remnants of who I used to be.

The storm intensified, its fury mirroring the turmoil inside me. The rain called to me, beckoning me to step into its embrace, to let it drown out the darkness that had taken root in my soul. I was done fighting it, done pretending that I could be saved. It was time to accept who and what I was.

Okay, let's dance.

I wiped the blood from my hands, stood up, and walked into the storm.

CHAPTER TWO
EMBRACING THE STORMS

My name is Aiden Storm, and I will guide you on this dark and fantastic journey that has become my life. So, before we get started, remain seated, fasten your seatbelts, and please don't feed what lurks within the shadows.

To fully understand my descent into madness, you must first know who I am. I am the middle son of three siblings: two boys and a girl. The oldest is Manuel Storm Jr., affectionately known to us as Manny. Back then, he was twenty-six years old, I was sixteen, and Sarah, the baby in every essence of the word, was fifteen.

Our family's heritage spans three continents, with Spanish, Native American, and Brazilian blood coursing through our veins. My dad was a towering, well-built man with dark brown hair, chiseled facial features, and light green eyes. Mom would say our dad was so attractive that calling him cute or handsome was an insult. Monkeys are adorable, and the actor Brad Pitt is gorgeous, but Dad, she would say, was beautiful. Dad wasn't amused with her calling him beautiful. He was a hardened "Frogman," and being called beautiful didn't sit well with a man who carried so many war scars.

Unfortunately, our dad died back in 1994. His plane was shot down during a so-called "routine" exercise over Iraqi airspace. His body was never recovered, and the details of his mission have never been revealed to us.

I vaguely remember my dad because I was so young, but his absence and its effect on me remained prominent. Sarah never got to know him because she wasn't born when we lost him. Manny and our mom took his death the hardest because they got to live with and understand our father and love the man he was. Manny wanted to be like our dad, so to honor his memory, he joined The Navy SEALs. My mom was so proud of him; we all were. He's always been like a piece of Dad left behind to look after us. On the other hand, Sarah and I are more like our mother because she's all we've known.

Manny has been our father figure for as long as I can remember. It was a lot to put on a teenager's shoulders, and he had difficulty adjusting over the years. Manny got into all kinds of trouble and rebelled over losing our father, but eventually, he overcame it stronger and more determined. Mom feels he pushes himself too hard sometimes, and they constantly argue about him being an individual and not a carbon copy of Dad. Manny couldn't stomach any more of their confrontations and decided to stay away as much as possible, only visiting during our birthdays and major holidays. Not having Manny around was hard, but eventually, you must adapt to change or fight it. We decided to adapt.

My mom was born in a small village about one hundred and twenty miles outside of Rio De Janeiro. The younger of two girls, my mom learned at an early age to never take anything for granted. Life was hard in a small village, and she vowed that one day she would escape and find a better life somewhere else. She did just that and after having a successful career as a super model, she met my dad and started a family. She has always taught us to take full advantage of life, never leaving any crumbs on the table. She always said to me "you can either participate in how your life turns out or be a spectator as someone else plans your life for you."

My grandfather would often say that Mom was a Brazilian witch who put a love hex on my dad. To a stranger, his description of her appeared to indicate he disapproved of her. But my grandpa had no ill feelings towards her. Grandpa was weird, and when he had a few drinks, he would rant on for hours about witches, warlocks, and other forces fighting for the souls of humanity. I thought this old man was going to the nut house in a straitjacket. But I would learn later in life that he was the sanest of us all, even while intoxicated.

Thinking back on the fall of 2009, when everything I believed was turned upside down, and the world became much darker, I had no idea how significant I would be.

On the surface, it would appear that we had a perfect life: wealth, stability, and family, even after the loss of our dad. But nothing is rarely as it seems, and what's on the surface usually covers something much darker. My family was no different. We had our secrets too. They just hadn't caught up with us.

Yet...

CHAPTER THREE
A NEW BEGINNING

Fall 2009

It was the first week of September and the start of the school year and with this came a particular change I wasn't looking forward to: Sarah joining me at Deerfield High. My mom initially wanted her to go to a private school in Lake Forest, but just like Sarah, she begged and pleaded until Mom gave in. She fed our mom this load of crap about feeling safer going to the same school as people she knew. The real reason she wanted to go to Deerfield started with a T and ended with a Y. Tony, my best friend, on whom Sarah has had an almost "stalktistic" (yes, I know that isn't a word but as a teenager, we always create our own words and here's my contribution) crush for years. For most, the attention from such an attractive girl would be heaven, but Tony wasn't having it.

As much as she tried, Tony made sure he was extra mean when she made any advances toward him. I knew he found her attractive—she's my sister and as much as she repulses me, I couldn't deny how beautiful she was. But to Tony, our friendship was so important that the thought of ruining it for Sarah made her ugly. I know it's strange for some to comprehend that kind of friendship nowadays, with people having lower standards and a higher tolerance for depravity…but there you have it.

Another major reason I wasn't looking forward to Sarah and me going to the same school was Sarah's bad temper and lack of patience. Combine that with her sensitivity and anything said that she didn't like could land her in the principal's office and the offender in the nurse's office. To this day, I can't understand how Mom controlled Sarah's temper the way she did. I knew with all of Sarah's issues, I was going to have my hands full trying to look after her and listen to all the complaints from lovesick boys and jealous girls at the school. Lucky me.

After getting up and preparing for the first day of school, I headed downstairs toward the kitchen to see what Mom had prepared for our "first day of school breakfast." The first day of school every year was a big deal for Mom because she never had the opportunity to go to school when she was our age. So, she would prepare a special breakfast for us. The house was filled with the delicious smells of waffles, eggs, and breakfast sausages. I didn't wake up hungry but now my mouth was watering. The closer I got to the kitchen, the stronger my hunger became, and by the time I walked into the kitchen, my stomach felt like it was pushing toward my back.

Mom was busy with a skillet of scrambled eggs and didn't seem to notice me, so I quickly tried to reach for a sausage from the plate on the island. Before I could get a good grip on the sausage, Mom quickly spun around from the stove and smacked my hand with her spoon.

"Ouch!"

"Good morning, Aiden!"

"Morning, Mom."

How is she that fast?

"Wash your dirty hands and have a seat. Where is Sarah?" Mom asked in her heavy Brazilian accent.

The sound of her name and the idea of her going to my school made me slam my hand on the granite countertop. The silverware on the island slightly jumped off the surface, sending the sharp sound of metal clashing together straight to my mother's ears. She quickly turned to face me while giving me a look that spelled warning; "eruption is imminent." I could imagine her blood boiling as her anger built up at my reaction to her question about her "baby." Sarah was fifteen for Pete's sake…but she was still Mom's baby and her fiery stare let me know that it wasn't going to change anytime soon. Her look should've given me the hint I needed but I was hard-headed and determined to try and insult Sarah.

"Mom, I don't know I can't keep up w—"

She quickly gave me another look that clearly said if I didn't want to play "dodge the cook's spoon," I wouldn't finish that statement. After seeing her look while holding the spoon in a way that appeared she was weighing it to see how far and hard she could throw it, I instantly grew a brain and changed my approach immediately.

"I don't know, Mom. She's probably still getting ready."

Smiling with a glow in her eyes, she turned back towards the stove, satisfied that she'd gotten her point across. But I knew she wanted much more from me. I knew the talk was coming. I could feel it…

"Aiden?"

"Yes, Mom?"

Here it comes…wait for it…wait for it…wait for it…

"Son, I really need you to keep a close eye on your sister…"

BOOM! The watch-your-sister speech.

"I don't want her getting into trouble with those fast girls at that school and I definitely don't want her getting involved with those hormone-driven boys, either."

"Mom, Sarah is a handful, and she doesn't listen to anything I say."

"That's because when you talk all I see is your mouth moving and garbage pouring out of it," Sarah cut in while she pranced into the kitchen. I gritted my teeth while shaking my head as she gleefully sat down on the stool next to me.

"You see what I'm talking about, Mom!?" I protested.

"Aiden, not even Mom knows what you're talking about, and she gave birth to you."

"Don't hate me, Sarah, because I wasn't born in a test tube."

"What?! Mom!"

"Hey, both of you stop it now! Sarah, you need to start respecting your brother and paying closer attention to your actions. Aiden can't clean up your mess at that school."

"Thanks, Mom! That's what I've been saying."

"I'm still talking, Aiden."

"Sorry, Mom."

"Aiden, you need to start being more involved with your sister. I know you've always been a loner but she's fifteen going on sixteen and she's going to need you now more than she cares to admit."

"Mom, I don't need Aiden babysitting me, it's embarrassing."

"Speaking of babysitting, I want you home at the same time during the school week, no exceptions!"

"What?!" We both protested.

"Mom, I want to try out for the girls' soccer team and practice is always after school."

"Really? Well, I guess Aiden will be your escort."

"Mom!"

"Wait, no!"

"No what, Aiden?"

"Why do I have to sit out two or more hours of my life for—
"

"Aiden!" My mom gave me that "watch it" look; she always could sense when I was about to say something to make things worse.

"Okay, wait for Sarah."

"Aiden, you have two options. Wait for her or try out for a team so that both of you are in practice after school together."

"Oh Mom, come on!"

"What, Aiden? You need to try something new. You're constantly working out, you're in great shape, you're an extremely fast runner, and I think you will do great in sports."

"Mom, that may be true, but the jocks at my school are not the nicest bunch to be around."

"Most jocks aren't, but you need to start learning how to work with others and thrive in a hostile environment. You never know when you'll need those skills. So just think about it; otherwise, you'll be watching your pretty little sister kick a ball around for two hours."

"Oh, God no! I'll look into football then."

"Great! Sarah?"

"Yes, Mom?"

"I don't want any games from you, do you understand me?"

"Yes, Mom."

After breakfast, I sat there in awe when I finally figured out what had just happened. My mom, for the longest, had been trying to get me into sports at school. I've always managed to get out of it…until today. I love sports and I play football at the park all the time, but I just didn't like being around the buffoons on our school's sports teams. Some of them were bullies and some of the people they bullied were pretty cool. They tried me once and only once during my first year with the starting senior quarterback.

I was only fifteen and while in the lunchroom, Adam the starting quarterback and "head bully of the buffoon squad" cut in the line right in front of me. Okay, so what, no problem. Then he kept reaching back over my tray. Now, he was pushing it. I didn't like people too close to things I was going to put in my mouth. After about three attempts of him reaching over my food, I could tell he was trying me, so I politely stepped out of line to avoid a confrontation. With my back towards him, he pushed me...hard. He was much bigger and stronger than me, but I knew even with his size and strength advantage I could seriously hurt him. So, I tried to avoid it, but he wasn't in the lunchroom to eat. His mission was to punk the new freshman; the attractive and quiet boy that all the girls were talking about. He wanted to make a mockery of me and put me in my place among the bullied. I can take a lot of things, but physical aggression is a big problem for me. So, after the push, I quickly turned and demanded he apologize.

I was less than a foot from him, staring directly into his eyes, waiting for his response. He smiled and told his crew I had heart and he was going to tear it out of my chest. I was in my comfort zone being this close to him. Close-quarter combat was always my strong point while training in Mixed Martial Arts. Something our brother Manny insisted on once he joined the SEALs. He felt if he couldn't be around to protect us, Sara and I should learn at an early age how to protect ourselves. I had been training since I was six and had Adam known this, he would've tried someone else, but me.

He pretended to walk away but suddenly turned, intending to push me in my chest and cause me to fall back onto the floor. A very old and lame trick—I saw through this from the beginning. I knew he had a reputation to keep up and he wasn't going to walk away from a "freshie" demanding an apology. Too many people were watching this exchange.

While spinning around and reaching out with all his strength to push me in my chest, I quickly and calmly stepped back to my left and placed my left foot directly in front of his shoes. The force behind his missed push, paired with my perfectly placed foot, propelled him down and across the lunchroom floor. The lunchroom immediately erupted in roaring laughter as they watched the starting quarterback glide across the lunchroom floor on his stomach.

Cherry-red with embarrassment, the quarterback decided to have another go at me. It never dawned on this dummy that if I was fast enough to avoid that push, I might know some things he didn't. But I guess he didn't see it that way. So, I calmly stood there waiting for him to dust himself off and try again. As he rushed towards me with violent rage in his eyes, I stood there contemplating how quickly I wanted to end this confrontation. Did I want to show off and completely embarrass this jackass? Did I want to instill fear in his buddies and other bullies to prevent future retaliation? Or did I just want to do all the above by ending this with one shot? I decided on the latter. As he got within range, I struck his throat with the outside of my left hand and punched him in his solar plexus with my right fist at the same time. I made sure the blow to his throat was a mere tap, not enough to kill him but enough to constrict his air supply.

The force of the air rushing from his midsection and his throat closing up from the tap, caused him to black out instantly. I quickly stepped to my right and let him crumble to the floor. Complete silence fell over the noisy lunchroom. No one moved as the entire lunchroom took a deep breath watching the toughest student go down in less than a minute at the hands of a freshman. I could feel the fear in the room; it seemed to make time stand still.

After about ten seconds, the "crumbled heap of stupid" on the floor came to, coughing and inhaling frantically. His teammates rushed over to help him to his feet while staring at me with disbelief. I calmly stepped towards them, looked them all over with a satisfied stare and said in the politest tone,

"I'll be in the principal's office. I'm sure he'll want to speak to me. You should help your friend over there too because he'll want to speak with him as well. You all have a nice day."

Mission accomplished. I didn't have another physical confrontation at Deerfield High again. But that confrontation was never forgotten, and now Big Stupid's little brother Brian was the new starting quarterback. He's never said anything to me, but he has given me some nasty looks from time to time.

So, you can understand my hesitation, but unfortunately, football was my only option. Basketball was out of the question. I was only six feet tall back then and the entire basketball squad were giants—the shortest guy was six feet four. I would look like a pigmy next to those guys. Soccer wasn't an option for me either; I just didn't care for it at all. So, football was my only realistic option to avoid having to watch my sister doing something I didn't like. I've always been great at the running back position because of my speed, strength, and agility. Our school's running back was a scrub, so I knew the coach was looking for a better alternative.

I was just hoping I wouldn't have the same kind of problems with Brian that I had with his older brother Adam. Actually, Brian was a great quarterback, light years better than his big brother and I knew it would be better to befriend him than beat him. He may leave the team and the team wouldn't win a single game without him. He was definitely NFL-bound, no question. But I wasn't ready to deal with him if he wasn't open to burying the hatchet on his brother's ass-kicking.

There I sat at our kitchen table feeling stupid because I had just been played by my mom and she used Sarah to accomplish her goal.

Suddenly the doorbell rang, and it could only be one person at our door this early, Tony Martinez; my only real friend. He just got back in town a couple of days ago after spending the summer in Israel with his dad. His parents were separated for about three years, but his dad tried his best to still be part of his life. My dad and his dad were both Navy Seals and the best of friends and that's how Tony and I met. We've been friends for as long as we both could walk.

We both started martial arts together, but Tony excelled drastically. He was a natural and he picked up on everything to perfection. Because of our friendship, our instructor never allowed us to fight against each other in any tournaments. I was grateful for that because Tony would have handed my butt to me easily.

Tony has always been considered attractive and he had a demeanor that just attracted attention from those of the opposite sex. So, to say he got a lot of play from the girls was an understatement.

Tony was extremely intelligent, so when they tell you never to judge a book by its cover, he was the definition of that warning. If you didn't know him like I did, you would expect him to be some athlete who didn't find academics very important. That would be an inaccurate assumption. Even though we both played football with some of the neighborhood kids, he didn't try out for any sports at school. He said he'd rather perfect his pimping than his punting. Tony was a natural comedian, and can you blame him? He was an African American teenager with a Hispanic last name, so he had to develop a thick skin, and he learned quickly how to give better than he got.

"Hey, dude! You're cutting it close this morning, huh?" I said while greeting him warmly.

"Aww, man, you know I got to make an entrance."

"Yeah, whatever, Casanova."

"You mean blacka-nova."

We both laughed at his crack on himself. Sarah heard Tony's voice from her bedroom and came running down the stairs screaming his name like a Beyonce fan, eyes gleaming with excitement.

"Boy, move!" she demanded, shoving me out of the way. Before Tony could stop her, she jumped into his arms, hugging him tightly.

"Tony, I missed you so much. Don't ever leave me like that again!"

I could see he was getting uncomfortable with her signs of affection, especially with my mom looking on. He tried to break away, but Sarah wouldn't let go. The look on his face while my mom gave him "the look" was priceless. I thought he was going to piss his pants.

"Okay, okay! Man, girl, give me six feet! Whew!"

He exhaled after she released her grip but not before landing a big juicy kiss on his cheek.

"So, you're kissing my baby right in front of my face?!" my mom protested.

"No! No! Mrs. Storm, it wasn't me...it was..."

"Are trying to say my fifteen-year-old forced you?"

"No!"

"So you *did* kiss her?"

"Oh no wait, please Mrs. Storm!"

My mom had the sternest look on her face, but Sarah and I knew she was teasing Tony. Tony didn't and after she stared at him with "the look" a little longer, he got so confused he started blaming himself.

Finally, none of us could hold it in any longer and broke out laughing.

"Aww, you guys are wrong!"

"Dude, you fell for it, you can't blame us," I said.

"Stop teasing my baby!" warned Sarah. "This is my future hubby."

"Uhh, no I'm not!"

"Please Tony, I'm fifteen now."

"Yeah, and you still got milk behind your ears. I'm not ever getting married. So, me being your 'hubby' is slim to none."

"You say that now, but we're going to the same school this year, so those rats you date are going to have to scurry along."

"What?"

I'd forgotten to inform Tony before that morning that Sarah would be joining us at Deerfield High. His eyes were bulging as he shook his head trying to make sense of what he just heard.

"Oh no, you are lying!"

"Nope."

"You *are* going with us?"

"Yep," Sarah answered teasingly, nodding her head. "So, you will be seeing a lot more of me," she said gesturing towards her body like it was on display at an auction.

"Jesus! Take me now," Tony yelled while looking up at the sky. "I'm ready to come home, lord! Oh well, Dick Cheney had Bush, Whitney had Bobby and crack, and I got you, huh?"

"Are you referring to me as a drug, Tony? Well, crack is addictive, so I'll be your addiction!"

"No, that's not what I'm trying to say! Mrs. Storm?"

"Nope, Tony, I got nothing."

"No help…nothing? It's because I'm black, huh? Can't a brother get any help? Ok, I guess that's how it is then. Come on, let's go, stalker," Tony teased.

"Whatever, Tony!" Sarah complained, pushing him out the door.…

CHAPTER FOUR
SOPHOMORE YEAR

eerfield High, what a wonderful establishment. Whatever. It was a good school but after being here for so long things got kinda stale and routine. Of course, it wasn't as bad as other schools for sure, but Deerfield still had its issues. Most of them were from overcompensating spoiled brats.

"MMM, mmm, mmm…the new possibilities," Tony said while looking at a few girls who walked past us in the hallway.

"Calm down Tony. Down, boy!" I teased.

Tony was already scoping out the new girls as we walked down the hall.

"Dude whatever, it seems like God poured a pitcher of beautiful all over this school and I'm thirsty, very thirsty."

Tony did have a point. There was an abnormal number of new students, and the girls were all very attractive. There were a few familiar faces, but it seemed like we had more "freshies" this year. A lot of the students we knew either graduated or had to leave

Deerfield because of the recession after 9/11. A lot of working families were losing everything and could no longer afford the high property taxes and cost of living in a place like Deerfield. We have watched over the last two years five families on our street alone, lose their homes to foreclosures. Families we knew and grew up with. It was sad, but I knew other families in less desirable areas were suffering even more.

The world was a depressing place to exist in. No one was living anymore. We were just getting by or surviving. Most adults don't believe teenagers think like this, that all we think about is sex, video games, and social media. And for the most part that's accurate; but even with all of those distractions, most of us still find a way to be aware of the world around us. It's called the Internet and YouTube. We just act out in front of adults because it's amusing to watch their reactions to our behavior. If adults knew how much free entertainment they provide teenagers, they would first be upset and then would likely start ignoring us. And that would be bad because attention is one thing almost every teenager needs in their lives to feel important.

"Hey, Aiden. I know you are focused and everything, but dude you need a girl for real."

"Tony, you know…"

"Yeah bro, I know but hear me out…"

Tony leaned towards my ear as if he had a secret that if revealed would mean disaster.

"Just because she's your girl doesn't mean you *have* to have sex with her. The thing is bro, the right girl in your life makes you a better man, completing your circle. They force us to grow up. I'm seventeen and you'll be seventeen in a couple of weeks. If not now, when?" Tony asked while giving me an assuring nod.

"Anyway, I gotta bounce bro, but I'll get at you during the second period."

While I watched Tony maneuver down the crowded hall, I realized that he might have just given me the most realistic and honest view of the relationship between men and women. But where the hell did he get that from? I just couldn't see that inspiration coming from the mind of a seventeen-year-old. At the time, I only partially understood the wisdom he bestowed on me. It wasn't until later in my life I fully realized his statement. I was only sixteen and had a very limited viewpoint on the connection between the sexes and why we needed each other. Later that day, when I asked him where he got that from, he told me his dad gave him that wisdom during summer vacation.

They were talking about women and what happened between his parents. His dad told him he fought his mom constantly when she was trying to get him to grow up. Tony said he made his dad feel like he was brushing off his advice, but it must have been important for him to share it with me.

I was going to be seventeen on September 16th. We were going to a club that Tony's cousin owned downtown not far from the Hard Rock Café. Tony's cousin started as a party promoter and soon opened his own club. He was a pretty cool dude and he always tried to give Tony whatever he wanted because of how much he looked up to Tony's dad. He was laying out the royal treatment for us on that night. It was eighteen to enter, twenty-one- and-over to drink nightclub, but he assured us entry wouldn't be a problem for either of us. I was nervous at first but then I thought, "What the hell." You only turn seventeen once.

I glanced over at Sarah to see how she was taking in this new environment and as usual, she had this "it's not all that" look on her face. She was such a troll. Ugh!

"Well, if this is all high school has to offer, then bring on college baby!" she yelled. "Okay, Lil' big brother, I'm heading to class, okay?"

"Try not to get into trouble."

"Yeah, me getting into trouble? Please, Aiden, this place is so lame it would be an insult to get in trouble here. I should have gone to Lake Forest. At least they have a little more class over there."

"Whatever Sarah. Now your class is—"

"Aiden, stop! This place is not that big, I'm sure I can just read the numbers on the doors and figure out where to go. This place seemed to be designed for idiots; did you need directions on your first day? Wait! Don't answer that. I don't want to think of you any less than I do now. Have a good day brother…don't get lost in this mental hospital, okay? Bye-bye now!"

As I watched her prance down the hall, I so wanted her to slip on something and fall flat on her butt. But Sarah was too graceful for that.

Oh well, to class.

As I looked around I began to notice a lot of things and even though I hated to admit it, Sarah was right. This school was designed as if we were not capable of thinking for ourselves. I must be coming down with the swine flu to agree with Sarah.

The day was moving pretty fast and before I knew it, lunchtime was upon us. I never got to meet up with Tony during the second period because I needed to sign up for football tryouts. When Coach Towers saw me walk through his office door, he looked at me like I was the IRS ready to probe his entire life and every opening in his body. When he inquired why I was there and I told him my intentions, he nearly fell out of his chair. I was well aware that word had gotten to him about my potential for the running back position and he was interested in me joining the team. But he also was aware of the lunchroom incident during my first year here with the starting quarterback's older brother. He would have asked me to try out a long time ago, but he didn't want to chance any confrontations that could disrupt the team's chemistry.

"Aiden, are you sure you want to do this?" Coach Towers asked. "You understand the commitment it takes to make the team and to remain on the team?"

"Yes Coach, I am aware, and about Brian…" I hesitated; I didn't want to say anything that would jeopardize my chances. "I will do my best to get along with him but he has to meet me halfway…"

"True. Very true," Coach Towers agreed. "Okay, I will make you a deal. If you can make the team, I'll personally talk with Brian."

"Thank you, sir"

"No problem, and to be honest, Brian's brother *was* a real prick."

We both laughed at the coach's revelation. Coach Towers was a great coach and one of the few decent mentors on campus. He kind of had a pulse and could relate to us teenagers better than the other teachers on campus. He normally came to our defense whenever we clucked up and we teens tend to cluck up a lot. So, we had him working overtime trying to keep us from getting into more trouble than we were already in.

I left the coach's office very optimistic about the chances of having a harmonious and exciting school year. If I could make the team and start at running back, maybe I could start having a lot more fun. My mom just may be right; maybe I needed to try new things. It's just that life seemed so boring to me. The world seemed so dull and lifeless or at least my life did. I found myself constantly asking; "Is this it?" My mom saw me backing into a shell and she just wanted more for me and enjoy life each day as if it was my last. Sarah was outgoing and aggressive so she took advantage of everything she could—so my mom didn't worry about Sarah enjoying herself. Actually, she was worried about Sarah enjoying herself too much. I was the total opposite. So, if I could make this football thing work, then maybe it would be the spark my life needed to revitalize itself.

CHAPTER FIVE
JASMINE

Tony texted me earlier in all caps, meaning he'd found another object of his affection. All the text read was, "OMG!! DUDE, IT'S ON!!" Walking into the lunchroom felt like entering a scene from a Black Friday shopping spree. There were a lot of new students this year, all scurrying around trying to look cool. Everyone wanted to be seen. I gritted my teeth at the thought of Sarah being right again. This was lame. I scanned the lunchroom looking for Tony in the crowd and quickly located him in the far-right corner.

He was surrounded, as usual, by a pack of shiny-eyed girls vying for his attention and phone number. I don't know how he did it. It was like his pores secreted sex appeal. He looked up, saw me, and immediately sent me a text to give him one more minute. He needed to close on a prospect. I shook my head and laughed. Tony was out of control. I decided to go to the line and grab something to eat. I usually didn't care for the food here, but the pizza was decent. Before I got into the line, Tony appeared behind me.

"Hey, bro!"

"What's up, playa?"

"Playa? No, Aiden, I'm not playing. I'm for real with this," he replied with a serious look on his face.

"Anyway, tell me about your text earlier," I asked as we started walking towards the food line. "Is she one of the girls you were talking to over there?"

"Oh no! This girl blows them out of the water. I saw her in my history class. Dude, she's unbelievable. Clearly, the finest girl in this school ever, and that's saying a lot, especially since Sarah goes here now."

"What?!" I protested.

"Wait, dude, I'm not checking out your sister like that, but real talk, your sister ain't ugly. I know she's your baby sister, but I'm just saying! But this girl is on a whole other level. I got the 411 on her too. Her family is from Iraq, I think, but she was born right here in Illinois. Her father owns a lot of real estate across the country, and they are pretty loaded, like Bill Gates."

"Bill Gates?" I asked, giving him a look of disbelief. "For real? And she goes to this school? A public school?"

"Okay, maybe not like Big Bill, but they are loaded. That is a fact."

"Are you sure this time, Tony?"

"Whatever! Let me finish. Her name is Jasmine, and she's already got everyone up here talking. The guys are baiting, and the girls are hating!"

"Is that so, Tony?" I mocked. "Because I haven't heard anything up until now."

"Dude, get real. How many students up here run to you and start talking about girls and stuff besides me?"

"You got a point there." I agreed. "Okay, so when are you going to make your move on the Iraqi princess?"

"Me? Hell no, not me... you!"

"What?!"

"Yep, you! Man, you have no idea how many girls ask about you. But they say you are too reserved, and they mistake you for the conceited type. Plus, a lot of them think you are a tad bit too pretty, and girls don't like their boyfriends looking better than them. And let's face it, you are waaaay too pretty."

"Tony, you shouldn't call me pretty in public. People may think you want me or something."

Tony immediately started faking like he was gagging.

"Okay, seriously, dude, that was gross. Now, what I was saying before you interrupted me with that horrible image? Oh yeah... this girl is right up your alley."

"And why is this girl right up my alley? Inquiring minds want to know."

"Well, for starters, she looks better than any of the girls up here. I mean, the girl is so fine she makes me nervous, and you know your boy isn't easily spooked by a girl. But I could build up enough nerve to facilitate a meet and greet between you two when you are ready. I usually charge for that kind of thing, but because you're my bro, I'll do it for you 'pro bro-no.'"

Pro bro-no? Sometimes Tony takes the comedy too far.

"Oh, so now you're hooking me up?"

"Naw, bro, it's not like that. You have to hook yourself up. I'm just making the transition easier for you. It's something to consider, though."

"Okay, Tony, slow down. I just signed up for football tryouts and—"

"What?! You did what?" Tony yelled.

"Ssh! Shut up!"

Tony started laughing until tears began rolling down his face. I could feel the skin on my face warming as I started to turn red.

"Dude? Come on!"

Tony was trying to control his laughter, but I could see he was losing that battle. He began to lean forward on me, still laughing.

"Get off!" I whispered as I pushed him off me. "Dude, is it really that funny?"

"No... wait... let me catch my breath... I'll explain. I'm not laughing at you. It's just when you told me you signed up for tryouts, an image immediately popped in my head of you smacking Brian around the field yelling, 'I got your punk-ass brother and now it's your turn.' Are you trying to beat the whole family?"

I gave him a really nasty and angry look.

"Oh, come on, Aiden. You are my boy. I wouldn't laugh at you like that. You got skills on the gridiron. You're gonna kill 'em out there, for real. I just can't wait to see how Brian is going to react to having you on the field. Oh, I just had another image of Brian talking smack to you and you punting his ass through the uprights! It's good! It's all good!"

Tony was holding his arms in the air like the referee in a football game, confirming a successful field goal attempt. Seeing him standing there looking silly made me laugh so hard that I started to tear up.

"Dude, you're slow."

"Seriously, though, that's great news you're getting into sports at school. It's about time. The NFL is calling."

"I don't know about all that, Tony."

"Okay, okay, fair enough."

"But like I was saying, that was a big step for me, and now you are suggesting I go after Helen of Troy? Come on! I need to take baby steps this year."

"No, you need to talk to her seriously because it's about time for you to..."

Tony suddenly stopped talking and began staring towards the lunchroom entrance like he was in a trance.

"What is it?" I asked.

"There she is. Look!" Tony said with excitement, never taking his eyes from the direction of the lunchroom entrance. I followed his gaze, and there she was, standing in the lunchroom doorway, looking over the room. Wow, Tony was right, she was absolutely amazing. She was about five foot seven and possessed a body that shouldn't be allowed around anyone under the age of eighteen. Curly, vibrant black hair ran halfway down her back, and her skin... my God, her skin... was so radiant and perfectly tanned. And to complete this amazing physical ensemble were the most captivating brown eyes I'd ever seen on a girl. Her posture was regal, but not arrogant, and you could immediately tell she was a girl used to a higher standard of living and expectations. As she stood in the lunchroom's doorway like a living monument of the queens of ancient times, her gaze slowly moved in our direction. My mind was telling me to stop staring, but I couldn't. She was so beautiful. It was like I was in a trance, caught in a spell with no antidote or cure.

As her gaze moved closer to mine, my heart began to race, my palms started sweating, and my temperature rose to almost feverish levels. Everything around me began to move in slow motion, and sounds became muffled like everyone was talking underwater in a fishbowl. Tony was saying something behind me, but I couldn't make out what he was saying. Is this what my mom meant when she said love at first sight? Was this the feeling of instant attraction? As her gaze got closer, the blissful feelings started to subside, and my emotions began to transform into anger and disgust, as a repulsive feeling engulfed my entire body. I felt like my skin was crawling with every disgusting critter imaginable.

Was I going to hurl? What's happening to me? And then, like a chameleon walking across a rainbow, my emotions changed again. A fire began to burn deep inside of me, causing me to clench my fists so tightly I could feel my fingernails digging into the flesh of my palms.

What the hell is wrong with me? Am I getting sick?

The fire began to burn into a fiery rage, and I noticed that I'd never been this angry. I felt like I wanted to destroy everything. Once her eyes met mine, I was shaking and sweating like crazy as the room morphed into a dark abyss that seemed to be void of all sound. I started to frantically look around for Tony or anyone, but no one was there. Everything and everyone was gone besides the darkness and her.

I could see her clearly in the sickening darkness, standing there beautiful and perfect while my body shook violently from the skin-crawling fear that had taken over me. As frightening as the darkness was, nothing was as terrifying as her, and my body reacted to her like she was a predator and I the prey.

But I felt she wasn't just a threat to me but an evil at the top of the food chain that threatened everything and everyone. The darkness itself seemed to harbor its own vengeful malice, and she was its master, controlling it to torment me. I was afraid to move one inch or be consumed by the evil that dwelled in the darkness, leaving behind nothing but bones. Time seemed to stand still, and I found myself trapped in an eternity of terror in this alternate dark reality. She appeared to notice my fear and smirked while looking into my eyes mockingly. I then discovered she knew what was happening to me and that she was the cause of my reaction.

Suddenly she broke her gaze, and immediately the room came back into focus, and all the sound rushed inside my ears, creating chaos and pain inside my head. When my eyes were able to focus, I noticed that she was walking towards the other side of the lunchroom as if nothing had happened.

"Aiden! Man, where did you go just now? I know she's beautiful, but you completely lost it, man!" Tony yelled in my ear. I pulled away from his loudmouth, trying to avoid my now overly sensitive eardrums from bursting inside my head.

"I don't know what just happened to me."

I kept my head down, afraid to look up and catch another glimpse of Jasmine. There was something not right inside of me, something was definitely off. The rage I felt was something new for me; even during martial arts tournaments, I never felt that angry and aggressive. And I've definitely never been teleported into a dark abyss with a beautiful girl before.

"I need to sit down," I said.

"Okay, you need my help?" offered Tony.

"No, I can manage."

"Cool, I'll get you something to drink and eat. What do you want?"

"Just get me an apple."

"Just an apple? But, Aiden, you kinda like this pizza…"

"Tony!" I interrupted.

"Yeah, okay, I'll get the apple."

"Thanks!" I had a seriously bad attitude at the moment, and Tony's constant questioning was annoying me to madness.

Sitting there at the table, I couldn't help wondering what would have happened if she hadn't broken her gaze. Where would that have led to? No one else in the lunchroom appeared to be going through what I just experienced. I looked around to see if she was anywhere near me, but from what I could see, she wasn't even in the lunchroom anymore. Why did she trigger that reaction from me? I was expecting some kind of reaction, but nothing like this. I looked up and saw Tony walking towards me with his lunch tray. As he sat down across from me, I noticed he didn't have my apple.

"Dude?"

"What?"

"My apple?"

"Oh damn, my bad. I'll go…"

"No, I'll get it."

"You sure?"

"Yeah, Tony, I think I can get an apple ten feet away without incident." I got up and started moving towards the fruit display.

I felt completely normal again. No uneasy feelings or nightmarish visions. The apples looked really ugly, some of them with brown spots and blemishes. Then, from the corner of my eye, I saw the perfect apple. Dark red, big, and it looked firm and delicious. My mouth started watering at the prospect of taking a huge bite and feeling the sweet and refreshing juices explode inside my mouth. I had to have that apple no matter what. Somehow, biting into that apple meant making sense of what had just happened to me.

As I reached for the apple, I started feeling the heat and rage build up inside of me again. I felt someone behind me—it was her! We were both reaching for the same apple. Being this close to her started an uncontrollable frenzy inside me. The terror was engulfing me, drowning me in wave after wave of uncontrollable fear. I was sinking fast and beginning to lose myself. Then I felt a surge of power run through my veins, giving me a godlike feeling.

I was ready for war, and one of us was going to get this apple while the other would end up with a handful of air. From the corner of my eye, I could tell my hand was much closer to the apple than hers, clearly indicating I would be the winner of this "Apple-Gladiatorial Contest." Then she did something I wasn't expecting...she gently brushed her arm and hip against me in the most seductive way.

(Sigh) Girls can be so evil...

Her touch sent unfamiliar urges and desires through my entire body. The contrast of the feelings of anger and sexual yearning caused an emotional chain reaction that I couldn't control. Before I could move away, it happened...

"Don't fucking touch me!"

The words exploded from my mouth like a nuclear blast. My voice was loud, rumbling across the entire lunchroom. It traveled above all the chatter, noise, and laughter. It drowned out everything and everyone. The room fell silent, and everyone's attention was now on me and Jasmine. They watched me snatch away from this beautiful girl, recoiling in disgust. I could feel a snarl forming on my face as my posture became aggressive. I slightly turned my head away from her, refusing to look her in the eyes. From the corner of my eye, I saw that same smirk she gave me in the darkness. I hated that she had this much control over me, but my reaction wasn't planned; it just came out of me naturally. I was losing control of myself, and I felt she was my enemy. I knew at that moment we would have a problem with each other for a very long time. But we were strangers, and there wasn't a rational reason why I felt that way towards her.

In an attempt to avoid our exchange from escalating, Tony ran over to me and began leading me out of the lunchroom. Halfway out, I turned to see Sarah looking on with shock and awe in her eyes. I then turned my head toward the fruit display and caught a glimpse of Jasmine, smiling back at me while taking a big bite out of the apple I wanted so badly. She had a look of triumph on her face, provoking me, and I suddenly wanted to run back into the lunchroom and snatch the apple right out of her hand. What was coming over me? I've never felt like this towards a girl before, well, besides Sarah, but she was my little sister. We were supposed to fight. But I've never hit a girl nor had any sort of confrontation with one. Nor had I ever dreamed of it until that day. I needed my head examined immediately.

CHAPTER SIX
THE AFTERMATH

After the scene in the lunchroom between myself and Jasmine, I began getting strange looks from everyone, even Tony. Once school was finally out, I waited outside for Sarah and Tony. I really didn't want to look at another person's judging eyes looking me over like I was a basket case. There weren't any after-school activities either; tryouts started next week. Tony walked out first, then Sarah followed, both of them cautiously walking toward me as if they expected me to pounce on them like a hungry lion.

"Oh no, I am not going anywhere with the psycho boy over there!" Sarah protested.

"Sarah, stop it," warned Tony. "Let's go!"

As Tony walked towards the bus stop, I could hear girls calling out for him.

"See you tomorrow, ladies," Tony responded and kept walking, clearly for their own safety. Sarah was with us, and if they got too close, she would not be polite. But most teenagers can't take a hint, and one such cute and flirtatious teenager suddenly ran up to Tony for a goodbye hug. Sarah immediately jumped between them.

"Uh, excuse me?" the girl complained.

"Yes! You are excused, and you can turn all that sexual energy down and carry it that way!" demanded Sarah, pointing in the opposite direction.

"I'm not even talking to you. Who are you anyway?" the girl responded.

Sarah hated being challenged in front of Tony. She took a step toward little miss "sexshine" and said, "You really want to know who I am?"

The girl, now curious, looked Sarah over quickly. Soon, the flirtatious smile disappeared from her face, and I could tell she was calculating her odds of being able to physically contend with my sister. Sarah was both physically attractive and intimidating. She worked out just as much as I did, and her well-defined arms and legs revealed to many, including this teenager vying for Tony's attention, that she wasn't to be taken lightly. After deciding against testing Sarah's patience, the girl took a few steps back and began rolling her eyes and neck.

"Whatever! Later for you?" the girl responded, flicking her hand in Sarah's face. "You and your brother are a bunch of weirdos anyway. Call me later, Tony, and make sure your guard dog is muzzled and chained before you do."

"What did you say?" Sarah jumped towards her, but Tony grabbed her before she could do the girl bodily harm.

"Sarah, chill!"

Then he yelled after the sophomore as she walked away, switching extra hard so Tony could notice her backside: "Hey girl, trust me, I just saved your life! Don't provoke this one!"

"Tony, you better check your tramps before I have to clean house!" Sarah demanded.

"Hey Sarah, you need to calm that down! I don't know how many times I have to tell you, I'm not your man!"

Then Tony turned to me, "Dude, what was that earlier? I mean, at first, you black out, then you burst out and snatch away from clearly the finest girl on planet Earth. What was that about?"

"He's been in that potato head training camp too long," blurted Sarah.

"Dude, I don't know what came over me," I responded.

"People are gossiping, bro. They're saying you're a racist!"

"Huh?" I said.

And then Sarah, while pointing at the both of us, broke out in a frenzied laugh, stumbling forward, trying to regain her balance.

"Aiden is a racist with a best friend who's black? Where do people get this crap?" she yelled out, still laughing.

"Well, they're saying because Iraqis killed your dad and she's Iraqi, you hate her."

"Dude, that's ridiculous!"

"I know it is, and then they're saying you are gay."

"Gay?" Sarah was laughing so hard, I thought she would collapse on the sidewalk and laugh until she fainted.

"A gay racist!? Oh, my Lord! If those are the things those brilliant minds at Deerfield High can come up with, then I was wrong. That school wasn't designed for idiots; it was designed for vegetables. I changed my mind—I want to go to Lake Forest! I feel the dumbness infecting me every second I remain on campus! Y'all too much! And they have the nerve to pass out A's up here? I wonder how dumb one would have to be to get an F?"

Sarah couldn't stop laughing, and we all started laughing as well. Again, though I hated to admit it, she had a point.

"Dumb enough to get kicked out of hell, I guess," Tony added. We started laughing harder.

On the bus ride home, Sarah kept looking at students from Deerfield High and giggling. I knew she was giving them all grades of her own. He's definitely an F right there. Then giggle. She was so mean. She would occasionally say out loud "F+," and the three of us would start laughing again.

Back at our house, Tony began to drill me in my room about the events from earlier that day. I explained everything to him, including my dark visions that included Jasmine. After I was done, Tony just sat on the edge of my bed, looking at me like I was Hannibal Lecter.

"Aiden, you got issues!"

"So, you don't believe me?"

"Yes, I do believe you. You've never had a problem before, no mental breakdowns, nothing. So, I believe you. But me believing you isn't the solution. The solution is to stay the hell away from that girl. And if what you're saying is accurate about her taunting you, she's not going to make it easy for you. But what I'm tripping on is that waking nightmare you just talked about. That doesn't sound normal on any plain of existence. Do you think she knows the effect she has on you?"

"Yes, definitely!"

"Okay, now you know how crazy this sounds, right?"

"Yes, I do. Being around her terrifies me to the point I feel like she's evil or something."

"Wow, dude, anyone else sitting where I'm sitting right now would be turning you in. Real talk! A girl that fine? Man, Aiden, you sure know how to stay focused, huh?"

"Hey man, that's not fair."

"Give me a little credit, Aiden. I am protecting my friend who may need his brain examined. So, I need to add a little humor right now to make me feel a little better about this."

"Oh, so that's what that was?"

Tony got up and walked over to the window, looking out across our backyard. I could tell he was very uncomfortable with my behavior concerning Jasmine. After staring out my window in silence for about a minute, I could tell by his uncomfortable stance he was ready to go home and think about everything I'd just shared with him.

"Anyway, bro, I gotta roll. I'll see you tomorrow morning, and we are going to figure this thing out together, okay?" He was shaking my hand while reassuring me that he had my back, and from his firm grip, I knew he meant every word.

"Thanks, man."

"No problem. Now let's pray she's not a Girl Scout and shows up at your doorstep selling devil's food cake cookies."

"Get out!" I laughed. As he walked out the door, I threw a shoe at his head. He ducked right before my shoe connected with the back of his head, then gave me the finger while doing a silly karate pose.

Out!" I yelled, laughing at his silly antics.

For the next four days, Tony and I tried to devise a system for me to avoid Jasmine as much as possible. It was easy at times, and other times it seemed she'd just pop out of nowhere behind me or next to me. I got the feeling of terror, but once I was able to move away from her, the effect on me diminished. Sometimes her presence felt threatening, and other times it felt sensual and inviting. The conflicting feelings were more than I could control, and my body would convulse and shake violently. Every time it happened, Tony would wait until I'd stop shaking and then ask,

"Need a cigarette and towel?"

Don't you dare laugh...it isn't funny.

I started searching online after school, trying to find out as much as I could about my condition and Jasmine. Nothing! Not a damn thing. It was very strange. You could find Bigfoot photos, porn, Elvis sightings, more porn, and 2Pac theories. Oh, and did I mention porn? But nothing about what I was experiencing. I began to second-guess myself, thinking maybe I always had these physiological imperfections that lay dormant for so long. Maybe that's why a teenage boy considered by many to be extremely attractive was a die-hard introvert. When I really thought hard about it, I discovered that I purposely cultivated my brooding behavior and did things to keep people at bay.

Maybe it was a subconscious protection mechanism to prevent me from harming anyone. But if that's true, then why her? Why now? And what about that dark vision? I just couldn't understand how something in my mind could manifest something so real and terrifying. And what about the power surge running through my body? I felt like I had about two million watts of power flowing through my veins that I could use at my disposal. I didn't even feel like myself when that happened. I felt lighter than air and I could do anything, be anything. The feeling was euphoric, like a drug. But not being in control of myself was terrifying and frustrating, to say the least. So, after trying so many different things and searching for hours online, by the end of the school week, we still had no idea what was going on between me and the new girl.

CHAPTER SEVEN
BOWLING NIGHT

The temperature rose considerably on Friday afternoon, so we decided to walk home instead of riding the bus to enjoy the beautiful weather. It was a pretty long walk, but it was the end of the week, and we were in no rush to get home. Walking home with the sun beaming down on me felt great. I felt re-energized, relaxed, and in control of myself. I was calm and loved it. The walk home was fun and uneventful without any of Tony's fans, nightmares, or Jasmine. It was a much-needed break from the chaos that had become my life since she arrived at Deerfield High.

Back at home, things were a little more hectic. My mom was scurrying around the house, trying to cook and get ready to go bowling. She would go bowling twice a month, or that's what she told us. My sister and I knew she'd met someone, and her bowling nights were really date nights with her new boyfriend.

The first time she told us she would be taking up bowling about six months ago, I knew she was hiding something. Sarah did too. There could only be a few things that could make Mom hide something, so it wasn't hard to figure out she was dating someone.

39

Dad had been gone a long time, and we both understood that Mom needed a social life too. We didn't want her to feel ashamed or guilty about it. She was very careful not to expose us to her adult life, and we appreciated that. We knew, but we didn't want it paraded in front of us either. So, for our appreciation of her motherly discretion, we went along with it. Sometimes, Sarah being Sarah would make a sarcastic remark about Mom trying out for the Olympic bowling team because of the time she puts into bowling. Her remarks would cause my mom to freeze, looking at Sarah for anything that showed the cat was out of the bag. But then Sarah would smile and say something to change the subject, leaving my mom wondering if Sarah knew anything.

"Bowling tonight, Mom?" Sarah asked.

"Yes, baby, and I'm running a little late. Aiden, do you think you could clean the kitchen for me?"

I hated cleaning the kitchen, and washing dishes was worse than torture. But that day, I was in a tremendously good mood and blurted out, "Sure, Mom!" before I knew what I was saying.

"Oh, wow," my mom replied. "It's usually a fight with you."

"It's okay, Mom. Have fun. I got it."

"Mom?"

"Yes, sweetie," my mom replied to Sarah.

"When are we going to meet him?" Sarah asked, never looking up from the magazine she was reading. The sound of the question coming out of Sarah's big mouth caused an uncomfortable feeling to take over the mood in the kitchen. My mom gasped, and I just turned away and closed my eyes. My mom hung her head down, searching for something, anything to say. I could tell she was trying to decide whether to come clean or keep the lie going.

She looked up, and I could sense she decided to choose the latter. I could only assume she wanted to keep it a secret to protect our feelings. But at this point, it would not be a smart move. I would understand, but Sarah wouldn't, and Sarah doesn't know how to let things go. So, I moved quickly to divert a disaster.

"Mom," I blurted out, "we've known for a while that you haven't actually been bowling."

"Oh my God!" my mom screamed.

"But...but..." I continued. "We are cool with it. It's cool you're dating someone. Of course, we would like to eventually meet him, but in your own time."

"We just want to size him up and make sure he's cute enough for you, Mom," added Sarah. "Because if he's going to be around us, then we need to match. We can't have three beautiful people and one ugly person. We have to coordinate."

"Ha!" My mom laughed. I could tell she was relieved at how we were taking it, and suddenly the mood in the room lightened.

"Yes, baby, he's pretty cute."

"What's the mystery man's name?" Sarah asked.

"His name is Jason."

"Soooo—"

"Okay," I interrupted Sarah's next question. Sarah was driven by impulses, and I didn't want her to make a bigger mess than she already had. "So, Mom, you get ready, and I'll clean the kitchen, and Sarah can do... well, whatever she does in her free time."

"Are you sure?"

"Yes, Mom! Now go and get ready."

My mom smiled at me, and I could see the appreciation in her eyes. She placed her hand gently on my cheek, smiled, and silently mouthed thank you. At that moment, I felt a wave of love come over me. Nothing mattered but seeing my mom happy and to see her appreciation for me stepping up was a great moment for both of us.

I waited till my mom was out of hearing distance before I went in on Sarah.

"Sarah, what the hell was that? Do you even know what you could have done to Mom? You are just unbelievable at times."

"Really, says who? You, Mom, or Manny? Whatever! Mom's been tiptoeing around here for over six months. When was she ever going to come clean? After a year? When they get engaged? Or better yet, when she got pregnant?"

"Sarah, don't you dare go there!"

"Oh yeah, I went there: 'Oh Sarah, Aiden, I'm going bowling tonight, and by the way, I'm getting married and having a baby!'" Sarah teased while mocking our mom's mannerisms and accent.

"Sarah, that's not fair at all!"

"Oh really? You were too afraid to push Mom to come clean, so I took charge. You should be thanking me instead of trying to get on my case. Big bro, you never take charge; you just cruise along. Well, I'm not a cruiser; I'm gonna say something. Now it's out, Mom feels better, and all is right in the world."

"Sarah, you think your no-holds-barred approach always works, but it doesn't. Tonight was one of those times. Yeah, you blurted it out, but you didn't see that Mom felt you were judging her, did you? You said what you said and then kept quiet. Not once giving Mom the respect that she deserves. You could've at least said something to ease her fear of us having a problem with her seeing someone.

Mom has always been here, never complaining or neglecting us for her agendas, and that's how you repay her?"

I could see my point was starting to sink in with Sarah because her usual arrogant and snobbish attitude started to disappear with every word. She began to hold her head down and play with her fingers. She always did that when she felt really bad about something, which was rare, so it wasn't hard to recognize.

"You're right. I messed that up big time, okay? I'm sorry. I just thought..."

"You thought? Sarah, were you even thinking?"

"Probably not, but I wasn't trying to hurt her feelings, not on purpose," she whined. "I have to admit, if you hadn't stepped in, it could have ended badly. Thanks for pulling my foot out of my mouth."

"Oh, anytime!"

"Well! I'm heading to my room now, big bro. Nice heart-to-heart," she said sarcastically while exhaling forcefully.

"I bet it was!" I snapped back.

I decided to head to my room as well to check my Facebook page and play some "Call of Duty" with Tony. Tony and I were breaking their backs on Xbox Live as a team. They hated to see us log in together. About an hour into playing, my mom knocked on my door to say she was leaving. No bowling bag or jogging outfit; she was dressed to impress. I could sense the relief she felt, being able to get dressed for a date instead of bowling.

"I'm leaving now."

"Okay, Mom. Have fun and make sure you're back at a decent hour, young lady," I teased.

"Oh, excuse me, big daddy," she played along. "I'll make sure I'm home before the rooster crows."

"Seriously, though, Mom, have fun and be safe."

"I will, sweetie. Bye and look after your sister."

"I will."

Saturday morning at breakfast, my mom told us she discussed the events in the kitchen the night before with Jason and wanted to know if it was okay if he came over one day next week to meet me and Sarah. It was kind of sudden, but we agreed because it was long overdue. The rest of the weekend was uneventful for the most part, besides the occasional argument with Sarah. I was looking forward to Monday and the tryouts for the football team. The prospect of being a "Deerfield High Warrior" was exciting. Back then, I didn't want to admit that I was intrigued by the thought of being popular. The cheering crowds, the extra attention from the girls, and all the other perks that came along with it. Yeah, I was more than intrigued. My only concern was Jasmine. I was just praying she didn't decide to become a cheerleader; that wouldn't be a good thing for either of us.

The very thought of Jasmine being a cheerleader whisked my troubled mind away to me playing in a championship game. I could hear the crowd's eruptive cheers from the stands encouraging me to run faster towards the end zone. I could smell the sweat from my jersey, feel the grit of the soil on my arms, and the turf beneath my feet. I imagined Jasmine on the sidelines in those short skirts with pom-poms in both hands. Smiling and cheering me on as I run down the field toward pay dirt. Her smile is so flirtatious and inviting, almost hypnotic. Nothing like the smirk she gave me in that waking nightmare on the first day of school. Then suddenly I decide to take a detour and run straight towards her with my arms outstretched like a child running towards its mother to be wrapped in her loving arms. Jasmine was now looking directly into my eyes, licking her shapely lips, enticing me to come in closer for big juicy kiss.

I'm running toward her at full speed. Just before our bodies collide, a shadow figure cloaked in black mist, reaches out from her chest with razor-sharp talons and wraps its hands around my throat. I immediately feel myself losing consciousness as it begins to choke me, scraping its talons across my neck, tearing the flesh away. I try to scream, but only blood pours out of my mouth as it pulls me closer to the spinning dark abyss that should be its face. Without warning, my ears are assaulted by a high-pitched scream erupting from the shadow figure's abyssal face. I close my eyes in terror, waiting for the shadow demon to devour me.

Just before I lost all sense of reality, I snapped out of my waking nightmare. What is wrong with me? Why are my thoughts of Jasmine so terrifying? This change coming over me was unnerving. What was I becoming, and why was she the focus of all my fear? Even my best friend was beginning to doubt me, and he knew me better than anyone. I could see the fear and confusion in his eyes every time I shared another nightmarish vision of the most attractive girl at school. He was terrified of what might happen if I didn't get a hold of these visions. It was only a matter of time before I started to lose myself and would be unable to tell what was real any longer. The knowledge of my sickness and his inaction would be a burden too heavy for anyone and could scar him for life.

I understood the magnitude of sharing my deepening madness with him, but he was my best friend—someone I trusted with almost everything, and he trusted me with the same. I quickly glanced around my bedroom, trying to make sure I was back in the real world and not still trapped inside my mind. I decided to divert my thoughts toward my upcoming birthday next week and away from my nightmarish visions.

For my seventeenth birthday, my mom promised me a car. I already had my license in preparation for my upgrade in mobility. She wouldn't tell me what make or model car I would get, but she assured me it would be brand-new. I was expecting something like a Ford Focus or a Chevy Malibu. Both cars are nice but not what I really wanted. My dream car was the 2010 Chevy Camaro. It had to be the most beautiful car on the road to me. When I first laid eyes on it in those Transformers movies, it was love at first sight. But the canary yellow was not my style; it was much too bright for my taste. I wanted a black and red beast of a Camaro, with matching black and red rims and a banging sound system. The SS model with a ground effects kit. I could just picture myself in that car rolling like a badass! The looks I would get driving to school in that car would be priceless. The roar of the engine turning heads as I pulled into the student parking lot, the smiles from the girls while they secretly plotted a reason to ask me for a ride home. YES! What a dream!

But it was only a dream. I strategically placed a picture of the exact model and color of the Camaro on my PC as a desktop wallpaper. From time to time when my mom would come into my room, I would say, "Hey, Mom, isn't this the most beautiful machine you've ever seen?" She would answer sarcastically,

"Yes, it is, and you can have that exact beautiful machine in your own driveway when you get a job and your own home."

Judging by the same response again and again, there was a very slim chance that my dream would become a reality.

Don't get me wrong; I was grateful for a brand-new car. No more bus rides and my weekends would be much more interesting now that I would no longer be confined to Deerfield. So, I was really looking forward to my birthday. Plus, the party that Tony's cousin was throwing for me at his club was going to be "off the hook," with VIP treatment and all the trimmings. I was planning on sneaking a drink or two in, but with my current mental state, I was reconsidering that. But I still planned on having a great time on my birthday, nonetheless. Well, that's if I make it to my birthday alive and free, because at the rate I was going, I may find myself behind bars or worse.

It's strange how we remember the events that change us or our perspective on life and the world around us, but we often forget the things we do that affect others. I remember my first kiss, my first R-rated movie, my first so-called girlfriend, and the first time I won a tournament. But I don't remember the first time I hurt my mom, the first time I insulted Sarah or the first person I was rude to. I don't remember any of those things. I guess each of us lives on our own secluded island in life. We are our castaways, and the only rain we see is the rain that drenches us directly. We never see the hurricane on the other island at the same time it's storming in our lives.

Nor do we care to see it. Back then, my life was one-dimensional; I saw things with my own eyes. Had I seen things differently, I would not have involved Tony in my mental troubles because his burden of silence was changing his life and would start events to unfold that would spiral out of control over the years to come. But again, I only saw my island being bombarded by a hurricane, and I needed help. I didn't think that by inviting him to my island, I was also inviting danger on his island as well. How selfish of me to assume he could and wanted to be involved in my descent into madness.

CHAPTER EIGHT
TRYOUTS

onday moved at a pace that made watching paint dry feel like a big-budget action movie. Each minute seemed like an hour, and an hour seemed like a week. I was extremely excited about the tryouts, and I couldn't hide it. Sarah teased me all morning, calling me a virgin schoolgirl on her way to the prom with the most popular boy in school. Yeah, she was trying to spoil my excitement, but I wasn't going to let her ruin my day. The more I thought about it, the more shocking it was to me how much I wanted to make the team. Aiden, the one who always believed that conforming to the popular crowd was worse than death, was now wanting the new experience and the limelight that came with making the team.

Finally! The bell rang, school was out, and it was time to head over for tryouts. When I got over to the field, Sarah and Tony were already waiting for me. As I walked on the field, some of the team began heckling the hopefuls. There clearly were some shockers on the field that year, myself included. People you wouldn't dream would try out, and they didn't hide their surprise.

"Wait! Is that Aiden, the same Aiden who broke down your big brother?" one of the teammates teased Brian, the starting quarterback, whose big brother and I had a previous physical confrontation.

"Yes, the same," he responded, gritting his teeth and trying to hold back the anger he felt seeing me on his field.

"Dude, that's just wrong!" one of them continued to tease.

"Okay, enough!" Brian demanded. "Let's just watch, I don't want to hear anything else about my brother!"

"Okay, cool, but do you think he wants to kick your ass, too? Maybe make it a family tradition? I mean like a generational ass-kicking. A rite of passage, if you will. You are not one of us until Aiden beats that ass!" Everyone besides Brian began wailing with laughter.

"I said enough!"

"No, you said nothing about your big bro dude, I'm talking about you now!"

"You know what? Keep it up, Stephan."

"Or what?" he interrupted. "You'll kick my ass?"

"Maybe worse," Brian responded.

Stephan, the team's resident clown, was always saying something or doing something to try to be funny. He always seemed to find the right opportunity to hone his comedic skills, so my presence on the field gave him all the material he needed. Most of the time, he was really funny, and he was also one hell of a linebacker. Often compared to some of the best linebackers in the professional leagues for his speed and strength, Stephan used it as motivation to excel on the field. He was a sophomore like I was, so if I made the team, we would be playing together for the last years of high school, which made me extremely happy to have such a talented linebacker leading our defense.

"If there's an ass you want to be kicked, go over to Aiden…I'm sure he can give you what you want. Just don't be surprised that it's your ass getting kicked in," Stephan joked.

"Kicked in like a police bust," added another teammate.

"Oh wow, it's Comedy Central at Deerfield High," scoffed Brian.

"Okay, quiet down," demanded Coach Towers.

Coach began to explain the process of making the team. There would be three stages. The first stage would be physical, to see if we were physically able to handle the rigorous and demanding sport of football. The second would be football talent per position. The third would test your IQ for the game. Depending on one's performance, you could fail, make the team, or even become a walk-on starter. Very few make the team, and someone rarely becomes an immediate starter. But I was optimistic, being how sorry the current person was in the position I was gunning for. The physical trials were simple for me. Running, speed, response, strength, and endurance—all of which I had in abundance. But I already knew this first part would be a breeze for me. It was the last part that worried me. It's one thing to play around the neighborhood, but it's totally different when it's structured and judged by someone who knows the game, and Coach Towers knew the game of football.

He played in the NFL for about ten years as a star running back before an injury cut a great career short. He was hard but fair, and he didn't accept mediocrity. If you were lazy and unfocused, he wouldn't even consider you for the water boy. I could tell I did great by the coach's look of excitement and Brian's look of utter disgust at my physical abilities. He should be happy I wasn't gunning for his spot.

Over the next few days, I maintained my focus on the task at hand: getting that starting position at running back. The second phase of the tryouts went by with ease as well. According to Tony's sources, I was ahead in every category and well on my way to getting that coveted starting position. Tony made sure word got around about my performance and standings during the team's tryouts. It was a major surprise to most because I wasn't known for sports. I was known for my looks, academic achievements, and being Tony's friend.

My status seemed to change overnight. I started getting a lot more attention and flirtatious looks from the girls who never paid me any attention before. I didn't even have to be around Tony anymore to get attention. It was a serious jolt to my confidence level. I became so confident about the final phase of tryouts that I started picking my jersey number. Even Sarah started coming around to the idea of me playing football. Sarah had already made the soccer team and took the starting striker position from the girl who tried to get Tony's number on the first day of school. I knew that was her intention once she found out that same girl played on the soccer team and plotted her way into the starting position. That poor girl had no idea who she crossed that day; I bet she knows now.

The day of the final phase of tryouts turned out to be the gloomiest day of the week. The gray skies seemed to loom closer to the ground, creating a depressing and claustrophobic atmosphere around the school. No one, and I mean no one, was looking forward to being out in that weather, but Coach wasn't about to postpone the final day of tryouts. Next week was our first game against Highland Park, and he wanted all positions filled. Surprisingly, the day moved along swiftly, and before I knew it, I was walking towards the field, preparing to take my place on the team. My confidence was at an all-time high; I just knew I had this in the bag. Coach planned to run some plays but allow things to be very one-sided. Only three linemen blocking for a running back but more defensive linemen to stop that running back. Fewer options for a quarterback to throw to but more defensive players to interfere with the quarterback's throwing lanes. The offensive line having more players than normal to stop a linebacker and a slew of other uneven scenarios. His purpose was to see us perform under extreme pressure and against huge odds.

He started with the defense, so I had time to sit on the sidelines and prepare myself. I was relaxed, confident, and ready for whatever Coach threw at me. The victory was mine. But then things took a turn for the worse. I started to feel a familiar feeling of fear, and at that moment I knew she was there! Every muscle and bone in my body began to ache. It got so bad I could barely hold onto my helmet or keep my arms from hanging down like the limp branches of a sleepy hollow tree.

Tony immediately ran over to me, "Dude!"

"Yeah, I know, she's here…"

"How the hell do you know that?" Tony asked while taking a step back.

"I can feel her."

"Wow! Just wow! Man, Aiden, you are really scaring me now. You feel her? Wait, dude, you don't look so good. Maybe you shouldn't go out there just yet."

"No, I'm here already, and I won't let this beat me."

CHAPTER NINE
BLITZ

oach blew his whistle, signaling for the offense to take the field. As I stood up, the entire field began to spin, and everywhere the field turned she was there, smiling with that evil look in her eyes. I started to feel my stomach convulse and vibrate, readying itself to expel my lunch all over the turf. Every step toward the line of scrimmage became more difficult. I felt like I had the weight of a car planted firmly on my shoulders. I started sweating uncontrollably, and my stomach flipped like it was in the Olympics, trying out for the gold in gymnastics. As I got into position, the field became as dark as the abyss of hell. I began to feel exposed and cold like everyone could see right through me. And then the field and everyone on it vanished except the darkness and Jasmine.

In the darkness, I could hear the faraway screams of terror and torment as I spun around trying to pinpoint where the sound was coming from. But it seemed the screams were coming from all around me. Through the screams, I could hear the faint sound of the quarterback giving the snap count. I strained my eyes through the darkness, trying to see where I was, but I couldn't see my hands when I placed them right in front of my face. I slowly started to fall deeper into a trance as the madness of the abyss started to consume me. Then all at once, everything came back—the field, the players, and...Oh shit!

The entire defensive line was right in front of me, running on a blitz. The sudden contact sent me flying back at least six feet. I'd never been hit that hard, and it felt like I'd just had two years of my life knocked right out of me. The pain was so intense I didn't even notice my helmet was no longer on my head. All I felt was the pain my entire body was going through. I could hear Coach blow his whistle and then yell, "Run it again! Aiden, wake up and get in the game, son, and focus!" Brian and his buddies were smiling now, pleased at the sight of me getting slammed. I slowly rose to my feet, nodding my head and inhaling deeply, trying to regain my composure. If only I had the power to do so.

There I was again, behind the line of scrimmage, behind Brian, and at the mercy of Jasmine. The nightmare came looming back at me as soon as the snap count began. It felt like Jasmine had a remote and kept hitting rewind repeatedly but adding more horrific images and sounds each go-round. By the time the tryouts were over, I had accumulated a whopping negative 135 yards rushing. The single worst tryout rushing numbers in school history, maybe even in state history. There was a look of utter confusion on Coach's face and a look of complete delight on Brian's. I began walking over to the bench to sit down, but before I could get there, I fell to my knees and started gagging uncontrollably. Tony and Sarah immediately ran to my aid. My chest was burning, like a fire was being lit inside my lungs. I couldn't breathe as the burning began moving up my chest towards my throat. The further up it moved, the hotter and more painful it became. At this point, my oxygen was completely cut off, and I started vomiting a black tar-like substance that seemed to burn the grass as it touched it. The taste was like pure abomination, and I looked up to see if Jasmine was still in the bleachers. By that time, she was slowly making her way off the field, never looking at me as she left. She had a rage-inspiring arrogance to her stride as she walked out of the fence towards the school's parking lot.

The further she got away from me, the better I began to feel. When I finally came to myself and was able to focus, I found myself surrounded by the entire team. The coach was kneeling next to me with his hand on my shoulder, looking over me for any injuries I may have acquired after the total smashing the defense put on me.

"Aiden, are you okay, son?"

I lied and told him I was okay. It hurt like hell trying to speak, but I had to muster up whatever dignity I had left because, at that moment, I felt lower than mold growing on crap.

I slowly stood up and made my way off the field. I didn't want to face the rest of the team in the locker room and hear all the jeers and dumb comments, so I decided to go straight home. I was so confident, so sure I would get that starting spot on the roster. This defeat was very hard to stomach because I knew I wasn't getting that starting position, let alone making the team. I tanked and tanked badly. Sarah looked at me with a concern I'd never seen from her; I was expecting her to take advantage of this to ride my nerves all the way home, punch line after punch line. But oddly, she didn't. She told me how proud she was of me trying to become more active in life and she was really looking forward to me doing more.

"Don't let this stop you, Aiden," she consoled. "It's just one bump in the road. Plus, you never know, you might still make the team."

I kept quiet; the embarrassment I felt demanded that I kept my mouth shut. I wasn't sure if I would make the team or how this would affect the newfound popularity that I had come to slightly enjoy. Who was I kidding? It felt awesome to be even slightly popular. With such a devastating failure, I began to question my ability to even do the simplest tasks without tripping out.

I began to even question my physical health after coughing up that black tar. It felt like it was poisoning and weakening my body while it was inside me. I wasn't sure if it was all gone, but the burning was still there. I was unsure about so many things besides one: Jasmine was a threat to me, and I was afraid of her. I was terrified because I didn't know who or what she was, and whatever she was doing to me, I didn't have the power to fight back. I was at her mercy, and I hated her for it.

There I was, retreating home with my tail between my legs, afraid to face the backlash of my failure to make the team. I just knew I had it, and I began to understand that Jasmine's intentions were to ruin me, maybe even kill me. I had a feeling her arrival right before I took to the field wasn't a coincidence. She was toying with me. How else could you explain that condescending smirk? How she always seemed to show up at the worst times and leave right before I completely lost it.

Tony and I just sat in my room, staring at the wall. Both of us were dazed and confused, not knowing how to discuss the events on the field and my chances, if any, of making the team. Eventually, Tony sighed and looked at me.

"Okay, dude, I'm not gonna just sit here in your room and say nothing. I gotta say something. So what happened out there?"

I wasn't sure I wanted to bring Tony deeper into my madness with Jasmine. But he was already halfway down the rabbit hole, so I decided to pull him the rest of the way. After I described everything I experienced on the field and my suspicions that Jasmine was the reason for it all, Tony sat there looking at me with his eyebrows raised as far as they could go and his mouth half open. He just stared at me like that for about thirty seconds.

"Wait, let me get this straight," Tony said with an uncomfortable chuckle. "You're telling me that every time she comes around you, she sends you to some kind of waking nightmare, and the reason why you choked out there today was because of her? Aaaand she's doing it on purpose? So now she's the threat? I thought before you were afraid of what you might do to her, but now you are telling me you are afraid of what she might do to you?"

"Yes!" I replied with the last bit of confidence I had left on reserve.

"Aiden, you are my boy, and I love you like a brother, but I can't cosign on this madness, bro."

"Tony, you didn't see my reaction on the field?"

"Yes, I did, and it looked like you froze up, got sick or something. Let's be honest, it looked like you couldn't handle the pressure out there. That's what I saw, that's what Coach Towers saw, and if we asked everyone else out there, that's what they'll say they saw. No dark abyss or little demons running in the dark on the field in broad daylight, dude!"

"Really, so explain to me the black stuff I was coughing up on the field."

"Huh? Okay, now I am sitting here having a WTF moment with you, Aiden. I didn't see any black stuff come out your mouth. You were acting like you were hacking up some nasty stuff, but nothing was coming up, dude. Not even spit!"

"What are you talking about? I argued. "I was throwing up this hot black stuff, and when it fell on the ground, it seemed to burn it like acid. It felt like it was burning and poisoning me."

"Sorry, dude, we may have been watching the same TV, but we were both on different channels on that field today," Tony sarcastically responded.

"How did she—"

"Okay, stop it! Stop it now!" Tony demanded. His confusion had turned to terror watching me try and rationalize my delusions.

"You have to listen to yourself. At first, you were afraid of these crazy ass visions you were having, now you are talking like she's doing it on purpose."

"She is! Not just to me either, but to everything and everyone!"

"Oh really, so now she's the anti-Christ?"

"No, but maybe she's some kind of witch or something."

"Right, Aiden, and she lives in a gingerbread house."

"Don't tease me, Tony!" I warned.

"I'm not teasing you; I'm trying to show you how crazy all this sounds. What do we know? First, that Jasmine is by far the most beautiful girl either of us has ever seen. Second, you are physically attracted and repulsed by her. I still can't wrap my head around the repulsed part, but to each his own. Third, her presence sends you into a weird dark nightmare that causes you to lose your grip on reality. And finally, you are becoming mentally unstable around a girl you want but may feel is out of your league, so instead of pursuing her like normal boys do, you created this entire delusion of her being evil just for being so beautiful and unobtainable."

"But—"

"No buts, Aiden. Just think about what I am saying to you."

Even though I hated to admit it, Tony had a point. But I've never heard of this kind of severe reaction.

"So you think I should talk to her?"

"Hell no!" Tony screamed. "You stay away from her, as far as possible until we figure this thing out. Aiden, you may need to speak to a professional if this continues and gets worse. I don't want anything to happen to you or her."

"Tony, I'm confused. It seemed so real!"

Tony let out a huge sigh and buried his head in his hands. This was taking a toll on him and our friendship, and I couldn't have that. So I decided to play along, but I wasn't fully convinced of Tony's logic.

"Maybe you are right," I said. "Maybe it's the stress of the new school year and all the changes."

"And the fact your mom has a new boyfriend too!" Tony teased while waving his hands in front of his face as if he was too hot and needed to cool off.

"Oh, don't get me started with that. I'd rather have violent intentions towards him."

We both laughed at my last comment, and the mood suddenly lightened up a bit in the room. I began to feel a little better seeing Tony was still comfortable enough around me to relax and have a good laugh.

"Oh yeah, your mom is getting her groove back, right?"

"You mutha—"

"What's his name?" Tony asked, interrupting me from finishing my curse.

"Jason."

"Jason?"

"Yeah, Jason."

"Does he come with a hockey mask and machete?"

"Asshole!"

Tony started laughing while watching me squirm at the very thought of Jason being a murderous, invincible demon in a hockey mask dating my mom.

"Okay, so why did you even lead your mom to believe that you were cool with it when clearly you're not?"

"Because I want her to be happy. My mom has been single for too long, and she seems to really like this guy...so..."

"Oh, I see. I gotta give respect, dude. Sacrificing for your mom...that's love right there. But wait, bro...how are you going to deal with him being around?"

"I don't know, but I will be giving him a hard time for a while to see if he's real. Then I'll lighten up on him a bit. Just as long as he doesn't try to replace my dad, I'm cool."

"Yeah, I hate that shit too. My mom dated this one clown a couple of years back who tried that crap."

"Yeah, I remember him, Reginald or something, right?"

"No fool, it was Greg."

Tony wasn't happy about me calling Greg "Reginald." Reginald was an ugly name, and Greg was just as ugly as the name Reginald, and I teased Tony constantly back then because I felt that Greg was so ugly his looks didn't match his name. He should have been named Reginald instead of Greg, and because Greg's parents didn't have the guts to do it, I volunteered my services. After the comment Tony just made about Jason and the hockey mask, it was only right I returned the favor. Payback is a bitch.

"But yeah, that fool, he tried to pull a Cosby Show at our house. Man, I had to get him straight. He didn't like that and tried to be on some 'I'm going to discipline you' shit and actually went and got a belt to hit me with it."

"Oh no!"

"Hell yeah... So after he woke up in the hospital to the beeping of the life-support machine..."

We both burst out in laughter that lasted well over a minute.

"Oh man, dude, you are crazy," I said, wiping the tears from my eyes. "So I take it didn't work out between your mom and Reggie."

"Punk!" Tony protested.

"Sorry, I meant Greg. But he did look like a Reginald."

We both fell over laughing again. It was moments like these that made it clear to me why Tony was my best friend and how valuable our relationship was to me. To be able to share a horrifying revelation one moment and then laugh uncontrollably the next was priceless. Our friendship was a rare one, and we both knew it.

CHAPTER TEN
HAPPY BIRTHDAY TO ME

My birthday rolled around before I knew it. I was finally seventeen! My mom had told me that after the age of fifteen, each year starts to feel very different, and she was right. I felt that things were going to change drastically from then on. I couldn't figure out if it would be for better or worse, but what I realized was that change wasn't coming; it was here. My birthday was also the day that I would find out if I made the team. I wasn't getting my hopes up after my performance in the final phase of tryouts. I still wasn't completely convinced that everything that happened that day was strictly in my mind, but I wasn't going to let Tony in on it. I'd involved him enough, and I didn't want to destroy our friendship, so I kept my doubts to myself. I didn't like keeping it from him, but I felt it was necessary at this point. So, I would just smile and behave as if everything was fine. But I was going to get the truth about Jasmine and her family because something just wasn't right about her.

The time had come, and more than half the school was standing outside the coach's office, waiting for him to post that year's roster for the football team. I didn't plan on showing my face over there. No one said anything to me about my performance in the last phase of the tryouts, but I could only imagine what they were thinking and what would be said once the list surfaced with my name absent from it. I decided, while everyone was occupied at the coach's office door, to head over to the library and pretend to be in deep study. Truth is, I was researching psychological profiles of serial killers. There were some very disturbing yet similar things in these books, and I discovered my condition wasn't rare or unheard of. Some of the most notorious serial killers believed their victims were a threat to them. They believed they were demons, witches, or possessed by some evil force, and by killing them in a ritualistic fashion, they were releasing the tormented souls of the possessed.

Experts really had no solid clues as to what triggered these dark fantasies. Some theories were troubled childhoods riddled with mental and physical abuse, but that didn't apply to all serial killers. The more I read, the more terrified I became. It was like I was reading how my life would turn out if I continued down the path I was headed. I became paranoid and started feeling like everyone in the library was watching me, and they were aware of what I was reading and, more disturbingly, why. I became anxious and unsettled as it became harder to focus on what I was reading. It got so bad I decided to put the books back and Google whatever else I needed in the privacy of my room. As I began to pack up the books, I noticed the area where I needed to put them back had suddenly gotten crowded with students looking for books.

It seemed like they were all just innocently looking for books, but I felt like they were waiting to see what I'd been reading. Once my secret was discovered, they would put the word out that Aiden was losing his mind and was trying to hide it. It seemed the longer I waited for the area to clear out, the more the traffic grew. I had to put the books back because leaving them was even worse. So I began to think up all kinds of excuses to explain why I was reading these kinds of books if anyone inquired or gave me any strange looks. The best one I came up with was research on Ted Bundy because of a special project I was given for the National Honor Society, of which I'd been a member for as long as I could remember. Everyone knew the N.H.S. always gave its members special projects and assignments, so it wouldn't be so far-fetched. Yeah, I think that would work. After sitting there convincing myself that the Ted Bundy story would fly, I mustered up enough nerve to make my move, but they were still watching me.

Nosey bastards! I should carve out their eyes and wear them as a necklace to warn others to stay out of my damned business.

Wait! What is wrong with me? That thought just popped into my head along with an image of myself wearing an eyeball chain, marching through the school's hallways. I was shocked that I felt no remorse or any hesitation that what I was thinking was wrong. Tony may be right; I may need to see a professional. They may be able to stop me and correct my mental breakdown before I lose all sense of reality.

Being that in a few minutes I would be the laughingstock of the school due to my major failure at getting on the football team, I thought a few months away from here would be fine by me. I'd rather sit on a shrink's couch than listen to the students talk about my choke session on the field. I knew if I told my mom everything, she would take me out of school and as far away from Jasmine as possible. Hey, she may even send me to live with my grandparents in Spain. Suddenly, coming clean didn't seem all that bad. At least with a head start, the doctors could help me. As I stood up with the books in my hands, I looked up to see Sarah and Tony standing in the library's doorway. Seeing both of them there startled me, and the books slipped from my grasp and fell to the floor. The sound they made seemed louder than gunfire, which was very strange because the library's floor was covered with carpet.

Then I swear to God, the books started yelling.

"He's a serial killer, look at what he's reading! Don't believe the Ted Bundy story! Look at us! Look at his books!" Louder and louder they screamed as they taunted me.

"Shut up!"

Before I knew it, I was stomping on the books as they began to laugh, saying, "Told you he's crazy, look at him assaulting and yelling at books!"

"Shut up!" I yelled at the top of my lungs.

"No, you shut up and fess up!" they continued to taunt.

At this point, I was in a rage, and someone had to pay. I reached down with plans to throw each book through the library's windows. Suddenly I felt Tony firmly grab my arm.

"Dude, what the hell?! Snap out of it, let's go!"

"Where?"

"To see if you made the team."

"No, I don't want to."

"So, you wanna stay here?" Tony asked while drawing my attention to everyone looking at me with fear and disgust.

"Oh. Point well made, let's go."

"Put those books back first."

I could see Tony glance at the titles of each book and then look at me with that worried look he gave me when I told him I felt Jasmine was a threat. I wanted to explain, but he stopped me and rushed me out of the library.

It took a lot of pushing and shoving to get near the board outside the coach's office. The energy in the hallway was explosive. I began to feel elevated and in good spirits. The excitement in the air was electric and powerful. I felt like I could touch the excitement, even taste it. I was alert and hyped like I just drank a gallon of sunshine and Red Bull. A smile formed across my face as I started to feel at peace and in control. After experiencing so much disappointment and fear over the last week, I didn't want this feeling to end. It was euphoric and personal. I felt directly connected to everyone in the hallway, like we all were one organism with one goal. Tony looked at me and started laughing.

"Dude, you look like you just got some."

"Some what?"

And then Tony gave me "the look"; it was the look he used every time he was referring to sex. It was the head tilting to the right and a look of mischief and confidence.

"Oh, whatever, I just feel great!"

"I'm glad you are better because that scene in the library has landed on my 'weirdest shit list.'"

"I know, but I'm good now."

And it was true. I was good, actually better than good. I felt like a brand-new car rolling off the assembly line, and not just any car, a Ferrari. I felt beyond any harm or fear, like a newborn in the arms of its mother after being pulled out of the darkness of the womb and into the light of this world.

As the excitement continued to build, so did my reaction. Again, I found myself bombarded with feelings of invincibility and endless possibilities at my fingertips. I felt like the world was my oyster, and I was ready to crack it open. I surprisingly found myself feeling more optimistic about making the football team. This godlike feeling that was moving through me was a welcome change from the shame and inadequacy I was used to feeling. Then the door to the coach's office opened, and Mr. Towers slowly walked out with the list in hand. The loud hall immediately fell silent, but the energy was still there. Everyone seemed to be holding their breath in anticipation of the contents on that list in Coach's hand. As he does every year, he stands there saying nothing, looking over the restless crowd, then he smiles and turns to pin up the list on the board. Then, without saying a word, he walks back into his office.

As soon as his door closed, the crowd rushed towards the board. As the crowd glanced over the list, you could hear above all the noise and chatter, yells of triumph followed by congratulations, and grunts of defeat followed by taunting and the occasional "better luck next year." When I looked, I noticed Sarah was already at the board looking for my name. Tony was standing next to me, waiting for the bad news. Sarah quickly turned to face me with gleaming eyes and the widest smile I'd ever seen on her face.

"No? No!" I yelled.

She nodded her head, yes. "Aiden, you made it!"

"Oh my God, no way!" I yelled and ran towards the board.

"You're not a starter, but you're second string, which is a miracle all in itself seeing how you performed the other day," Sarah teased.

I didn't care, I made it; I was a Deerfield High Warrior! My excitement was on full tilt, and I just stood there smiling. The Warriors were in their best shape in years, and a lot of sports analysts labeled the Warriors the team to watch.

Happy birthday to me!

Nothing mattered but that moment. Before I knew it, the three of us were pumping our fists in the air yelling "what!" until everyone in the hallway started to yell along. It was one of those moments you carry with you throughout your life. When you feel like a failure and nothing seems to go your way, you will remember moments like these. These moments inspire miracles in all of us. They make the impossible seem possible. Remembering moments of success and victory when failure seemed the only option makes that loser reach for his place among the winners. This was our moment, and we celebrated with all our hearts.

CHAPTER ELEVEN
JASON

The day went by fast after the roster reveal, and soon we were walking home, talking about all the "what ifs" and what I should expect this coming season with the Warriors.

"So how does it feel to be a Warrior?"

"It feels great, man, it really does. Hopefully I can get some playing time and show the coach my worth."

"Tony?"

"Yes, Sarah," Tony sighed, answering with stress in his voice for fear of the question he would have to answer.

"Why don't you play sports?"

"I do, it's called pimping, and only champions need apply."

"Uhh! Tony, sometimes you can be such an infant," she complained.

"Hey, you asked."

"I'm sorry I did now!"

"Good! Next time you'll stay out my business!"

"Good luck with that," I laughed.

Sarah rolled her eyes and walked ahead of us.

"Now Aiden, what was that in the library?"

"Dude, don't ask, let's just leave that alone for now."

"You're right, bro, my bad. Let's bask in your victory and look forward to tonight's festivities."

"Is everything in order?"

"Dude, my cousin's gonna have the whole club clicking. VIP treatment all the way. But the big thing is will your mom come through with the ride?"

"She'll come through."

"You sure? It's a recession, you know."

"Tony, you of all people should know my family isn't hurting for money."

"True, true. Dude, it's gonna be off the hook tonight!"

"Yes, sir." I agreed.

"Happy Birthday again, brother."

"Thanks, man!"

As we approached our house, I saw another vehicle in the driveway, which I figured was Jason's. I inhaled deeply, preparing myself for this meet and greet. I could tell Sarah wasn't all that enthused about meeting him either. Jason's car was a beautiful black-on-black 2009 Bentley coupe convertible. The license plate read "SHDW 36." Even though I didn't want to give props where they were due, the license plate name was dead-on for the kind of vehicle it was attached to. From his car, I could tell Jason had taste and money and had no reservations in showing them both off. So at least my mom didn't land a leech.

"OOOO WEE!" Tony yelled, admiring Jason's Bentley while doing a silly dance next to the driver's side door.

"Aiden, you have to admit the dude has got great taste in cars; those black 22s are banging!"

I quickly glanced over the car. It *was* badass, I nodded in agreement.

"Wait! You know most of the time dudes with cars like this are butt-ugly. I mean, can you imagine your mom dating a white Flavor Flav?"

Sarah was standing next to Tony, admiring Jason's car. When she heard the Flavor Flav comment, she immediately punched him in his shoulder.

"Ouch!"

"Hurt, didn't it? So did that comment," she complained.

"My bad! I'm just saying let's hope he looks as good as his car."

"Dude, stop!" I warned.

"Stop? Remember Reginald? Yeah, playa, payback's a bitch in a badass car."

Sometimes Tony could be such a dick.

"Well, I'm heading home. See you in a minute."

"Aw, hell naw! You are coming in too, Tony," I demanded. "Clearly, Jason is rich, and rich people aren't always the most tolerable, so walking a black dude in might throw him off his game."

"Oh, so I'm the bait?"

"Yep, that's you. If he doesn't like black people, he's gotta go," Sarah advised.

"I agree…hmm. You know what, you're right. Let's see what's up with Mr. Bentley," agreed Tony.

When we walked through the door, we were greeted by possibly the most handsome older man I have seen outside of a movie. He possessed a regal yet inviting aura. My defenses immediately lowered, and I found myself pleasantly surprised to be smiling at him. Sarah's eyes were sparkling with admiration, and Tony was equally impressed. He greeted us all warmly and by name. His voice was deep and penetrating yet possessed a gentleness in it that seemed to massage all the apprehension from inside of us. I felt like I could immediately trust him with my life.

Was I under a spell?

Sarah and I agreed to give this guy a hard time for at least ninety days. It was rare that we agreed on anything, and this was one of those occasions. But there we both were, totally forgetting our pact. He seemed perfect, not too perfect, but everything I would want in a father figure physically. No one wants a beautiful mother and an ugly father or father figure in their lives. Again, impressions are important to most, but to a teenager, it's everything.

So, for your single mother to find a very attractive man to date is a win on many levels. He was about six foot two, tanned, with a well-groomed haircut. He had some gray sprinkled here and there, but it added to his appeal. Blue eyes, and from his accent, he sounded like he was Greek or maybe from somewhere else around the Mediterranean. I could see my mom looking on with a huge smile on her face, watching our warm exchange with Jason.

"I've been anxiously waiting to meet you," Jason revealed. "All of you. I'm so happy to finally get this chance. Thank you, Aiden, for allowing me to share this special day with your family."

"You are welcome," I answered.

"So, Aiden, did you make the team?" Jason asked.

"Yes, I did," I answered with complete surprise.

"Your mom told me about you trying out for the team. I've never played any sports when I was your age. Always wanted to but never got the opportunity. In my village in Greece, we didn't have much time to play sports…"

Gotcha! I knew it, I thought.

"But I love sports, and I try to go to as many games as my time allows. Congratulations again on making the team. I've heard the Warriors have a real chance of winning the state championship this year."

"Yes, I've heard that too."

"Well, with you on the team, I'm certain their chances just got better."

"That is a beautiful car you have out there," Tony interjected.

"Ah yes, the Bentley. Thank you, Tony."

"So, Aiden," my mom interrupted. "I guess it's time, huh?"

A huge smile grew on my face. Yes! I could barely contain my excitement.

"You've kept your end of the bargain and even exceeded my expectations with your academics. So, since you went that extra mile, I did too. Let's all go to the garage."

We sprinted towards the door leading into the garage from the kitchen. As I opened the door, I got a glimpse of something I needed to wipe my eyes to believe. I nearly fainted when the garage door opened, revealing a most beautiful sight. There it was in all its splendor, the car of my dreams exactly as I dreamed it would be: the 2010 Chevy Camaro, and it was the SS model with the sickest ground effect kit on the market. The exterior was jet black with blood-red graphics. The Camaro sat on twenty-inch rear rims and custom nineteen-inch rims in the front. The rims were jet black as well with a blood-red two-inch lip.

I took a step back as tears immediately started filling my eyes. I slowly walked over to the car and opened the door. The interior was black and red leather. It came equipped with a seven-inch touch screen entertainment unit. It was perfect in every way. As I slowly sat in the driver's seat, tears kept rolling down my face. I placed my hands on the steering wheel and exhaled. This day couldn't get any better. How could it? The keys were already in the ignition; I glanced over at my mom and she nodded, giving me the

O.K. to turn the ignition. The roar of the engine filled the garage and the house. It was beautiful.

"Mom, I…I don't…thank you so much."

She walked over to the car as I got out and held me in her arms, crying as she whispered in my ear, "You're welcome. No mother could wish for a better son."

"Man, this is so emotional," Tony protested. "I can't be crying like this."

We all started laughing at Tony's silly ass.

"Thank you, Mom. This is the best birthday gift ever!"

"You're welcome, but there is one more thing," my mom said. "Look in the glove compartment. There's something else there for you."

I quickly hopped back in the car and reached over to open the glove compartment, and after a quick pull of the handle, the door swung down and out popped an envelope. Opening the envelope revealed a birthday card with a Visa gift card worth one thousand dollars.

"Oh sh…" I quickly looked at my mom, catching myself, and from the look on her face, I just sidestepped a disaster.

"Okay, be careful. Don't get grounded on your birthday, Aiden," she warned.

For several weeks prior to my birthday, I was trying to figure out what I was going to do concerning spending money for this night. I wanted to buy something new to wear and also have some money to spend at the club. I didn't want to ask my mom for any money because I was preparing to get a new car, and I knew she would be spending a lot on it, but nothing like what I was sitting in now. This was well beyond what I was expecting. Yeah, I was dreaming about this car, but realistically I wasn't expecting it.

"Mom, can we…?"

"Yes, Aiden, you can take it for a spin," my mom answered before I could get the question out fully.

"We're gonna go to the mall real quick to get some clothes for tonight."

"Okay, be careful. The insurance papers are in the glove box. Don't lose them. And do you have your license with you?"

"Yes!"

Then from behind me, I heard Sarah ask, "Can I come with?"

I was in a really good mood, so I replied she could. I was feeling too good to actually tell her no.

"Yes!" Sarah yelled and quickly hopped in the back seat. As we pulled off, we all yelled our byes and nice to meet you to Jason. I put my foot on the gas pedal slightly, and the Camaro responded like the jewel she was. The roar of her engine could be heard loud and clear down our street.

On the way to the mall, we discussed Jason and how cool he seemed. Tony expressed caution, citing it was still too soon to give him the keys to the kingdom. Tony had a point, but we all had to admit being around Jason made us feel uncannily comfortable.

CHAPTER TWELVE
AN UNFORGETTABLE NIGHT

fter a whirlwind evening of showboating and shopping, we headed home to prepare for the night's festivities. Downstairs, I could hear the laughter and playful banter of Mom, Sarah, and Jason as they played on the Wii. Their joy was infectious, and I found myself grinning as I looked in the mirror. The outfit I'd chosen fit perfectly, and I exuded confidence. That night, I felt unstoppable.

Tony called to say he was on his way. It was around 10:30 p.m., and the club was a good forty minutes away. Tony's cousin had pulled some strings to ensure we'd get the VIP treatment. My mom, although uneasy about letting us go, knew it was better to allow us than to force us to sneak. She just reminded me not to forget who I was while having a good time.

The doorbell rang. Tony had arrived, and I heard him boasting about his gaming skills as he joined the others in the media room.

I took one last look at myself, decided against popping my collar, and headed downstairs.

Jason was trouncing Tony on the Wii. "I see you got skills, Jason," I said, impressed.

"I have a little something," he replied with a grin.

"Oh, I see I'm gonna have to school you because Tony isn't a challenge," I teased.

"Oh, is that so?" Tony shot back.

"And you know this!"

My mom and Sarah were sharing a loveseat, a sight that warmed my heart. It was rare to see Sarah so affectionate, and Jason seemed to be the missing piece that completed our family puzzle.

"Mom, did he call?" I asked, hoping for a birthday message from Manny.

She shook her head no, but smiled. "Listen, I'm sure he has a good reason. Don't let it ruin your night. Have fun, baby. And behave! I don't want to bail you out of jail tonight."

"Yes!" we chorused. "Okay, we're gone! Good night, Jason."

"Good night, Aiden. Have fun. It's been a real pleasure finally meeting you all."

"Thank you!" I said, genuinely touched.

"Ah, Jason, stop sucking up," Sarah chimed in. "Come on, so I can beat you again."

"Oh, a challenge?" Jason responded with mock seriousness.

"Yep!"

"You're on."

I loved seeing Sarah this happy. Even Tony was surprised by her behavior.

"Okay, we're out."

"Happy Birthday, baby!" Mom called after me.

"Thanks, Mom."

When we arrived at the club, the security guard recognized Tony and valet parked the car. We walked straight in, no lines, no charge. Just awesome.

Inside, the energy was electric. The music, lights, and people created an intoxicating atmosphere. I felt like a kid in the world's biggest candy store. Tony's cousin, Chris, was an imposing figure who ran his club with a blend of charm and intimidation. He greeted us warmly.

"Hey, cuz!"

"What's up, Chris!"

"You see what's up! It's jumping in here tonight. What's up, birthday boy?"

"Hey, Chris! Been a long time!"

"Yeah, about three years."

"Yep. Well, tonight's your night. Let's make up for lost time." Chris gestured toward the bar and summoned four of the most beautiful women in the club.

"Ladies!"

"Hey, Chris," they said in unison.

"Listen, why don't you escort these two gentlemen over to VIP? Take real good care of them for me, okay?"

"Sure!"

"And special care of this one, it's his birthday."

"Oh really? Happy Birthday!" they chorused, kissing me on the cheek, one by one. The shock and awakening desire made my knees tremble. Tony almost fell over laughing at my reaction.

"Dude, I should've taken your picture just then," he teased, mimicking my stunned expression.

In VIP, the girls waited on us hand and foot, occasionally sitting on our laps and keeping us company. Tony ordered drinks, and I hesitated when he handed me a shot.

"Dude, you think I should?"

"Why not?"

"You know."

"Damn, Aiden, is Jasmine here? No. Okay, we are forty-five minutes away from her. Let's get it in, bruh. It's your night!"

He was right. I made the team when everything seemed lost. I got my dream car, and my mom's new boyfriend was actually a cool guy. A celebration was in order. You only live once, right?

After hours of countless drinks and dancing with stunning women, we were having the time of our lives. The DJ was killing it, and every woman looked like a supermodel. I was drunk and it felt incredible. The room's energy was intoxicating, more forbidden and sexual as the alcohol flowed. Before I knew it, I was on my back on a couch in VIP, passionately making out with one of our vixen waitresses. Her touch was electrifying, and I could hear Tony shouting, "Look at my boy getting it in!"

The room spun as we spiraled out of control. Her hands roamed under my shirt, her touch sending my nerves into a frenzy. The DJ sent a shoutout, wishing me a happy birthday, and the whole club joined in. The unified energy hit me like a truck, dizzying me with lust. I wanted more.

"Are you ready, baby?" she whispered in my ear.

I nodded, lost in her touch. I wanted her so badly, and she knew it.

"Mmm, baby. Yes…" she whispered.

Her hands moved down to my belt buckle. The music grew louder, the lights flashed faster, and I felt the energy building inside me. I looked into her eyes, filled with desire, and then—darkness.

CHAPTER THIRTEEN
THE ABYSS

Where am I?

he world was pitch-black, with rain pouring down so heavily I could barely see my hands in front of my face. Massive stone hedges surrounded me, and I was already soaked to the bone. The raindrops seemed to glow eerily, falling with force and purpose. They hit the ground silently, adding to the unsettling quiet.

A terrifying thought crossed my mind—Jasmine. Was she here? Was this another waking nightmare? But this felt different, like it had a purpose beyond fear and malice. I felt compelled to see or experience something crucial. I moved through the night and rain, trying to navigate the maze of stone structures.

What is this? Where am I? And how did I get here?

The last thing I remembered was being in the VIP section with the waitress, about to receive an exhilarating birthday gift. The deeper I moved into the maze, the more the rising waters sent me into a frenzy. I opened my mouth to call out for help, but no sound came out. The more I tried, the tighter the grip around my neck. Panic set in as my air supply was cut off, causing me to collapse to my knees. Tears filled my eyes as my chest burned with an unbearable pain. My stomach spasmed, and the same acidic black filth from tryouts exploded out of my mouth like a volcano. It spread, infecting everything it touched, growing like a living plague.

The night grew darker and thicker, a sense of hopelessness and doom suffocating the air. I broke out in a feverish sweat, desperately trying to inhale. To my surprise and relief, I succeeded, and I collapsed on my back, coughing uncontrollably. The air was hot, getting hotter as the black filth consumed everything. The confusion in my mind was nothing compared to the chaos around me.

In the distant blackness, I heard the screams of life being consumed by the filth from within me. I had to get out of there. I tried to call for help again but decided against it, not wanting to risk another bout of torture. The rain turned to black filth, covering me with a smell like raw sewage, moving along my skin as if searching for a way inside. But for some reason, it couldn't penetrate.

I felt a vibration beneath my feet, growing into a thunderous rumble. The ground began to give way, splitting and cracking like porcelain. Through the cracks, I saw a glowing light from the earth's core. The black substance poured into the earth, extinguishing the light and destroying the planet from the inside. The final glimmer of warmth vanished, and the earth trembled violently, accepting its fate.

This was it.

I wanted to believe it was a nightmare, that I would wake up on the club's VIP-room floor. But everything had been bizarre and out of whack lately. I had to think of a way to escape or accept my fate. The ground buckled, and I braced myself for the worst. I saw a protruding edge within reach, my only chance at salvation. Leaning forward, I swung my arms and prepared to jump.

One, two, three…

As I jumped, the ground disappeared beneath me into the abyss. I misjudged the distance and barely grasped the edge with my fingers. Pain shot through my hands as I struggled to support my weight. I was losing hold. In the deafening roar of a dying planet, I heard footsteps approaching.

"Please, God! Help!" I screamed.

There was no response, just the sound of footsteps. I looked up and saw the most beautiful little girl I'd ever seen. She stood above me, clearly visible in the pitch-blackness. Her long, shiny black hair and big brown eyes were mesmerizing. Her caramel-brown skin was perfect, but her eyes were filled with sorrow and pain. She cried, but no tears fell—only the same black filth that consumed everything around us.

The black plague seemed to yield to her, bowing as if it worshipped her as its goddess of destruction. I began to think that this little girl was the cause of all this devastation. How could something so innocent and beautiful be responsible for so much destruction?

I started to wonder if she was here to help me or push me into the abyss. Strangely, she looked at me as if she knew me, and her gaze was filled with pain and regret.

"Help me, please!" I begged.

She seemed oblivious to my pleas and just stared at me. Then suddenly, she broke her gaze and began weeping uncontrollably.

"I miss you so much," she cried. "I'm so sorry for all of this. I just wanted to make you proud."

"Huh? What are you talking about? I need your help! Is there anyone else that can help?"

"No," she answered, her voice suddenly changing from a sweet little girl's voice to something dark and sinister. "No one can…because you're already dead!"

Those last four words cut through me like a razor. Without warning, I lost my grip and began falling into the emptiness beneath me. I looked up at the last moment to see her put her hands over her eyes, screaming while the darkness that once worshipped her began consuming her. The agony she felt watching me fall outweighed the pain of being swallowed whole by the evil that had become the ruler of our planet. I should have been screaming, but I wasn't. I just closed my eyes and accepted my fate. It seemed like I'd been falling forever, and I could hear the earth's crust being shattered and torn to pieces by this darkness. If this was the end of the world as we knew it, I couldn't escape this fate. No one could.

Then suddenly, silence. I felt a surface beneath me and slowly opened my eyes. There was still darkness all around, but I could clearly see I was in some kind of deep ravine, and the night sky was above me, the stars gleaming like tiny diamonds. A light came from the left side of my face, and I slowly turned toward it. The image I saw sent chills through my entire body. I tried to move but couldn't; I was restrained by an unseen force. I tried to turn away from the horrific image, but I couldn't move my head. Whatever was holding me captive wanted me to see this disturbing image, and it felt like a hand was pushing my face down, preventing me from moving. Tears poured down my face as I was made to endure watching the nightmare unfold.

What my eyes beheld was an moment that has forever been burned into my memory. I didn't fully understand what I was experiencing until much later in life, but by then it was too late. I was being forced to watch my father being tortured by cloaked assailants in black. One second, they weren't there, and then the next, they would reappear, slashing and clawing at my father's flesh. They were more like shadows or a dark mist that took a form similar to the Grim Reaper. They repeatedly tortured him until he died, then brought him back to life to start over again with new and brutal ways to murder him. He screamed in agony with every cut, every broken bone, and every torturous extremity they inflicted. They enjoyed toying with his life, inflicting enormous amounts of pain on an already weak body. The last time I remember seeing my dad alive was him smiling at me on his way out to his final mission before he was killed.

That memory was my last cherished moment with him—a ray of light and a positive memory of my father. Now, these evil entities had taken that from me and replaced it with this depraved memory. I continued to struggle to break free as anger built inside me, watching my father's tormentors carry on with their task.

"Dad!" I screamed. "Dad! Daaad!"

Then everything stopped. His tormentors turned to me, staring and hissing.

"He is a danger!" they exclaimed in unison, their voices sounding like air brakes struggling to halt a semi-truck out of control. Their many voices seemed to speak in unison but in different tones. The sound was terrifying.

"He must be destroyed before it's too late." "Yes," they agreed. "Destroy the boy."

"Dad?" I whimpered.

My father looked at me and managed a smile through the extreme pain he was feeling, before saying, "Aiden, don't save me. Let me go. It's better this way."

Before I could try to make sense of my dad's request, the cloaked shadows began to screech like chalk dragged across a blackboard. The sonic pulse of their screams was so powerful I could feel my ears bleeding. Suddenly, they began flying towards me at an alarming speed. They were more menacing than I thought, possessing five-inch fangs and talons; I could only imagine the horrors they were about to inflict on me. I tried to break free but couldn't move. I could only watch as they drew closer to tear me to pieces.

"Dad!"

"Aiden!" I heard my father yell as I closed my eyes, waiting for the torture to begin. Then I heard screams, but they didn't come from me, the shadow figures, or my dad. They sounded like little girls—frightened little girls. I reluctantly opened my eyes to find myself standing in the darkness on a staircase in a strange house. I quickly tried to get my bearings.

Where am I now?

I looked at the top of the stairs and saw the glow of a light suddenly illuminate the hallway and the staircase. The girls were still screaming, and I heard a clicking sound, a sound all too familiar to me, having lived in a house with two military men with a fondness for firearms.

It was the sound of a gun, safety off, and ready to bring the pain. I heard footsteps coming towards the top of the stairs from the right. I had to get out of there fast! As I sprinted down the stairs, I noticed numerous pictures along the wall. In my panic to get out of the path of whatever firearm was going to appear at the top of the staircase, I knocked one of the pictures down. It fell right in front of me, and the image within the frame almost made my heart stop. There she was, beautiful, flawless, and smiling back at me. It was Jasmine.

I was in her house! WTF?!

How could I get from downtown Chicago to Jasmine's house without a car or even remembering how I got here? At the bottom of the stairs, I could see what appeared to be the front door. I sprinted towards it as fast as I could. God, I hoped the lock on this door didn't need a key. Unable to stop because of my forward momentum, I slammed into the front door and, what do you know, staring back at me was a lock that needed a key! The gunman was at the top of the stairs now and had a clear aim at me. I quickly shifted my weight and direction to the right before I heard the loud boom of the gun go off. The top half of the door immediately shattered. From the damage the shot caused, I knew it had to be a double-barreled shotgun.

Whoever was wielding the weapon meant business and wasn't looking to injure—they were shooting to kill. He was aiming for my head and nothing else. The screams intensified from upstairs at the sound of the shotgun going off. I ran towards what appeared to be the dining room. Behind me, I could hear my pursuer reaching the bottom of the stairs and preparing for another go at my skull. I looked to the right and saw a window, with no security bars, and the glass seemed thin enough.

As I ran on the far side of the dining room, I saw another picture of Jasmine on the wall, smiling back at me as if to say, "You're dead now!" Through the reflection of the glass on the picture, I could see the gunman aiming and readying himself for the kill shot.

Oh shit!

I shifted my body quickly to the left before another boom went off as the bullets shattered Jasmine's picture.

Ha! Smile now, bitch.

I ran as fast as I could towards the window. I could hear my pursuer's footsteps as he tried to catch up with me before I escaped. Wow, he was fast—too fast. He cleared the entire area on foot in less than five seconds. Who are these people?

I jumped towards the window and stretched my arms in front of me, closing my eyes, bracing for the impact of my body going through the glass. The sound of the breaking glass filled the air, and I could hear my pursuer swearing as I dove out the window. I quickly rolled as I hit the ground and, without missing a step, was on my feet, running away from Jasmine's house as fast as my weary and drunk legs could carry me. After running for about twenty minutes, I decided to stop and rest. I glanced at my watch; it was 2:20 a.m. Where was my car? Where was Tony? That nightmare seemed so real and vivid. How did I get all the way out here this fast? By foot, it would have taken at least eight hours. The last time I glanced at my watch at the club, it was 1:35 a.m., and I knew I had been on that couch with the waitress for at least thirty minutes. How did I get here so fast without a car? My head was pounding, and I reeked of alcohol. I could only imagine my mom's reaction when I got home, smelling like a walking bottle of vodka.

I needed to keep moving. They must have called the police, and I had no idea if anyone got a good look at me. Being out this late by myself would definitely put me on the prime suspect list with the Deerfield PD. I started heading home, taking short cuts to avoid busy streets and patrolling squad cars. I checked my pockets and found my cell, trying to call Tony. No answer. Where was he? He had to notice my absence. The confusion fueled my fear. What was I planning to do in Jasmine's house? What would have happened if I hadn't yelled out, waking everyone up? My impulses toward Jasmine were spiraling out of control. I needed help, someone besides Tony, before I did something terrible.

I was about two miles from home and beginning to relax. I heard a car coming and quickly moved towards some bushes alongside the street. If it was the cops, I was done for, my life ruined with charges of breaking and entering, among other felonies. I ducked behind the bushes, out of sight from the street. The car slowly pulled in front of my hiding place.

The car door shut, and I heard footsteps approaching. A beam of light invaded my hiding place through the bushes.

"Aiden? Dude, I know you're in there."

It was Tony. I immediately jumped up and ran towards the car.

"Hey! What happened with—"

"Tony, not now. I have to get home, now!"

Tony just stood there, watching me get into the passenger side of the car. He didn't move or flinch, confusion and concern etched on his face. He looked beyond scared.

"Dude! Come on, we got to go," I urged.

"Okay!" Tony responded, looking at the ground. He couldn't look me in my eyes anymore. Things were changing between us, and there was nothing I could do about it. But at that moment, I was only concerned with getting home without running into the cops. Tony got in the car and began driving. We both stared ahead, saying nothing. I was trying to avoid questions I had no real answers to, and Tony was afraid to ask because the answers would force him to make a hard decision. The radio was off, and the drive was depressingly slow.

"You know what? I can't do this!" Tony yelled.

"Do what?" I asked, pretending I had no clue what he was talking about.

"This! Acting like nothing is wrong. Listen, I know where you were. You were at Jasmine's house. Now I'm telling you this so you can avoid lying to your best friend. I know you're wondering how I could possibly know that, right?"

I turned and looked at Tony. He was still looking straight ahead, avoiding eye contact. Fear gripped me. How could he know? Tony was getting borderline hysterical now, ranting about how he couldn't remain quiet anymore, about how he climbed through my bedroom window while we were downstairs eating dinner and installed GPS tracking software on my cell phone. He had been tracking me since I told him about my reaction to Jasmine on the football field during tryouts. He knew every move I made since then. Once the reality of this revelation sank in, I became overwhelmed with shame. Shame turned to fear, fear transformed into anger, and anger gave birth to rage. My entire body heated up, and I began sweating profusely. Tony kept ranting about how he had no choice because he couldn't live with himself if I harmed Jasmine and he could have prevented it by acting sooner. His words were muffled by the roaring waves of rage smashing against my head.

Everything was spinning now, and my mind struggled to process what Tony had just said.

"Stop the car," I said, calmly at first, trying to hold back the obscenities dancing on the tip of my tongue. Tony was so engrossed in his rant that he didn't hear me.

"Stop the car!" I repeated, more forcefully. Still no response. By now, those obscenities were no longer dancing; they were hanging on for dear life.

"Tony! Tony! Stop the fucking car and get the fuck out!"

Those damned obscenities were now escaped convicts, and they had already done a world of hurt. Tony immediately stopped the car and looked at me like I'd lost my mind. The truth was, I'd lost my mind weeks ago.

"What did you say?!"

"Get out of my car," I demanded. "Now!"

Tony looked horrified. "Look, you left me no choice. You—"

"Get the fuck out of the car right now, Tony. I won't ask you again!"

"Ask? You call that asking? Fine, whatever, I'm out. I was only trying to help," Tony protested as he got out of the car. I quickly moved into the driver's seat.

"Aiden, hear me out. I only did it bec—"

I floored the gas pedal and raced off before he could finish his statement. As I sped off, I looked in the rearview mirror, watching his reflection disappear into the night.

CHAPTER FOURTEEN
THE HANGOVER

The sunlight hit me the next morning with a cold burn I'd never felt before. When I opened my eyes to greet the day, the events of the night before hit me harder than my throbbing hangover. Last night was a nightmare I would never forget. It was a night of firsts: being shot at, betrayed, and feeling a darkness within me that I couldn't shake. Tony's betrayal cut deep. I had trusted him with my darkest secret, and he had crossed a line by secretly tracking me. He made his choice, and now I had to make mine. I needed to cut ties with Tony until I could sort this out. If someone had told me Tony was capable of this kind of betrayal, I would have laughed in their face. But now, everything had changed, and I would have to navigate this mess without him.

I turned and looked at the clock; it was 1:15 p.m. Normally, Tony would be here, invading my room and waking me up to play a few rounds of "Halo 3" on Xbox Live before finding something to do outside later. But that day, there was no Tony, and I realized

I would have to get used to this new normal. Despite my pounding headache, I forced myself to get up and face the day. It felt like it was going to be a long, boring day, but I was wrong—very wrong.

I didn't eat anything until around 3:30 p.m., and all I could stomach was a banana. I still smelled like alcohol, so I avoided contact with my mom and Sarah. Finally, around 3:30, I decided to leave my room. My room felt like a tomb, cut off from the rest of the world without my best friend. I tried chatting on Facebook with some new fans I'd gained since making the team, but it was boring.

When I finally went downstairs, my spirits lifted. The sunshine felt good, even though my headache persisted. I was getting ready to go outside and try out some new things in the car when a huge banging sound erupted in our home. The sudden noise sent shockwaves through my body, and my headache returned in full force. The sunlight seemed to diminish, and I felt like I was back in my tomb-like room. I looked out the window to see who it was. It had better not be Tony because I had nothing to say to him. But who it was made me wish it were Tony banging on the door instead.

In front of our house were six Deerfield police cars, and four officers were standing outside our door. My heart raced, and a cold sweat covered my back. If the gunman had seen my face, they would have been here last night. Deerfield PD didn't have much to do in our secure and well-to-do township. Very little crime happened here, and a lot of times, Tony and I would see officers in their parked squad cars surfing the web on eBay or Facebook. Most of them were cool, but some were action junkies, always looking to create a movie-inspired traffic stop. They would provoke people and then crash through any opportunity to act. You could tell which breed of cop you were dealing with within three minutes of a routine traffic stop.

The banging started again, then the doorbell, then more banging. These guys were relentless. They kept ringing the bell and pounding on the door. It even sounded like they were kicking it.

"What the hell?" I heard my mom yell from upstairs. "Aiden, who's at the door?"

Somehow, in my youthful ignorance, I thought maybe, just maybe, my mom wouldn't hear the door, and the police would leave. Boy, was I wrong.

"Aiden!"

"Yes, Mom?"

The bellringing and knocking had become frantic. It seemed like they were going to take the door off the hinges.

"Who is that banging on the door like that?"

"The police, Mom," I answered.

"The police?"

"Yes!" I said, walking toward the door.

By now, my entire body was covered in sweat. My head was pounding as hard as the police banging on the door. If the gunman didn't turn me in, who did? Then a thought crossed my mind that made my anger explode. Tony; he had finally struck the killer blow. The police were here to take me in. I was terrified at what awaited me outside that door, but this was inescapable. Time to face the music. My hand was reaching for the door handle when the phone began ringing. My mom was now coming downstairs.

"Aiden, you get the phone. I'll get the door."

"But, Mom, I'm right here."

"No, I'll deal with the police, and you answer the phone."

I didn't want to get my mom involved. I wanted to open the door, extend my hands, and let them slap on the cuffs and carry me away. Hopefully, my mom would be on the phone while I was taken away. That was my plan, and, yeah, I was only seventeen then, so don't expect me to have many common-sense moments.

"Mom, I can get the door and—"

"Aiden, you've been down here the entire time, and you haven't gotten the door yet. So I'll get it, and you get the—"

At that moment, the phone stopped ringing.

"You see, Mom, I can get the door now."

Then my cell phone started ringing. I looked at the display, and it was the coach.

"Who is it?" my mom asked.

"My coach."

"Well, son, answer your phone, and I'll get the door. Now go in the kitchen and take the call."

"Mom…"

"Now!" I could see any more protesting would be met with a strict punishment. So I decided to yield and do as I was told.

"Hello?"

"Aiden?"

"Yes, Coach, it's me."

"Thank God! We have a serious situation."

My heart dropped. A serious situation? Did everyone know now, and I was being kicked off the team? Damn Tony. He's going to get what's coming to him. And to think I considered him my best friend and trusted him with my dark secret. Needless to say, my second day as a seventeen-year-old wasn't going too well.

"What's going on, Coach?" I asked, bracing myself for the bad news. I could hear my mom unlocking the door and swinging it open.

"Ma'am! Didn't you hear us at your door?" scolded the cop. "Why didn't you answer sooner?"

His tone was very rude, and he was yelling at my mom in anger. This must have been his first time meeting her because if he knew her like I knew her, he would have watched his tone and conduct.

"Wait a minute! You are at my house…Officer Rude Ass! You are banging on my door, ringing my doorbell like you have no home training or respect. And then when I open the door, you are yelling at me? Do you have any warrants or national homeland security issues with my residence?"

"No, ma'am, but…"

"But my ass! Don't you ever come to my house again in this manner. I have children here, and you are making them uncomfortable, and unless your name is on the deed of this house and on their birth certificates, you have no right to make them feel that way! Now you can either apologize, correct your tone, or leave my property right now. Your badges don't intimidate me!"

Boy, I was hoping he decided to leave, but that was never my luck. They had a job to do, and they weren't going to leave until it was done. I could hear the officer clear his throat and humbly apologize to my mom for his behavior.

"Also, I don't believe all of you need to be here."

"No, ma'am," they all answered.

"Well, I'm sure some of you can leave my doorstep now."

"Yes, ma'am."

"Thank you," she replied.

"May I come in?"

"Sure."

"Thank you, ma'am." The officer was now speaking as if he had his manhood removed and displayed for all to see. She'd just totally punked him. During all the commotion, I forgot about the coach on the phone, and he was still talking, but I had no idea what he was saying.

"Aiden?"

"Yes?"

"So, I need you to start for us next week."

"Huh?"

"I need you to be our starting running back next week. Were you listening to a word I've been saying?"

"Yeah," I lied. "So how long will I be starting?"

"Indefinitely, unless you choke like you did during tryouts. Then I will have to replace you. Can I count on you?"

"Yes, Coach."

"Good. So, I'll see you at practice Monday?"

I paused. Would he?

"Yes, Coach, I'll be there."

"Okay, I know it's going to be a rough few days ahead, but try to have a good weekend anyway."

Without thinking, I responded, "You too, Coach."

I should have been ecstatic after talking to the coach, but I had other pressing matters. Being arrested for breaking and entering was at the top of the list.

"Aiden!" my mom called.

"Yes?"

"Come here!"

Here we go. When I walked into the foyer, the officer was standing there, hands on his belt, waiting for me.

"Aiden, this officer has some questions for you."

"About what?"

"Last night."

My heart froze.

"Last night, your mom called the station to inform us that you and your friend…Tony, correct?"

Friend? I thought. Yeah, right. Ex-friend.

"Would be coming home after 12:00 a.m. curfew for under-eighteen-year-olds with her permission. Just to look out for you and make sure you were okay. She gave us your GPS tracking code so we could keep an eye on things, being that it was a brand-new car and all. Anyway, last night there was a break-in, and we saw that your car was around about twenty minutes after the perp escaped on foot. Did you see anything while on your way home? Your car stopped momentarily when you got near your home."

Wait—my mom too? Everyone was tracking me! Geez!

"No, Officer, I didn't see anything."

"You sure? Your car stopped momentarily when you got near your home."

The officer was staring into my eyes, searching for any sign of deceit.

"Why did you stop?"

"Me and Tony were arguing, and…that's why we stopped."

"Strange, Tony said you two were trying to talk to some girls."

"What?"

"Yeah, we talked to him earlier."

My mom turned and looked at me with that "you better come clean" stare.

"Yeah, yeah, we were showing off and trying to get their numbers."

"Were there any guys with them?"

"No, no, not that I know of."

"And you didn't see anything else?"

"No, Officer," I exhaled.

"Okay, well if you remember anything else, give us a call."

"Okay, will do."

"Thank you for your time," he said as he left.

I walked to the living room and flopped on the couch, allowing my entire body to sink into the leather. I peeked out the window, watching the officers get in their vehicles and leave, but not before they mocked the rude officer for being checked by my mom. I could hear some of them comment on how hot my mom was and making silly animal noises. How these morons ever passed the entry exam for the police academy was beyond me; somebody must have been high on something when they graded their papers. It was like watching frat boys at a party talking about a hot teacher. And to think men who could legally carry firearms behaved that way was even more disturbing. But I was happy to see them leave. To say I dodged a bullet was an understatement. More like dodging a freakin' freight train. My mom walked over to me with a concerned look.

"Aiden, I'm sorry I didn't tell you about the tracking device on the car. But with how the city has gotten lately and that car being so...how you kids say it? 'Off the hook.' I needed to be careful and make sure you and Tony were safe. I know you're angry and surprised, but just know I did it to keep you safe."

"Aww, Mom!" Sarah and I yelled in unison. Sarah had joined us downstairs after the police left.

"C'mon, you used our slang. Now it's tainted. We can't use it anymore," I protested.

"What?"

"Yeah, the rules are if your parents start saying things like 'off the hook,' 'real talk,' 'that's a good look,' 'fo-shizzle,' 'holla back,' or any of our slang, we have to stop using them immediately," explained Sarah.

"And now that you've used 'off the hook,' we are forbidden to use it again in this house. And I really liked that one too," I complained.

"Me too," agreed Sarah.

My mom was standing there, smiling at both of us.

"Can I say it though?" she asked.

"Yep, you can use it. It's yours now."

"Oh wow! I'm so fortunate to be the proud owner of the 'off the hook' phrase. I should call my publisher," she said sarcastically. "Seriously, Aiden, are we okay?"

"Yeah, Mom, it's cool. I get your point," I lied. "I may not like it, but I understand."

"I'll change the code right now so those idiots can't track you anymore. I don't trust them; they are way too high-strung to be police officers. But I won't take it off until you turn eighteen."

I didn't like the idea of my mom being able to track my whereabouts in my car. But I knew if I didn't go along with her terms, I would be without my car until I was eighteen. No supervision equals no car. Supervision equals car. I'll take supervision for 500, Alex! Sometimes we have to make hard choices. This wasn't one of them.

"So, how was your night?" my mom asked with a probing stare.

"It was great! We had a lot of fun."

"That's great, Aiden. I'm happy you had a great time and made it home safe without incident."

Ha, without incident? If she only knew I was well on my way to claiming my first victim. I could feel myself changing—becoming more aggressive, self-centered, and paranoid. I was starting to care more about how I was viewed by others than how I viewed myself. At first, I thought it was just a teenager thing, but after last night, I knew things were different inside me. I still couldn't explain how I got inside Jasmine's house without setting off the alarm. Also, getting there faster than Tony in a car was even more disturbing. After discovering my mother was also keeping tabs on me, I should have forgiven Tony. But I was too arrogant and proud. I allowed my fear and anger to control my actions, and I justified to myself that forgiving my mom was acceptable, but forgiving Tony was out of the question.

"Who was that on the phone?" Sarah asked.

"Oh, it was the coach."

"What did he say? You're fired!" she teased, mimicking Donald Trump's reality show.

"Actually, Cruella Deville, he told me I would be starting until further notice."

"Wow, so the starting running back died?" Sarah began laughing at her own joke, but my mom wasn't laughing.

"Actually, Sarah, yes, he did die last night. They said he had a heart attack. Eyes wide open with a look of horror on his face. Whatever he saw was so terrifying that it caused a seventeen-year-old's heart to stop cold in his chest. I was upstairs talking to his mother when the police started banging on the door. She's on the parent-teacher board at the high school. Very sweet lady, a little detached from reality, but sweet."

Sarah's face went white. "Mom, are you serious?"

"Afraid so, baby."

"Aiden, I'm sorry, I didn't know."

She didn't know? Neither did I! As my mom told the story of the starting running back's death, I replayed the phone call with the coach in my head. I had overheard him mention a tragedy, but I was so focused on the exchange between my mom and the officers, that I didn't process what he was saying. So, I pretended I knew about the student's death.

"What's his name?" Sarah asked.

As I sat there, I realized I had no idea what his name was, nor did I have any emotional investment to find out. His death opened the opportunity for me to start at running back, and not knowing his name was okay with me. Had this scene played out three months ago, I would've reacted differently.

"Steven Gray," my mom answered.

"Where did they find him, Mom?" Sarah asked.

"His body was found less than a block away from the house that was broken into last night. The police suspect the break-in and his death may be related."

I felt myself go cold with the revelation that my intrusion at Jasmine's home and Steven's death were somehow related. There is a sense of total and complete hopelessness that overcomes you when you fully understand that you are no longer in control of your actions. And fear—fear so deep and thick, it feels like a part of you, like an extra organ growing inside of your body. Did I kill Steve? I couldn't remember anything after I blacked out besides that horrible nightmare and waking up at Jasmine's. How I got there and everything in between was a blank space in time, like someone removed that portion of my memory. But in light of the current circumstances, I didn't know if I really wanted to recall my actions.

CHAPTER FIFTEEN
WHAT HAPPENED TO STEVE?

he weekend went by in a blur. To this day, I can't remember specific details after that Saturday afternoon. The following week was the same; I was on autopilot, trying to cope with having such a dark secret inside me and my best friend exiled from my life. The funeral for Steven Gray was being held on Friday, and Saturday was our first game of the season. The entire team had pledged to attend. I wasn't looking forward to it, but I had no choice. The police were still looking for the intruder, and they believed Steven's untimely death was related to the break-in. I needed to keep a low profile to avoid drawing any unwanted attention. I remained wary that Tony might speak up one day, so I tried avoiding him at school as much as possible. I figured if I wasn't on his mind, he would forget about Friday night. I'm not sure how insane I was becoming, but that line of thinking made me feel like I was well on my way to being a stamped and certified nutcase.

I still felt like there was a slight chance my activities on the night of my birthday celebration and Steve's death weren't related, and a good medical explanation would be forthcoming. I held on to that hope, and it kept me going during the week leading up to the funeral and our first game. But like all things, that hope had to end, and it ended after practice on Friday in the locker room. The funeral was scheduled for that evening to allow the students to attend. So we decided to have one last practice before the game on Saturday. Ronald Brice, the starting safety, was the son of Deerfield's coroner, and he always had the scoop on deaths and details concerning someone's demise within our city's limits. I overheard him on the other side of the locker room, discussing Steve's death. I tried to ignore him, but when I heard him say that the police purposely lied about Steve's death, I had to find out what he was talking about.

"What do you mean 'they lied'?" one of my teammates inquired. "They said he had a heart attack."

"Dude! C'mon! Steve? He was only seventeen and he was an ox. No way that healthy dude died of heart failure and he didn't have any history of heart problems. It's not even in his family's history."

"So, tell us what happened to him then," one of the teammates said.

"You really wanna know?"

"No, not really," I responded without thinking.

"Well, the truth needs to be known, so, Aiden, your request is denied. He had his throat slashed till his head was nearly severed."

The entire room broke out in a roaring laugh. I even found myself chuckling at Ronald's revelation.

"Aw, ya'll think it's funny? You don't believe me?"

"No!" We all responded in unison.

"Dude, this is Deerfield, not Chicago, Elm Street, or Crystal Lake. Things like that don't go down here," Brian said. "And I think it's extremely disrespectful to Steve's memory for you to make up that kind of story about his death."

"Okay, now have I ever led any of you astray?"

"Well, yeah, that time you said the police found a body behind the school and it was half-eaten, and the teeth marks couldn't be identified," Brian responded.

"That was true, they covered it up."

"Oh, so little Deerfield has conspiracies and cover-ups? C'mon, Ron, I can say most of the time your info is on point, but Steve's head getting cut off?"

"Almost, I said almost," corrected Ron.

"Okay, almost cut off. But, Ron, this is Steve, and it's disrespectful to his memory to lie about his death like that. Not cool, dude. You lost a lot of cool points with me on this one."

"I'm not lying!" Ronald screamed. You could see the frustration and seriousness in his eyes, and I wanted and needed to hear more of what he had to say because inside, I knew the heart attack story made no sense at all.

"Okay, okay! Let's hear him out," I interjected. "But, Ron, this better be actual, or you have a good team-hazing in your future. Deal?"

"Deal!" he agreed without hesitation.

"Wait! I am the captain of this team, not you," challenged the quarterback. "And I don't want to hear this crap. Steve was my friend, and I don't want to remember him this way."

"Well, you may be the captain on the field, but you have no say on what we want to hear off the field," I snapped back.

"You wanna go?" Brian challenged with anger in his eyes. "I'm not my big brother. I won't just fall on the floor!"

"Wait! Wait! C'mon, guys, this is stupid," Ronald protested. "We shouldn't be fighting. Steve wouldn't want this."

"Steve's dead, Ron. He doesn't want anything anymore," responded Brian. "Listen, if ya'll want to listen to this crap, you can, but I don't have to. I'm out of here!"

As the quarterback turned to leave, I could see Ronald becoming desperate. Whatever he had to say was extremely important to him.

"They suspect a serial killer is on the loose in Deerfield and the surrounding areas!" he yelled out behind the quarterback.

Brian stopped dead in his tracks.

"They lied because they don't want us to panic, but that's real," Ron continued. "There were markings all over Steve, carved in his flesh, patterns they can't explain. His body isn't even in the casket. The FBI has it, studying it for clues. They want to keep it hushed, and they are hoping the killer was just passing through."

Brian turned and charged Ronald with the intent to knock him to the floor, and Ronald just stood there waiting for the impact. I quickly jumped in Brian's path to prevent him from pounding Ronald. Brian stopped and stood face-to-face with me. Now his rage was concentrated on me, and I could tell my presence made him want to erupt in a fury of violence.

"Get out of my way!"

"No! Beating on Ron doesn't change that what he says makes sense."

"I swear," Ron protested. "It's the truth. I'm not happy having this news, but we need to be careful because any of us could be next. If you still don't believe me, look at the funeral service program. It says, 'This is a closed-casket funeral, please don't touch the casket.' Look, I got a copy of the pamphlet." He pulled out the program for the funeral service and began showing everyone. And just like he said, there it was in bold capitalized underlined letters:

THE FAMILY RESPECTFULLY ASKS THAT EVERYONE REFRAIN FROM OPENING OR TOUCHING THE CASKET!

"Okay, stop! This doesn't prove anything," protested Brian. "Maybe the family is in too much pain to see Steve lying there, so they want a closed casket. And what if the police said he had a heart attack because that's what happened? Ever thought about that? And why would they keep this from us anyway? How can we keep ourselves out of harm's way if we have no idea that there is a serial killer on the loose?

"Aiden says this makes sense? No, it makes no sense whatsoever!"

"It does!" Ronald yelled. "The FBI wants to flush out the killer. They know that this kind of serial killer usually has some kind of purpose, or they feel like they are a tool for a higher power. So, they need their work to be known. They need their victims to be identified, and if they don't get credit for their work, they begin to act out of character, which makes them easier to catch. So they haven't mentioned anything to prevent panic and to flush him out. There will be FBI agents at the funeral just in case the killer shows."

The mood in the room immediately dropped from excitement to gloom. I could tell that the team began to accept Ronald's explanation. Even Brian dropped his head in submission. No one wanted to admit that the story of Steve dying from a heart attack sounded suspicious, but it was definitely hard to believe a healthy seventeen-year-old died from cardiac arrest.

I was too busy trying to keep Brian from beating Ronald's ass, so that I hadn't had time to process what was revealed in the locker room. Did I murder Steve? But there was no sign of blood anywhere on me, and that kind of violence produces a huge amount of blood. But somehow, I felt responsible, and once this new information got to Tony's ears, he would surely come forward.

I felt like I was on borrowed time, that soon my life would take a 360-degree turn, and the world that I knew would transform right before my eyes. I would no longer see things the same way again. After listening to Ronald, I really didn't feel like being in the same room with Steve and the federal agents.

But if I didn't show up, it would not reflect well on me. His death allowed me to start in his place, and also, I was out at the time of his murder. Murder—wow! To even let that concept enter my mind was terrifying. I prayed I had nothing to do with Steve's death. Because without a shadow of a doubt, I had no intentions of turning myself in if I found out I did, and that thought sent chills down my spine.

CHAPTER SIXTEEN
THE FUNERAL

ater that evening, I was standing in the doorway of Steven Gray's funeral, and the atmosphere was suffocating. Grief and pain filled the room, making it hard for me to breathe. It felt like the collective sorrow was draining the life out of me. I knew I couldn't stay long; the environment was too intense. Scanning the room, I searched for any signs of agents or plainclothes detectives. I needed to either confirm or disprove Ronald's story about a possible serial killer on the loose and since the serial killer could be me, it was crucial to be sure.

With my family's strong military background, I had a keen eye for spotting armed forces or public safety personnel. It wasn't hard to identify them scattered across the room. Stern looks, rigid postures, always observing and calculating. They seemed to look right through you, assessing threat levels. I counted six agents and eight detectives. Ronald was on point, and I would never doubt him again. Their presence made it even harder to stay.

I decided to quickly express my condolences to Steve's family, pretend to look at the closed casket, just as Ronald had predicted—and leave. I didn't care who saw me, and if questioned about my hasty departure, I would say I needed to prepare for tomorrow's game to honor Steven. It was a plausible excuse. I could already imagine people buying that lie and showing pride in my supposed dedication. It was all bullshit, but only I knew that.

I made my way through the crowded room of mourners, speaking only if spoken to. I was in no mood for lengthy conversations. I just wanted out. I could feel the agents' and undercover cops' eyes on me. I might not be a suspect yet, but I was definitely a person of interest. It's rare for someone my age to be a potential serial killer, and my age was likely the only reason they hadn't aggressively pursued questioning me. With Tony and I at odds, and my memory lapse, I had no solid alibi. These men could sniff out weakness like sharks in the water. My best bet was to act as if I didn't know they were there, watching me. I avoided direct eye contact but didn't shy away from looking in their direction occasionally.

While in line to give my condolences to Steve's family, I noticed the "suits" moving closer, subtly shifting to more tactical positions. It was strange and terrifying to go from being an introverted teen with no social status to a starting running back, potentially guilty of murdering his teammate with a serial killer flair. I was on the radar of both local authorities and the Feds.

Oh, what a difference a few weeks can make.

After what felt like an eternity, I found myself face-to-face with Steve's mom. Steve was never particularly handsome, and looking at his mom, I could see why. To say her looks were average would be an insult to average-looking people. She was hopelessly unattractive, and grief only made it worse. Steve wasn't a total loss in the looks department, so I assumed his dad, whom he never met, must have been decent-looking to counteract his mom's unfortunate appearance.

Steve *had* to be the by-product of a drunken one-night stand. After my first night of drunken passion, I could only imagine how that night went. Steve's dad had to be wasted beyond reason to consider bedding the woman before me. The hangover the next morning would be nothing compared to the realization of his mistake. Her kind of unattractiveness should have been labeled a toxic waste. Because of his shortcomings in the looks department, Steve pursued sports vigorously to gain attention and popularity. He was a decent running back but NFL-bound? I didn't think so. Maybe a college scholarship at a school with a good football program, but unless he improved his speed, he would ride the bench for most of his college career and return home to his mother.

His ugly ass momma. Maybe his murder was an act of kindness to prevent him from waking up another day looking at this modern art masterpiece.

What is wrong with me? I've never been this mean before. Yes, Steve's mom was unattractive, but to mentally rip on her while she grieved the loss of her only child? The mournful atmosphere was having a negative effect on me, and I needed to get out fast. It was hard looking her in the face, not because I felt responsible for her grief, and not because I grieved with her. She was just too unattractive in my eyes, making it unbearable to look at her for more than ten seconds. She reached out her hand for me to shake. I caught myself pulling away, feeling like her touch would somehow transfer her unattractiveness to me.

I was truly losing it. I touched her hand briefly and made a mental note to disinfect thoroughly when I got home. I immediately got in line to view the closed casket. Impatience gnawed at me. Who wants to look at a closed casket? I was sure, like Ronald said, Steve's body wasn't even in there. Finally, I stood in front of the casket, seriously wondering if he was inside. I moved closer, tempted to tap it to see if it sounded hollow. From the corner of my eye, I saw the "suits" moving closer, waiting for any reason to intervene.

They had made it clear while entering the funeral home: under no circumstances were we to touch the casket. They figured the killer would want to confirm his work and wouldn't resist touching the casket. I felt an uncontrollable urge to tap it, to see if it held my first victim. I moved closer, feeling the "suits" tense up. I didn't feel in control anymore. I was all rage, passion, desire, and lust. I couldn't take it anymore.

Just before I touched the casket, I felt a familiar presence beside me. It was Tony. I hadn't seen him when I walked in.

Where did he come from?

He stood next to me with his hands in his pockets, staring ahead. He calmly said, "What are the odds?" and then turned and walked out. I quickly followed him outside to confront him. The last thing I needed was for him to torment me for his amusement. After navigating through the crowded room, I finally made it outside, exhaling forcefully, feeling like myself again.

I looked around but couldn't find Tony. If he wanted to play cloak-and-dagger, he could do it alone. I was not in the mood. After searching a bit longer, I decided it was time to go home. I noticed several "suits" posted outside, pretending to smoke. I knew why they were really there. I decided to head home before something else happened.

I barely slept that night and got up early on Saturday. My nerves were shot, and I had no appetite. Jason promised to come to my first game with my mom and Sarah. Strangely, the thought of Jason being there eased my worries. I decided not to dwell on it. I had a game in a few hours, and something inside me felt that how I performed today would affect my life for years.

This game was important to everyone in Deerfield after Steve's supposed untimely death. I would be the center of attention, taking over his position. If I messed up, I didn't think I'd get another chance. Everything was riding on this game. Time moved quickly. One minute I was getting out of bed, the next I was in the team's locker room, trying to listen to the coach's speech about winning and good sportsmanship.

From the locker room, you could hear the roar of the crowd. The sound was amazing. I was anxious to get out of the locker room and was the first to jump out of my seat once Coach Towers told us it was time to head to the field.

The walk onto the field was incredible—the crowd, the energy, the cheers. I felt at home. All the jitters were gone, and the more they cheered, the stronger I felt. I felt invincible. I belonged here, and my only regret was not getting here sooner. I looked for my family in the stands, hoping to see them cheering. But I couldn't find them. Maybe they were late. No matter; nothing could spoil my mood.

Or so I thought. Just as the offense was about to take the field, I saw Jasmine on the sidelines, staring me down. I immediately felt weak. Every step felt like I had two five-hundred-pound weights tied to my legs. The field began to spin, and I felt faint.

Not now.

The entire field spun, and I began to lose my balance.

I can't let her do this to me.

Jasmine began smirking at me, the same smirk from the lunchroom.

God, I hated her.

If this became a disaster and I lost my spot on the team, my first order of business would be to expose who and what she was. Because whatever she was, she wasn't human, and everyone needed to know.

CHAPTER SEVENTEEN
INZONE

The next two quarters were horrendous. I fumbled constantly, rushed for only fifteen yards, dropped easy passes, and even assisted in an interception. The boos and taunts were unbearable, but the looks from the coach and team were worse. My mom and Sarah arrived five minutes into the first quarter and witnessed my terrible performance. I thought Steve had no chance of an NFL career, but I wouldn't see a career past today.

The mood in the locker room at halftime was hostile, and all the anger was directed at me. The team wouldn't sit next to me, and a few players made choking gestures. The score was 36 to 7 in favor of the away team. Highland Park High had a great team, so a comeback was unlikely. Many people started leaving during the halftime show and dedication to Steve.

Coach called me into his office after going over our strategy. He looked exceedingly frustrated.

"Coach, take me out. I'm costing us the game."

"No, we need to show dignity and poise. You wanted the starting position, so you got it. You're finishing the game. I don't coach quitters. You might redeem yourself. If not, maybe next time."

"But, coach, I'm not cut out for this."

"Son, you were amazing during tryouts and practices. You have great skill and potential. Suck it up, focus, and show me what you're capable of."

Arguing further was pointless. We both exited the office, and Coach announced I would finish the game. The team protested, and Brian stormed out, kicking over a water cooler. This was going to be a long day. Minutes later, I was back on the field, welcomed by boos. A few people threw cups and garbage, and security escorted them out. Jasmine stood on the sidelines, taunting me, intensifying whatever she was doing. She smiled, filled with joy at my failure. Why me? What did I do to her to deserve this?

Tony thought my feelings came from within, but I was sure they came from her. I began to second-guess myself, thinking maybe it was me who murdered Steve. Did I just admit to killing Steve? I was confused and afraid. My life was a nightmare I couldn't wake from.

After a dynamic series of plays, I watched our defense work hard to get the ball back. They forced a turnover, and it was time for the offense to take the field. I had given up hope. I just wanted it to be over so I could go home and hide. I planned to play sick to avoid school for a few days. I needed to prepare for the slaughter from my teammates and students that awaited me for my failure that day.

As I walked to the field, I heard a familiar voice.

"Aiden! Aiden!"

I turned to see Jason calling me. Jasmine turned too, and the strangest thing happened. A look of pure horror came over her face at the sight of Jason. She immediately left the field. I couldn't believe it. Jason hadn't even looked at her. He was focused on me. I watched Jasmine sprint off the field, feeling better as she distanced herself. Jason stood by the benches, gesturing for me to come over. I called a time-out and ran to him. Coach was furious and stormed over.

"What are you doing? And who are you?"

"I'm sorry, Coach, my name is Jason. I'm a good friend of the family," Jason said, extending his hand. Coach hesitated but shook it. Coach calmed down the moment their hands touched.

"I need to speak with Aiden. It's important."

"Okay, fine. Nice meeting you."

"Likewise, Coach."

Jason grabbed my shoulders firmly, looking into my eyes.

"You can do anything if you believe you can. Whatever happened before doesn't matter. What matters is now. Play your game. Forget the boos and laughter. Have fun and show them what you can do."

His words sent a surge of confidence through me. I was ready to win and believed we could.

"Now go. Play your game!"

I turned to the huddle, ignoring my teammates' taunts. I listened to the next play—a run. Determined, I was ready to prove myself. We lined up, and I saw the defense going for a blitz. The quarterback changed the play, hoping I would fumble. But this time, I was alert, strong, and confident.

Nothing would stop me. I saw the surprise on Brian's face when I caught the toss and moved upfield. Everything moved in slow motion, and I was at super speed. Breaking through tackles, I reached the secondary and ran toward the end zone. As I continued to run, I heard the coach yelling,

"Go! Go! Go! Goooo!"

The crowd roared as I crossed into the end zone. The announcer yelled touchdown, and the crowd went wild. My teammates and the defense were in shock. I hadn't noticed we snapped the ball from our end zone. I ran the ball from one end to the other. It was impressive.

I handed Brian the ball, smiling. He looked down at the ball in his hand and then back at me. He looked amazed.

"Next time, let me know when you change the play."

"Sure, Aiden. My bad."

"It's cool. Let's win this for Steve."

I held out my hand to Brian, an invitation to become teammates and maybe friends on and off the field. He looked at my hand, smiled, and shook it firmly.

"Cool, let's do this," he agreed.

The next two quarters were like a video game. By the end, I'd rushed for 302 yards, 108 receiving yards, and four touchdowns. We won 42 to 36. It was a glorious feeling.

The crowd rushed to the field to celebrate. The local news was there to cover the game, and I was interviewed. Nervous, I kept it short. I didn't want to say too much that would make me look arrogant or stupid. As I was answering the reporter's questions, Coach walked over to me and handed me the game ball.

"I don't know what Jason said but thank you. You were amazing. You honored Steve's memory. You deserve this."

I looked at the ball, frowning. I was here because of a murder that I may have committed and that didn't sit right with me. I looked up and, in the stands, I noticed Steve's mom sitting alone, sobbing with her face buried in her hands. She was devastated and rightfully so, she would never get to see her son play on this field or any other field again. Inhaling deeply, I walked away from the reporter before she could ask me for a closing statement.

I walked to her, hoping no one would ask where I was going. Honestly, I didn't want to give her the ball. It was mine and I went through hell to earn it, but if I was remotely responsible for her son's murder, it was the least I could do. It would also throw off the suits at my display of empathy for Steve's mother. I climbed up and over the railing and stood in front of her. She was leaning over in her seat, so she didn't notice me standing in front of her, holding out the game ball.

Damn, I wanted to keep that ball.

"Ms. Gray?"

"Yes?" she responded, looking up. Her grief was heartbreaking.

I kneeled and handed her the game ball. She broke down, and I hugged her. The crowd fell silent, watching our exchange. I could hear some people in the crowd sniffling and weeping the longer we held each other.

Amazing.

The feeling of influencing others was intoxicating. It was at that moment I knew what I wanted to do with my life, and football was it.

CHAPTER EIGHTEEN
A BAD CALL

The rest of the weekend was like a dream. Newspaper articles, interviews, and the attention of new fans surrounded me. I couldn't go to the store in Deerfield without being bombarded by people congratulating me on my game performance. It was overwhelming and a bit annoying without my best friend, Tony, by my side, cracking jokes and guiding me through the crowds of girls vying for my attention. Tony had always been around during significant moments in my life, either teasing me or giving advice. But at this crucial juncture, he was missing in action, and I didn't know how to fix what was broken between us.

The start of the school week seemed like it was torn right out of a teenage fantasy novel. I was the center of attention, and everywhere I went, people smiled and congratulated me. Even Sarah became a fan, calling me "Aiden Peyton". It was strange and hard to get used to, but it was a nice break from her constant badgering. The most noticeable change was that Jasmine stayed away from me completely. A few times, I noticed her taking immediate detours when she saw me coming. She looked afraid of me, but there was something more—a look of deep concern in her eyes as if she knew about a disaster looming in my life.

I should've paid more attention to how concerned she looked, but everything seemed to be going great, and I didn't want to ruin it with thoughts of Jasmine and her change in attitude. The coming weekend we had another game against the number one ranked team in the state, and I was planning on having another great game, hopefully delivering the upset. No one expected us to win, just to put up a good fight against a team that had too many weapons, including the number one quarterback and running back in the Midwest. Coach drilled us extra hard all week to get us sharp and used to me in the backfield instead of the recently deceased running back. Coach Towers made it clear he wouldn't accept anything less than our full potential, especially from me. No more disastrous first halves; we had to make the top-ranked team fight for every yard. We were motivated and ready to bring the pain.

Friday rolled around faster than I expected. Before I had time to relax, I was packing my gear Friday evening to head over to the school for our game. Jason was there again, and this time he was going to ride with me to the field. Being around Jason made me feel at ease, like nothing could go wrong. He always said and did the right thing, as if he could read our minds. He was different around each of us, never offending the other. He was great with Sarah, great with me, and my mom adored him. I tried to find or create a reason to give him a hard time, but I couldn't; no matter what I said or did, he always had the best response to shut me down completely.

I was running late, so I rushed downstairs burdened with my gear, with one thing in mind: winning! Instead of meeting Jason,

Mom, and Sarah, I was greeted by two suits at the foot of the stairs, staring at me like lions ready to pounce.

"Aiden, these men would like a few words with you," my mom informed me. I froze, gripped with fear. My palms started sweating immediately.

I really don't need this right now.

"Mom, I'm late!"

"It will only take a minute, son," responded one of the suits.

"I really don't have a minute, Mr...?"

"Smith," the lead agent responded.

"Smith?" I asked.

"Yes, Smith."

Am I in the Matrix or something?

"No first name?"

"Well, since you're pressed for time, let's skip my name and get into your whereabouts on the night of your birthday."

Smart-ass, I thought.

Only a minute turned into fifteen, with Mr. Smith asking the same five questions in different ways over and over again, while the other nameless agent just stared at me and scribbled in his notepad. All the questions were pretty standard except one that startled me and made all the agents stop writing to focus on my response.

"Are you seeing things you can't explain?"

The question threw me off guard, making me wonder if they knew about Jasmine.

Noticing my hesitation to answer the question, Agent Smith requested everyone clear the room, but Jason stepped in, insisting an adult needed to be present. Noticing that Jason wasn't going to budge, the agents decided it was enough questioning for one day. His assertiveness shocked me because I expected my mom to step in. But what was even stranger was how the agents loosened up with Jason, shaking his hand and laughing it up with him. With me, they were all business. But with Jason, it was like they were old college buddies. I needed whatever magic he had because they weren't warming up to me at all. After they drove off, Jason turned to me and said,

"Don't let that rattle you, Aiden. Stay focused. Your team needs you."

His words calmed me immediately, and I felt a surge of power flow through me. My focus returned, and I felt like I could rush for a thousand yards if needed.

The scoreboard read 31 to 31. I was closing in on 250 yards rushing and three touchdowns, but the other team wasn't giving up. Their quarterback and running back were amazing. We were all exhausted as we approached the two-minute mark at the end of the second half. Neither defense was giving an inch, and both offenses were at a stalemate. It took a team effort to stay with our opponents. They were good, very good. Our defense held them to three-and-out, and we were back on the field in the huddle. All of us were exhausted but proud of our level of play. Brian looked at me and said,

"Aiden, we need you to tear them to pieces now! Going into overtime or tying won't cut it. We need to win, right here, right now!"

As we walked to the line of scrimmage, the crowd was on its feet. The rumble of the crowd was so loud, that I was sure it woke up God himself. The energy from the crowd surged through me. I never fully understood the importance of home games and how the crowd could change the outcome. But that day, against the best team in Illinois, it made sense. Their energy fueled our ambition to win. We played harder, were more focused, and believed in our ability to beat this superior team.

We only had time for one more play. If we blew this play, we would go into overtime, and we were too exhausted to contend with the opposing team. They would surely win if we did. Most of us were prepared to expend every ounce of energy for this last play. After this play, I wouldn't be surprised if the entire team passed out on the field.

Everything moved in slow motion as the snap count sounded like a slow song. I was focused, ready to give my last ounce of energy for the win. We had to win this to send a message that Deerfield High had arrived and was headed to the championship. I kept my eyes on Brian, reading his every move. I wanted to be in the right spot to make a play, whether rushing, blocking, catching, or running interference. All that mattered was being where I was needed at the exact moment.

"HIKE!"

Ball in hand, Brian stood straight up, surveying the field. It was a pass play, and I sprinted downfield toward the end zone. As soon as I crossed the line of scrimmage, I was flanked by three defenders. I'd been hurting their defense all day, and they weren't going to let me do it again. Not on this play, not at this moment. I glanced back to see Brian readying for a Hail Mary pass. I picked up speed. No one on their defense could keep up with me, so I quickly found myself alone. I glanced over my shoulder and saw the ball heading my way. Brian had overthrown it, and I needed more speed to reach it.

I gritted my teeth and willed my tired legs to move faster. I heard the defenders breathing behind me, trying to catch up and break up the play. I saw the goal line in front of me and glanced over my shoulder. The ball was just a few feet ahead, crossing the goal line before I did. I dove forward, stretching my hands out.

I wasn't sure if the ball would land in my hands, but it was my only chance. As I dived across the goal line, the ball landed in my hands. It seemed like it would fall from my fingertips, so I pulled it towards my chest and curled up in midair. The landing hurt, pain shooting through my body as my back hit the turf and I slid, scraping my arms and elbows. The pain was intense, like a hot iron running across my skin, but I kept the ball against my chest.

I rolled and came to a stop. The crowd was quiet. I heard myself breathing and felt the rumble of players running towards the end zone. I looked down at the ball cuddled against my chest. We did it! We won! I jumped to my feet, raising the ball in triumph. The crowd went insane, rumbling like an earthquake. I started walking towards my teammates, smiling and pointing at Brian, acknowledging his great pass. Then, out of nowhere, a referee blew his whistle, claiming an incomplete pass!

The time on the clock had expired, and the opposing team celebrated. Coach was furious, demanding an explanation from the ref, who quickly turned his back. I couldn't believe it. I knew I caught the ball; it never touched the ground. I dropped the ball, placed my hands on my knees, and leaned forward, boiling with anger. I wanted to smash my helmet across the referee's face.

The ref's words felt like daggers: "He dropped the pass!" My anger surged, and I snatched my helmet off. It wasn't the helmet making it hard to breathe, it was my blood-boiling rage. All I could think about was breaking the referee's face with my helmet. And each time he repeated that I dropped the pass, the urge to shut the referee up permanently grew.

Hearing the ref again, I couldn't take it. I rushed towards him. He must have seen the look in my eyes because he fled towards the stands. Coach was too busy arguing to see me give chase. Brian tried to warn me, but I was too engulfed in anger to listen.

"I didn't drop that pass, and you know it! You're a liar and a cheat! I'll break your neck!" I yelled.

The ref frantically climbed the stairs, thinking the crowd would protect him. But no one could protect him from my wrath. I started up the stands, teeth gritted, thinking about the damage I'd do. Before I got halfway, four suits surrounded me. I recognized one from the visit to my house. He smiled, leaned in, and spoke in my ear.

"What is it with you young people today? So quick to turn to violence. Now, why are you chasing this man? What are your intentions once you catch him? Are you planning to do to him what you did to Steve?"

His question froze me in place.

"I may not be able to prove it yet, but I know you had something to do with Steve's death. I won't stop until I have you in custody. Now, if I were you, I'd turn around and go about my business while you still have the freedom to do so. Soon, you'll be the property of the Federal Government."

I looked at the agent and smiled. "That's a lot coming from someone too afraid to look me in the eyes when he throws down a challenge."

The agent chuckled. "Don't worry, you'll see my eyes soon enough, but not in a football uniform. Something less fashionable."

"Well, make sure you get me the right size, Agent Smith. I know how you guys hate things not fitting the description."

What was I doing?

It was like I was watching myself challenge and stare down a federal agent without fear. I was outnumbered, but I had no reservations. I had officially lost my mind.

By then, the ref noticed I'd been stopped by the suits and came down the stands. "Young man, you are reckless. I'm ejecting you from this game and recommending you be suspended for the season."

The agents moved away, but not before the lead agent gestured that he was watching me.

Douchebag.

"Now, step aside, young man, or I'll have you arrested."

I moved out of the ref's way, not taking my eyes off him. Brian had caught up in time to hear the ref's decision. As he walked past me, the ref bumped my shoulder, leaned over towards my ear, and said,

"In what world did you think you could beat this team? You lost before you stepped on the field, and I'm here to make sure you understand that."

His admission to cheating was more than I could bear. I wanted to break his neck but couldn't with the agents watching.

"Now, get off this field immediately!"

I waited in the locker room for the game to be over. The crowd's groans told me the game was slipping away. We lost by three points, and I faced a season-long suspension. The locker room atmosphere was tragic, and Coach was in disbelief at my actions. He informed me of the referee's intentions to suspend me for the season and ban me from playing high school sports in the state. I'd put my future in the ref's hands with my hot-headedness.

I didn't tell Coach what the ref said. What's the point? How could I prove it? Coach was concerned about my aggressive behavior, and I promised to get it under control. He assured me he'd fight the suspension and ban, but he had little pull. Still, he'd do what he could to help me.

I went home, needing time to calm down and figure out my next steps. The agent made it clear how he felt about me and my possible involvement in Steve's death. So now, I had a cheating referee and Agent "Smith" from The Matrix aiming for me. Both situations could turn out bad, and I had no answers. If Tony were around, he might have advice, but that wasn't an option.

On my way home, Brian called, asking me to meet him at his father's store. The team was there, and he wanted me to join them. I didn't feel like being around anyone, but I needed support, so I agreed. When I arrived, half of them were already drunk, and the other half was almost there.

Brian's father's store had become an upscale establishment with a café, bar, and spa. Brian kept a key, so even though the store was closed, he had access to the door and the booze. As I walked in, he handed me a glass. With my mood, I didn't care what was in it; I just wanted to escape.

By the second glass, some cheerleaders started walking in, and things got fuzzy. The last thing I remembered was being handed another glass and a cheerleader suggesting I drink my next shot off her chest. Then, nothing… darkness. I hated blacking out just before I was about to get lucky.

CHAPTER NINETEEN
PRIME SUSPECT

I awoke the next afternoon in my bed to the sound of sirens and flashing lights. My mom burst into my room with a look of terror.

"Baby, get up and come downstairs now!"

"Mom?"

"Now, baby… please!"

She only called me baby when she was terrified. I sat up and looked out the window. Four police cars and FBI SUVs were parked in front of our house. Had the agent decided to bring me in for questioning? If so, things were moving fast, and maybe I could get to the bottom of what was happening to me. This was a terrifying time because I thought I knew my boundaries and principles, but everything was changing. I decided to face whatever they had in store.

Downstairs, the scene was dramatic. At least ten regular officers and six suits filled our living room. Agent "Smith" watched me walk down the stairs with an arrogant smirk.

I was really beginning to despise smirks.

"Have a seat, son," the agent commanded, pointing to an armchair across from him.

"I'm not your son," I snapped.

My mom, standing by the front door, looked terrified. She didn't recognize me.

"Okay, you're not my son, but we have questions for you."

"We?"

"Yes, me and my associates."

"Associates…" I chuckled, rolling my eyes. "Okay, shoot. What do you want to know?"

"Where were you last night around 8:30 p.m.?"

"I was hanging out with friends."

"Where?"

"At Brian's parents' store."

"At 8:30 p.m.?"

"That's what I said."

"Well, that's strange because they claim no one was at the store after 8:00 p.m., and you left around 7:45 p.m."

"Really?"

"Yes, we corroborated their stories. So again, where were you around 8:30 p.m.?"

"I don't remember."

"You don't remember?"

"No, I don't. Is there an echo in here?"

"How could that be?"

"Because I was drunk."

My mom gasped. Her look spelled doom for my social life until I was forty.

"So, is it customary for you to not remember anything while partaking in underage drinking?"

"I don't know because I don't customarily partake in underage drinking. But given the day I had yesterday, I figured, what the heck. So, are you gonna arrest me for drinking?"

"The drinking part is the least of your worries."

"Excuse me? How is that the least of my worries?"

"This is a murder investigation."

"What?!"

"Yes, the referee you threatened was killed last night."

"How?"

"Someone broke his neck."

I immediately felt sick and wanted to hurl all over Agent Smith's smug face.

"Are you okay, Aiden? You look like you need water or something."

"I'm fine."

"You sure? I can have one of my associates get you water or aspirin?"

"No, I'm fine."

"You seem on edge and annoyed, Aiden."

"Really? Do I? Well, I have a killer hangover, and the cold breeze from the open door isn't helping."

"No one twisted your arm to drink."

"No, they didn't, but that doesn't change the fact I have a hangover."

"Young man, I don't have empathy for your current state because your irresponsibility led you here."

Going back and forth with Agent Smith wasn't helping. He was calm and calculating, unmoved by my sarcasm. This guy was good.

"So, what now?"

"We need to figure out your whereabouts and if you had anything to do with the victim's death."

"Why would I have anything to do with that?"

"You were the last person that threatened him. And his body was found with a broken neck. Isn't that what you said you would do to him? As an investigator, I thought, 'Hey, why not ask the out-of-control teenager a few questions.'"

His sarcastic tone and smug attitude were getting to me. I wished I could dropkick those glasses off his face.

"Threatening people isn't a crime, is it? I was angry because of the crappy call."

"Yes, we saw that. But threatening someone can be a crime... just for future reference."

Just then I had an epiphany and decided to use my newfound wisdom to get out of this mess.

"Really? So, your threat to me at the game was a crime?"

"Wait!" my mom interjected. "You questioned my son without my authority? And you threatened him?"

"Ma'am, it wasn't really a threat... my team and I stepped in when your son had the referee cornered. We wanted to prevent a situation."

"Yeah, true," I said, "but your comment had nothing to do with the ref. You told me you knew I had something to do with Steve's death and soon I would be the property of the federal government."

"What the hell!" My mom was upset, and Agent Smith looked uneasy. Jackpot!

"Your threat drove me to drink because I couldn't take the pressure. I needed to forget the visuals you put in my head about what the government would do to me in jail," I whined, laying it on thick.

"Wait, did you tell my son he'd be thrown in jail? And I thought Steve died of a heart attack. How could Aiden have anything to do with that?"

"Well, ma'am. That's not entirely accurate. I alluded to him being thrown in jail and being responsible for the student's death. But…"

"But what? You alluded to it?"

"Something like that, ma'am, but I was trying to…"

"Okay, that's it. Allude your asses out of my house right now!"

"Mrs. Storm, you're making a big mistake."

"A mistake for protecting my son? Agent, I'm asking you and your team to leave my home and property. If you need additional information, we can arrange for my lawyer to contact your office. But you're not allowed to communicate with my son without my consent. Good evening, gentlemen. Now get out!"

My mom cleared the living room in less than five minutes. As Agent Smith walked out, he looked upset. He turned to me, shaking his head. I gave him a huge smile and a thumbs-up. As he walked out, I slammed the door behind him and whispered, "Bitch."

As I listened to the sound of their footsteps walking away from our front door, I peered through the peephole and saw him staring back. Seeing him that close startled me, and I jumped back. He laughed and walked away. How did he know I was looking through the peephole? Before I could figure it out, I felt two sets of eyes staring at me. I turned to see looks of disgust from Sarah and rage from my mom.

"Aiden, in the office now!" my mom demanded.

I'd never gotten an ass-chewing like the one my mom gave me. She was so angry I thought she might get "old school" and get a belt. Of course, the conclusion was punishment: no car, no fun, no TV, no video games, and kitchen-cleaning detail until further notice. My mom didn't even consider that I could be guilty of murder, but she couldn't tolerate me drinking and driving until I passed out. I hated disappointing her, but it felt like my life was spiraling out of control. No matter how much I tried to hold onto the boy I was, he kept slipping through my fingers, and I didn't know how much of the old Aiden was left. And to be honest, I didn't miss him. The old Aiden would've pissed his pants at the idea of being questioned by an FBI agent. With all my martial arts skills and physical ability, I was soft and timid. But the new, more aggressive Aiden? I liked him. I just wished this new Aiden wasn't a possible serial killer but only a social badass. But I guess you can't have summer without a bitter winter.

The referee's murder was all over the news that evening, and I could hear my mom watching it in her bedroom. His name was Mark Hampton. Father of two and an alumnus of the school that beat us. Now I understood why he would cheat for them, but it wasn't an excuse I was willing to accept. But was I angry enough to break his neck? I was angry, and if I'd caught him, I wanted to give him a good pounding with my helmet. But would I have done that? No, not likely. But drunk off my ass… no telling what I was capable of. I tried to convince myself I didn't kill him, but without much information, I wasn't convinced. And if I was guilty of murdering the ref, then why not Steve?

Steve had something I wanted, and short of a career-ending injury or death, he wasn't giving it up without a fight. That night I didn't get much sleep, thinking about how I was a prime suspect in his murder. Who chases down a referee with intentions to helmet-pound him into the ground? Damn, I was out of control.

The next morning, Sarah was in the family room watching TV when a breaking news report came on. It seemed multiple recordings of the game showed I caught the ball. Even though I wasn't allowed to watch TV, I needed to see this. The news speculated it was an angry fan who was distraught about the call, but I wasn't implicated in the murder. Another video showed the altercation between me and the ref, recording him admitting he cheated. The audio was clear, and the video was crystal clear. It must have been one of the kids sitting nearby. No video of me chasing him, just us standing shoulder to shoulder, and him making that comment about the reality of the world. Watching it again angered me, so I walked away just in time because my mom walked in, asking what we were doing. We lived in the age of YouTube and online catalogs of everything people did in their lives. Before today, I hated it. Now, I am a fan.

At school the following week, the coach had a meeting with the team and then a private sit-down with me. He stared at me for about a minute and then said,

"Well, I guess you'll be playing for the rest of the season. It's horrible how it played out, but we have to move on. You can't flip out every time something doesn't go your way, Aiden. Life is full of disappointments, and if you can't handle them, you'll never mature. You'll be left behind."

He saw great potential in me, but that same potential unrealized could lead to horrible things. There was a fine line between being famous and infamous. It was a lot to think about. The coach was genuinely concerned, and I respected that. I promised to behave better. I wanted to confide in him about the six agents stalking me, but it was better for his safety to keep him out of it.

Over the next few days, tension and uncertainty lingered at school. Several law enforcement agencies came to talk about the recent deaths and how to stay safe. The days were getting shorter, and soon most of us would be going home in darkness. They gave us the "travel in groups" speech and encouraged us to catch a ride with family or friends instead of walking. It should have been a standard safety presentation, but the six suits were present at all the presentations. They sat strategically around the students: two on the left, two on the right, and two at the back. No one seemed to notice them but me. I knew why they were there and for whom.

I noticed them in different places around Deerfield as well, just sitting and watching, waiting for me to slip up. Sometimes they were even on the bus coming home from school. It was extremely odd and intimidating. I couldn't figure out their strategic purpose. Did it help them survey better? Did it cut off all exits I might try to use? I wasn't going to mention it to Sarah or anyone else. That would open a conversation I wasn't willing to have.

Jason came over the following Friday with Chicago Bears owner's box tickets in hand. Jason knew a lot of wealthy and powerful people, and great seats at all sporting events were one of the many perks he enjoyed. My mom protested because I was still on punishment, but after bringing Jason up to speed on recent events, he convinced her to let me go. After that, Jason came every weekend with tickets to a sports game. Sometimes it was all of us; other times, just me and him. Jason was known by so many people that going places with him was like being in the president's entourage. Special treatment, exclusive access to locker rooms— nothing was too exclusive for Jason.

During our times alone, I found myself bonding with him more, talking about my newfound aggression and insecurities. His advice was priceless and always made sense. Speaking with him and watching the games made me a better football player and gave me the confidence to control my emotions. Being around him became like a drug habit, and I relied on him for emotional support and mental stability.

I never thought I'd bond with another man who wasn't my father, but Jason made it difficult not to. Sarah also grew attached, and we trusted him so much that having him spend the entire weekend wasn't uncomfortable. Actually, if he didn't spend the weekend, we would get upset. He was becoming a huge part of our family, and we were happy to have him.

The closer I got to Jason, the less I saw of Jasmine. Even when I did see her, I didn't react the same way. It was like Jason gave me a protective shield. At first, she smirked, but when she saw I wasn't reacting, she walked away. After a while, she avoided eye contact altogether. With Jasmine and those dark visions out of the way, my confidence soared, and my performances on the field became legendary. I averaged over 250 yards a game, and Deerfield Warriors had eleven wins and one loss. We were on our way to the state championship.

Reporters and sports broadcasters made me a household name. By midseason, several top-tier college programs were interested in giving me a full scholarship. It was a great time in my life, and I enjoyed all the perks of popularity. Brian also gained exposure and received several full scholarship offers. Brian and I quickly became good friends and hung out regularly. He was fun to be around, but fun with Brian wasn't the same as with Tony. I still saw Tony up to his old antics with the ladies, but we didn't speak. We acknowledged each other and broke eye contact immediately.

The downside of hanging with Brian was his irresponsibility. He drank too much and had too many girls coming in and out of his bedroom. Tony was a player, too, but he handled his affairs with tact. Brian was all over the place. When he was drunk, he didn't care about a girl's looks; if she was willing, he was game. Sometimes he'd be so drunk he wouldn't remember the girl the next day. His behavior made him the person he was, and nothing we said could change that. On the field, he was a beast; off the field, he was a problem.

After the fiasco with the ref getting killed and my blackout from drinking, you'd think I'd stay away from alcohol. But like most teenagers, I succumbed to peer pressure and drank again. Each time, I'd black out. Sometimes I'd wake up the next morning with no incident. Other times, I'd wake up in Jasmine's bedroom standing over her while she slept. Needless to say, those nights were not the best for trying to leave her house without waking anyone. If it weren't for those situations, I would have forgotten about my dark visions and Jasmine. But every now and again, things like that reminded me the darkness was still there, waiting to take over. After a couple of times waking up in Jasmine's bedroom, you'd think I would remove alcohol from the equation, right? Problem solved. But not me. I loved the way I felt when I drank. It was like all my inhibitions were taken away. I felt free, but that feeling came at a cost, my sanity.

After weeks of hype, the Deerfield Warriors were heading to the state championship to face the only team that beat us earlier in the season. It was going to be a hard-fought battle, and hopefully, this time we wouldn't have another referee making erroneous calls in favor of the other team.

Almost the entire suburb of Deerfield was going to Soldier's Field to watch the game. It was going to be televised on ESPN 2, giving us more exposure. I was excited and scared at the same time. This was a big deal, and the last thing I needed was any distractions. Coach took us all out for dinner the night before and told us how proud he was of us and the season we had. He talked about winning and how it wasn't always about winning. At that point, I tuned him out because I knew better. It was *always* about winning. Only those used to and accepted being losers said, "It's not always about winning."

What was the point of a contest if not to win? I understood the journey, integrity, and sportsmanship, but the goal was the big "W." If winning wasn't important, practice, sportsmanship, and integrity wouldn't matter. But we were in this contest to win, not lose. I understood his reason for saying it, but I didn't believe it.

Playing at Soldier's Field was different from watching a game there. Things seemed bigger and more intense. The view from the field into the stands was breathtaking. I felt like a gladiator in an ancient Roman arena, engaged in mortal combat with a formidable adversary. Make no mistake, our competition came to win. The stadium was almost filled to capacity, and the noise was insane. Our small high school field's noise was but a whisper compared to Soldier's Field.

Both teams were equally represented, and every play brought boos or cheers. It was very cold, and the wind from Lake Michigan made it worse. This hostile environment made each play more important because there might not be a second chance.

By the fourth quarter, our opposition was up by a touchdown, and Brian's arm was tired. He had thrown for over four hundred yards and four touchdowns. I could tell by his body language that throwing more passes would be a problem. But Brian was a true warrior. He never complained or whined; he just played the game. Say what you want about his off-field antics, but on the field, he was a joy to watch. In the huddle, I looked at Brian and the rest of the team and said, "I think it's time to run this ball down their throats."

Coach had been calling passing plays to keep up with their high-powered offense. But their defense was tired. I felt like a million bucks, fueled by the crowd's energy. Some of the team protested, warning me about how Coach didn't like us calling our own plays.

"Is the coach out here, or are we out here?" I asked.

"We are," they responded in unison.

"Look at them over there. They're tired, and their defensive line is worn down. We need to give Brian's arm time to rest. We're down a touchdown, and I'm not looking forward to overtime in this weather."

They nodded in agreement.

"We came to win, not take second place. We have to play like next year isn't coming. We have to win today, right now!"

Brian looked at me, nodding in agreement. He was ready to do whatever I said. The rest of the team trusted me because Brian did. With all in agreement, we moved to the line of scrimmage. As we moved into position, I noticed the look and body language of the other team showed they were exhausted and unprepared. Big mistake on their part. Very big mistake.

CHAPTER TWENTY
JUDAS

onfetti, horns, music, fireworks, screams of defeat, and tears of triumph. This was just a small portion of the chaos that erupted on the field as the Governor of Illinois handed our coach the state championship trophy. I stood there with the game ball in hand, voted high school player of the year and MVP of the championship game. I rushed for 110 yards in the final quarter alone, scoring four touchdowns. Brian didn't have to throw another ball the entire quarter. The final score wasn't even close: 58 to 34. The other team was taken by surprise when we decided to run the ball while we were down a touchdown. Both coaches were open-jawed the entire quarter, watching us tear into their defense over and over again.

It was a glorious win that solidified our claim to the top spot in the state and hopefully the nation. We were gods of Olympus that day, and no one or anything could bring us down.

It took about two hours after the game for us to get out of Soldier's Field and on our way home. From the fans and interviews, it was madness and impossible to leave. The team headed back to the school for a meeting with Coach Towers. Sarah asked if she could tag along with me. I was on cloud nine, so it didn't matter. A lot of students decided to go back to the school to celebrate with us. Though it wasn't supposed to happen, the school board was okay with it because of the big win. After the meeting, I decided to head straight home to celebrate with my family and watch our game on TV. My mom set the DVR to record the game on ESPN 2 so we could watch it again later that night. I was anxious to see how I looked on camera and how awesome I was in the fourth quarter.

When I got home, Jason and my mom were in the kitchen, laughing and joking around. They ordered pizza earlier, and it must have just arrived because it was still piping hot. Watching them together brought a smile to my face, and a warm feeling vibrated through my body. This is what a family is supposed to feel like. Safe, warm, inviting, and fun. I quietly sat on one of the stools and began to dig into the pizza. Boy, was I hungry.

"Great game today, Aiden," Jason congratulated me. "You were incredible out there, and to do all that in the final quarter was something amazing. Where did you get all that extra energy from?"

"I don't know, really. I just had it and wanted to win, so... I took care of business."

"Yes, you did," my mom agreed.

"I saw a few scouts out there today, and I can assure you if you apply yourself, the NFL will be waiting with open arms. You could become a Hall of Famer one day. But it takes work, and you have to be focused and consistent with a great work ethic."

"Yeah, I know. After today's game, I see exactly how focused I have to be because even though I had a monster fourth quarter, that game wasn't easy. We just caught them off guard, and they were too tired to respond."

"True," agreed Jason. "Whatever you need, I am here for you, Aiden. Just let me know."

After eating until I was nearly bursting, I looked around and noticed Sarah wasn't home.

"Mom, where's Sarah?"

"Oh, she said she got held up, but she's on her way home now. She called me about ten minutes ago, letting me know Tony is dropping her off."

"Tony?"

"Yeah, go figure, huh... By the way, why doesn't Tony come over anymore?" my mom asked.

"Are you two... umm... what do you guys call it these days... oh, beefing," said Jason. "They call it beefing now."

"Yeah, are you two beefing?"

An awkward silence followed the question, casting an uneasy feeling over the kitchen. I wasn't even going to try to answer that question with the truth, and lying was out of the question, so my only option was to pretend the question didn't exist. Just before things got really weird, I heard the front door swing open. It was Sarah, and for the first time, I was grateful for her presence.

"Mom... Mom, I need to talk to you," Sarah said.

Sarah sounded strange—her voice was anxious and subdued, which was very uncharacteristic of a girl so confident and defiant. She sounded scared; worse yet, terrified and unsure. I could hear her voice shaking as she spoke. The first thought that ran through my mind was that Tony did something to her on the way home. If he did anything to my sister, I would kill him, I thought. I turned to face her as she walked towards the kitchen. I needed to get a look at her condition. I was scared because whatever shook her up, it seemed she would never be the same again.

She had scratches on her face and a bloody nose. Her shirt was bloody and torn at the sleeves. Her knuckles were bruised from punching something or someone. She looked like she'd been in the toughest fight of her life. Through all the martial arts tournaments we participated in, she never came out of them looking the way she did now, and she'd been in some tough scrapes before. My heart started pounding in my chest, and I felt a sick, icky feeling build up in my throat. I kept saying to myself, "Please don't let this be rape," over and over again. No matter how annoying Sarah was, she was my kid sister, and no one had the right to put their hands on her. A fight would be bad, but a sexual assault would be devastating.

"Sarah, what happened to you?" my mom screamed as we both ran over to her.

"Baby, are you okay? Who did this to you? What happened?"

Sarah grabbed my mom and started clutching at her clothes, sobbing uncontrollably.

"Please tell me you are okay... please!" my mom kept pleading.

I saw tears roll down her face as she kept whispering, "My baby, my baby." I held Sarah's hand and looked her over for signs of what kind of assault this was.

"Baby, tell me what happened, please."

After a long silence that seemed to last forever, Sarah loosened her grip on my mom, inhaled, and said she got into a fight with Jasmine.

"What? Who is Jasmine?" my mom asked, looking over at me for answers.

If anyone in this house knew who Jasmine was, it would be me. She was evil, and something bad lived inside her soul. Now, since she couldn't get to me anymore, she decided to attack my sister. Tony, the suits, the police, or God himself wouldn't stop me from doing some serious damage to her bodily functions. This was the last straw.

"Why were you two fighting?" my mom continued to probe Sarah.

"She said something very mean and crazy about Jason, and I got so mad that I hit her. Then we started fighting. But that's not what's wrong. She did something else to me."

"What did she do?"

"I don't know… during the fight, she held me down on the floor, placed two fingers on my forehead, and said…

'AWAKE!'"

An icy chill traveled through my entire body at the sound of the word echoing through the air. But it wasn't the word that startled me; it was who said it. The word "awake" came out of Jason's mouth first, and then Sarah whispered it after him. But it wasn't just the word that turned my blood into ice water; it was also the way Jason said it that was alarming. He always spoke in a very calm and melodic tone, but when he said "awake," it was like the word came out of another person's mouth. His voice was loud, aggressive, and filled with hate.

"How did you know?" Sarah asked, peeking over my mom's shoulder to look at Jason.

The scream that came from Sarah's mouth sent sharp vibrations and more chills up my spine. I noticed my mom tensing up and looking at Sarah, trying to figure out what was wrong with her. There was a look of terror on her face that I'd never seen before, like she was looking at her own death unfold right in front of her, a menacing horror that was just an arm's length away. How could this be? She was looking directly at Jason. I slowly turned to see what scared my sister, and what I saw was a sight I would never forget for the rest of my life.

142

Standing in the place of Jason was a dark entity, formless like a smoky mist one second and then taking the form of a faceless cloaked figure the next. I would be lying if I said this entity was foreign to me, but it looked exactly like the things that tortured my father in the dark vision I had on the night of my birthday. But that was a nightmare. This was actually happening, and every hair on my body stood straight up. The nerves on the back of my neck were vibrating so fast it hurt. Tears began to fill my eyes from the fear of looking at something so menacing.

There was an ominous sound coming from the entity, causing a whirlwind of terror to blow through our kitchen. It sounded like people screaming and wailing from some unseen torture or hellish reality. When the mist retook shape, I could make out talons at least twelve inches long where its hands should have been. The talons were illuminated with a neon-white light that made them appear transparent. There seemed to be something alive inside them, moving like tiny worms made of light. I swallowed hard, thinking about what those things would do inside the human body if someone were unfortunate enough to be attacked by this thing's talons. Suddenly, the lights above the island started flickering and exploding one by one, spewing glass shards all over the kitchen. The sound of the lights exploding caused my mom to scream and turn around to see what was shattering in her kitchen. Before that moment, my mom hadn't turned around to face the island or this "thing" that had invaded our kitchen. She was still on her knees, holding Sarah in her arms. At the sight of the entity, my mom started shaking uncontrollably while picking Sarah up off the floor. Sarah was wailing, asking our mom, "What is that?"

I was expecting to see the look of a fish out of water in my mother's eyes. A look that would show me she was unfamiliar and ill-equipped to answer Sarah's question, but to my surprise and horror, it appeared she was well aware of what this thing was. Just like me, this wasn't her first time seeing something this horrifying. And it was that look that made me very afraid because I could tell she knew exactly what it was, and she was more terrified than either of us. Meaning "we were royally screwed."

It suddenly began screeching at a pitch so high it caused us to cover our ears to stop the head-shattering pain that was now vibrating in our skulls. Sarah was screaming at the top of her lungs, and we were all frozen with fear. We were paralyzed, helpless to do anything but stand there in terror as this nameless horror filled our home with demonic sounds that seemed to pour out of its faceless form. The screeching slowly started to lose its volume and pitch until it started making a humming sound, and then it spoke. Its voice was the sound of multiple voices in different tones, slightly out of timing with each other, trying to speak while inhaling. It was also hissing as it began to form words from the dark void that should have been its face. The sound of it trying to speak was even more terrifying than its appearance.

"I am your ending."

Those four words sent shards of fear through all of us as we jumped and took a step back.

"I am Lalartu, and I have been sent by Alal to feast upon your fear and scatter your flesh until your bones are bare and the walls are weeping red with the stain of your blood."

"Oh God, no!" my mom screamed and grabbed my arm, pulling me away from the kitchen towards the back door.

"Run," she grunted at me.

I tried to run, but my legs felt weak and heavy as if something was pulling me down and back, making every step I took seem like I was sliding backward. The more energy I expelled, the harder it was for me to move. It was terrifying because I refused to look back to see if that thing was getting closer. My mom was holding Sarah while pulling my arm, but we weren't moving fast enough, and I could tell my mom was feeling anchored and exhausted. But she kept running, and when I looked towards the back of the house, the hallway seemed so long, and the door seemed so small, like the back door was a mile away. I was covered in sweat, and my mom's grip on my arm started slipping. But she refused to let go, and I suddenly felt her fingernails dig into my arm to get a better grip. I gritted my teeth from the pain but refused to let out one sound. The house was completely dark, and I didn't want this thing to find me in the darkness.

The pounding of our feet on the hardwood floors seemed to echo throughout the house, giving away our exact location to this evil being, sent to murder us. Sarah was still crying in my mom's arms, and my mom was slowing down, so I began pushing her. The added weight of her and the hardship we had trying to move was almost too much to handle. My legs were dripping with sweat and shaking like wooden stilts with too much weight on them. I was afraid my knees were going to shatter from the weight, but I kept pushing, still refusing to look behind me for fear of seeing those talons slashing across the darkness, emitting the only light in the black void that was now our home. I suddenly felt light-headed and started choking. The air I inhaled was burning my throat, and my insides felt like they were on fire.

"Mom, keep moving," I pleaded, and then suddenly, we ran into the back door. It just seemed like the door was over a mile away, and now we were slamming up against its hard exterior. What kind of illusions was this evil capable of? I began to realize that if this thing could manipulate our perception of reality, then what else was it capable of? My mom was fighting with the door locks, and from the corner of my eye, I saw the glow of the talons moving through the darkness. The glow was beautiful and almost hypnotizing as it floated closer to my mom's...

"Mom, move!" I screamed and pushed her head away just before the talons ripped through the back door, shattering wood and metal everywhere. The door was oak with a steel interior for security, and those talons went through that door like a scalpel through flesh. We were all on the floor, scrambling, trying to get away from the door. The entity was still swiping at it, tearing it to pieces while it hissed and screeched in enjoyment at the destruction it was creating.

"Upstairs! We have to get upstairs to my room and call 911," my mom said.

It seemed that while the entity was occupied with the door, its spell of illusion on us was gone, so we quietly and quickly made for the stairs. Halfway up the stairs, the sounds of the entity screeching, and the destruction of our back door stopped. The sudden silence stopped us in our tracks as we tried to listen to where this thing could be. After about five seconds, my mom grabbed my arm, signaling me to follow her upstairs.

I started moving slowly up the stairs, still straining my ears to listen for anything, but all I got was silence. My muscles were exhausted from shaking with fear, and I could barely keep a firm foothold on the steps in front of me. As I lifted my leg to reach the next step, the wood bent beneath my weight, releasing a faint but unmistakable squeak as it strained under the pressure. I gritted my teeth as the sound of the squeaky step echoed throughout the house. Never before had this step made one peep in all the years we'd been living in this house, and tonight, when we were fleeing from a force beyond our comprehension, this step decided to betray me. At that moment, I vowed if we got out of this alive, I would be replacing and burning this squeaky step the first chance, I got.

CHAPTER TWENTY-ONE
THE AWAKENING

hrough the suffocating darkness, we finally made our way up the stairs and into my mother's room. It was as dark as a tomb. Usually, through the huge windows in her room, light would shine through from the streetlights or the moon, but tonight, the window offered no light or comfort from the outside world. We were trapped with this thing, and the darkness it brought with it refused to let us find any hope of escape. We stumbled around in the darkness until my mom found her cell phone. As she fumbled with the phone, trying to get the display to turn on, I found myself praying that the phone would work and that we would get out of this situation alive and unharmed. I tried to get my thoughts together, but the darkness and silence made it almost impossible.

We were all terrified, and our fear acted like an inhibitor to proper brain functions. We were like toddlers given a task more suitable for college graduates, and we were failing miserably. My mom kept pressing the power button on the phone, but it wouldn't turn on. After about eight to ten tries, she began to cry and cursed the phone for not working. I could feel her shaking while she knelt on the floor next to her bed.

"Take the battery out and put it back in," Sarah whispered.

My mom nodded her head and began to take the phone battery out. After listening to her fiddle with the phone for what seemed like forever, I finally heard the click of the phone's back plate being reinstalled, and then she pressed the power button. The light from the phone seemed to light up the entire room. I looked around quickly to get a good look at the room and noticed the darkness was reacting very strangely. The light from the phone didn't dilute the darkness; it seemed to fight it. The darkness was cowering in each of the corners of the room and moving like black waves crashing on the shores of a beach. Also, the longer the light from the cell phone remained, the less terrified I felt. My nerves were slowly relaxing, allowing my mind to expel the chaos that was raging inside my head, and I began to regain control of my thoughts. I started to assess our situation and that thing downstairs and its relationship with Jason and my mom's familiar reaction to it. Suddenly, I felt Sarah pulling on my arm, and I turned to see Sarah pointing towards the ceiling.

She had a look of confusion and fear on her face, and when I glanced towards the ceiling, I understood her expression. The ceiling light in my mom's room was on and had always been on, but the darkness was so thick and invading that it covered it up like a thick black sheet covering a window to keep out the afternoon sun. The cell phone's light seemed to have pushed the darkness back from the ceiling to reveal this strange spectacle, but what was even stranger was now that the darkness was pushed back and the ceiling light was revealed, its light still had no effect on the room.

The only light that had any effect was from the cell phone, and I knew that once that light went out, the darkness, the terror, and more than likely that thing would return. By now, my mom was dialing 911, and through the phone's ear speaker, I could hear the dispatcher answer...

"Nine-one-one, what is your emergency?"

Silence... my mom said nothing. The dispatcher repeated her greeting, and still, my mom remained silent. The dispatcher again repeated her greeting, and my mom was sitting there frozen.

"Mom? Please answer her," I pleaded.

My mom was looking around the room frantically, realizing that once she put the phone to her ear, the light from the cell phone screen would go out. Then the darkness and that thing would return, and we weren't sure what new horrors were waiting for us once my mom began speaking into the phone. She continued to look around the room, and then I noticed her staring at the closet on the other side of the room. She pointed to both of us and then towards the closet. I shook my head in protest; I was not going to leave her alone out here once the light went out. She looked at me, and in her eyes, I could see pain; the thought of her answering the phone and harm coming to us was too much for her to bear. I knew she was ready to give her life for us, but she didn't want us anywhere around if it was to come to that.

As much as I wanted to stay, I knew I needed to keep Sarah safe. I would be the last line of defense, and whatever might come through that closet door would have the fight of its life; if I was going to die protecting Sarah, I was going to make it count. Nothing was going to come easy for my attacker that night. I leaned forward, grabbed Sarah's hand, and pulled her away from my mom's arms. Sarah was still crying and didn't want to leave her either, but after a few hard pulls on her arm, she kissed Mom on the cheek and turned away, walking towards the closet. I headed towards the closet after Sarah, and right before I closed the door, I looked back to see my mom looking back at us. Tears were falling from her eyes, reflecting the cell phone's light, making them appear like streams of silver running down her face. Through all the terror of what would possibly come next, she forced a smile and whispered the words, "I love you."

I made Sarah sit on the floor towards the back wall of the closet while I got on all fours in front of the closed closet door. It was very quiet besides the faint sound of the dispatcher still saying, "Hello, are you there?"

Then the light went out, and it felt like the air was suddenly sucked out of the room. I jumped back when I saw the darkness starting to pour in under the closet door like a weightless goo. I quickly grabbed one of my mom's coats and covered the space under the door, trying to keep this diseased darkness out. I could hear my mom through the darkness pleading with the dispatcher to send help. She was sobbing now as the dispatcher tried to calm her down with no success. Then there was a loud boom that shook the entire room, and I could hear the bedroom door exploding. Pieces of wood slammed up against the closet door, making loud banging sounds and violently shaking the hinges on the door. My mom began screaming at the top of her lungs, followed by the high-pitched screech of the dark entity trying to speak again.

"Where is she?" the entity asked. "Where is she?"

My mom was still screaming, but the entity's voice could still be heard clearly over her screams.

"Tell me where she is, and your death will be quick. Toy with me, and I will savor your death for hours. Tell me now; I won't ask you again."

Its questions were answered with louder screams of terror. I wanted to kick open the closet door and protect my mom, but doing so would jeopardize Sarah's life, and I loved her too much to leave her defenseless against this evil thing.

"You think you are strong, and the love for your children will keep you silent. I will show you how wrong you are; I will show you a level of pain and suffering you can't possibly imagine, and

150

right before I take your life, I will make you betray them. And before death takes you, I will make you watch the pain your silence brought on your children. Yes, I can feel your fear; I can taste it. Its flavor is wonderful. I will enjoy feasting on your pain."

Then I heard the agonizing screams of my mom as that thing began to attack her. It was clawing into her flesh with those talons, and all I could do was listen to my mom die a horrible death to protect me and my sister. Over her screams, the entity moaned and laughed in enjoyment at the pain it was causing her. It was almost like it was experiencing some kind of sensual rush from her suffering. Sarah was overcome with grief, crying while constantly whispering, "Mom, Mom, Mom," over and over again. The coat I placed under the door started to dissolve right before my eyes, allowing this strange darkness to seep inside the closet. The situation was devastating, and normally I would be frozen with terror, but miraculously, I was far from that. The feelings of determination and purpose began to build up inside of me. Something was awakening in me, and slowly, things became clearer than they've ever been.

The room felt like it was spinning as my fear began to subside, giving way to a more potent and powerful emotion. Tears rolled down my face as a warm feeling came over my entire body. Suddenly, I felt a deep emotional yearning for my sister and my mother. Hearing my mom's screams and listening to my sister's heart breaking as she listened to our mother being tortured sent a tidal wave of empathy through my body. I wanted to protect them and see them safe and alive from this ordeal. Their safety and well-being became more important than my own.

I didn't care what happened to me and how much pain I would have to endure saving them both; all that mattered was keeping them alive. It felt like waves of fire were hitting my chest over and over again, engulfing me in an emotional state I'd never experienced. I moved towards the back of the closet, held Sarah's head in my hands, and kissed her on her forehead. I knew what I had to do, and I was willing to do it. As I placed my hands on the closet doorknob, I realized exactly what emotion I was feeling. It was love, pure and uncorrupted, and this love sent waves of energy through my body. This love I felt was so intense it shook the very foundations of my being. This love was so potent and engaging that it seemed to take on its own consciousness, and soon it would materialize into a power that I'd never known.

Walking out into the room, I immediately felt my body temperature rise, covering my entire body in sweat. The heat coming from my body became so intense the sweat on my arms started to boil and turn to mist.

What's happening to me?

My body temperature was rising drastically as I felt my fingertips become numb; and then I saw it. The entity was astride my mom on the bed, clawing at her with those glowing weapons of evil. The closer I got towards the bed, the hotter my body became, until my skin began to give off a glow similar to the light that the entity's talons emitted. I was becoming light-headed, but unlike previous times, I didn't feel faint. Actually, I was more focused than I'd ever been. By the time I was at the foot of the bed, the light and heat coming from inside me were so bright, the entire room was engulfed in it, and the darkness that covered the room was dissolving and peeling away like the outer skin of an orange.

The glow from my skin began to surround the form of the dark entity, but it was so consumed in torturing my mom it didn't notice me. Somehow, even though I'd never experienced this kind of power coming from inside of me, I knew exactly what I needed to do next. A bright light blasted from my hands, and I held them out in front of me, reaching out to grab this evil and expel it from this room, from our home, and away from my mother. The light flashed across its face, and it turned suddenly and screamed,

"It was you! It was you all along! I thought it was the girl!"

And then it began screeching again, trying to move away from me, and then another blast of energy shot out of my body towards the dark entity, causing the entire room to be engulfed in flames. Soon the heat inside me was so intense my clothes burst into flames, but the fire didn't burn me; rather, it seemed to become an extension of my body and consciousness, and the fire began moving and burning the darkness at my command. The entity cowered in the corner by the windows, trying to move away from the light and fire that was burning through the room. It coiled like a snake, hissing as it tried to get out through the window. When I saw what it intended to do, I commanded the fire to prevent its escape, and suddenly the window burst into flames, blocking its only way out. It began hissing again as it ducked back into the corner and kneeled down in fear.

I could hear my mom screaming for Sarah, but her voice seemed far in the distance; a mere echo in the bright light and fire that had become the controlling environment in the room. I was still moving towards the evil that had now become the prey and not the predator. In the light, this thing wasn't so menacing anymore, and now it seemed like a small matter to deal with. Its dark and misty form slowly began dissolving in the light, and what was left was a shocking revelation. Once the cloak of evil was shed away, what remained was a man I came to trust, a man I decided to love as a father despite my initial reservations. Kneeling before me was Jason, but he wasn't the same man I knew, and his eyes seemed to harbor a deep hatred and fear that sucked the love I felt for him right out of me.

To see that hatred in his eyes was even more devastating because his deception was so complete he made us all believe he loved us, that he loved me as a son, giving me the father I never knew and the love I've always yearned for. But we were all wrong. During the terror and chaos, I assumed that this thing had killed

Jason, taking his place where he was standing at the island in the kitchen. It never crossed my mind that this thing and Jason were the same person.

As I walked towards Jason with the intention to end his reign of deceit and terror in our lives, I vowed to never make that mistake again. I began to feel another surge of energy build up inside me. This energy was hard to control, and the fire in the room started to burn more intensely as it concentrated all its energy towards the corner where Jason was kneeling. I started to lose consciousness right before I heard Jason scream in agony as the energy shot through my body, and then... darkness...

CHAPTER TWENTY-TWO
SARAH'S REVELATION

I hate hospitals. I hate the smell, the sterile atmosphere, and the oppressive sense of death that hangs over everything. Hospitals feel like the waiting room to the afterlife, where operating tables are the ticket counters to the beyond. Now, here I am, sitting in a waiting area, terrified that this hospital will be the one to send my mom and my brother to the afterlife. My mom is in serious condition from blood loss and shock, and Aiden is in a coma. Today will forever be etched in my "weird shit is afoot" book. I can't begin to rationalize how this all started or how it's playing out. It's way too much for a fifteen-year-old to handle.

I'm trying to relax in this uncomfortable chair, but at least Tony is here next to me, making things a bit more bearable. We both reek of smoke and sweat, but Tony is covered in soot and ash, even his hair has some in it. Despite everything, I almost giggle at how funny he looks. Tony is always so put together, so seeing him like this is strangely amusing. But laughing feels out of place with all the worry about my mom and brother.

"So, tell me what happened in there?" Tony asks, his eyes wide with concern.

He looks like he has some idea of what went down, but I know he can't possibly fathom the truth. His concern is sweet, but there's nothing he can say to make this better. My mind is a mess, and I'm sure I'll be dealing with the trauma for years to come. I just hope I'll be able to sleep with the lights off again someday.

"Sarah? What happened?" he repeats, more insistent this time.

Why do guys do that? Keep asking questions even when they know we're not ready to answer. But Tony did run into a burning house to save my brother, so I guess I owe him something. But do I tell him the truth or make up a story about a faulty socket or an iron left on a bed? I don't want him to think I'm crazy. The last thing I need is my crush thinking I'm one screw shy of a straitjacket.

I take a deep breath. "I don't know," I finally say.

Tony looks annoyed, but I can't give him the weird truth about what happened. Not yet. I fidget in my chair, trying to avoid thinking about all the supernatural horrors I've witnessed today. The fight with Jasmine, the dark entity that attacked us at home, the sight of people with ghostly attachments—it's all too much.

It all started in the school hallway when I heard someone call my name. I turned around, but no one was there. I felt someone watching me, following me, but the hallway was empty. The whispering voice echoed through the corridor, bouncing off the walls and lockers. I felt the hairs on my arms stand up, and my skin crawled as if bugs were moving under it. I tried to brush it off as a trick of the air conditioning, but then it happened again. When I turned back around, Jasmine was standing right in front of me.

I'd always heard guys talk about how beautiful she was, but looking at her up closely, I felt she was overrated.

Ok, I might have been hating a lil bit. Truthfully, the girl was flawless.

Her smirk made me uncomfortable, and without thinking, I let out a quiet yelp at her sudden appearance in front of me. She seemed to enjoy my discomfort, and that made me angry. She tried to make small talk, but I cut her off, telling her I didn't have time for chit-chat. She ignored my hostility and kept talking. I couldn't even remember what she said—I just wanted to get away from her.

I tried to walk past her, but she grabbed my arm with a grip colder and stronger than it should have been. Now, I was livid. Just as I was about to punch her, she said, "Jason isn't who you think he is. He's done horrible things, and he will do the same to you and your family."

How dare she say that about Jason? She didn't know anything about him. Enraged, I slapped her, really fucking hard. The sound echoed through the corridor. But then she did something I wasn't expecting. She kicked me across the face. I don't even know how she managed it from such close range. The next kick to my stomach knocked the wind out of me, and I fell to my knees. She stood over me, smirking, but I wasn't done. I executed a sweeping kick that missed but followed it with a spinning kick to her chest that sent her flying.

I stood up and looked at her across the hall. That smirk was gone from her face and replaced with a look of surprise. I could tell she was too confident in her fighting skills and didn't expect me to be as skilled as I was.

Stupid, arrogant bitch.

Looking at her I wanted to pound her face in until nothing was left but mush and bone fragments.

She staggered to her feet, clutching her chest, her breathing ragged. Once she regained her balance, she inhaled deeply and then charged toward me, her eyes blazing with fury. I wasn't about to back down. I met her head-on, and when we were within striking distance, we unleashed everything we had on each other. She was much stronger than me, and every blow that slipped past my defenses landed with punishing force, leaving me reeling. My strikes, on the other hand, seemed to have little effect on her. Realizing I couldn't win this way, I shifted my strategy. I backed off, letting her come to me, and focused on countering her attacks instead of merely reacting. Each time she struck, I quickly repositioned myself to her side or behind her, making her pay dearly for every miss. It wasn't long before she was screaming in frustration, cursing every time she failed to land a hit, and I took full advantage, landing blow after blow to her head and body.

But then I got greedy. I stuck to the same tactic for too long— a mistake my sensei had warned me about countless times—and she made me pay for it. When I tried to slip behind her again, she anticipated my move. She bent low, stepped back, and suddenly, I found myself in a vulnerable position as she grabbed a handful of my hair. She wrapped it around her arm and yanked me backward, slamming me to the floor with brutal force. The impact was so hard I bit down on my tongue, the sharp pain nearly bringing tears to my eyes as the bitter taste of blood filled my mouth. But I refused to give her the satisfaction of seeing me break.

I knew I was in trouble. Despite the damage I'd inflicted on her, she had won the fight with that one decisive move. Lying there, I braced myself for the onslaught, expecting her to exact revenge for the beating I'd just given her. But when I looked up at her, I was shocked to see a different expression in her eyes. Instead of the anticipated fury, there was a strange look of compassion. She seemed to be checking me over, almost as if she were concerned for my well-being.

As I lay there, vulnerable, waiting for her to pound on me, she placed two fingers on my forehead and whispered, "Awake." Then she walked away. I laid there on the floor for about a minute, trying to gather myself and make sense of what just happened. When I finally stood up, I felt different but couldn't pinpoint why. I felt a draft blowing through me that wasn't there before, like something in me was now exposed. I checked myself to make sure I was fully clothed, and everything seemed to be there; but at the same time, I kept feeling like I was missing something or something that was once heavy was now much lighter.

When I walked outside, there were hundreds of students celebrating with a few teachers overlooking the chaos to make sure things didn't get out of hand. As I searched the crowd for Aiden, I glanced over at Mrs. Palpachek, the school's nurse, watching a group of students that was further away from the rest of the crowd.

They were clearly up to no good and I could tell she knew it. As she walked towards them, I saw something move behind her. At first, I thought I was tripping and seeing things; a result of hitting my head on the hard floor, but when I took a second look, I was sure I wasn't. Whatever it was seemed to be attached to her and it was moving around and through her. It was ugly and disfigured like an old doll left in a fire. It appeared solid but was able to move in and out of her body like a ghost. As terrified as I was, I couldn't keep my eyes off it. Suddenly, it noticed I could see it and it growled at me, revealing a mouth full of jagged teeth. Mrs. Palpachek immediately turned around and gave me the evilest look, like I'd invaded her privacy or caught her cheating on her wealthy husband. Which, if rumors were correct is something she did regularly. She was a very beautiful woman with an amazing body and because of that she got special treatment from the male faculty as well as the principal and took full advantage of it.

She wasn't a nice person and whatever was attached to her wasn't nice either. It was threatening and aggressive, constantly scratching at the air in my direction. Mrs. Palpachek also seemed agitated by the way I was looking at her and she decided to go elsewhere and out of my line of sight instead of checking on the students.

What was happening to me?

Was it the knock on the head from hitting the floor? Was I going crazy? I was losing my cool and it got worse once I started looking closely at everyone and noticed they all had those misty things attached to them.

Some were similar to Mrs. Palpachek's, and others were different and not as aggressive. They seemed peaceful and their forms were beautiful and serene. Some were a mixture of the two, like the arms would be disfigured while the rest of the body wasn't so deformed. It was strange and terrifying to see everyone have these entities clinging to them as if these things wouldn't survive without the host they were attached to.

All kinds of things popped up in my head from alien invasions to demonic possessions. But none of them made sense or seemed to describe what I was seeing. As bad as I wanted it to be an illusion, something inside me told me these things were real and I began to understand the feeling I had in the hallway. Jasmine had done something to me, but I didn't know what or how. I just knew I was different now and I didn't see my life going back to how it used to be anytime soon.

I ran back inside, trying to escape, and that's when I ran into Tony—literally. He helped me up, and I hugged him, seeking comfort. But then I saw his entity, and I screamed and immediately jumped away from Tony and pointed at it. He looked around himself to see what I was pointing at. Tony's little visitor was hiding behind his head. I carefully looked at it and I realized that his little creepy visitor wasn't disfigured or aggressive. Actually, it was very shy and cute like a koala bear, but it didn't have any animal features, nor did it look anything like Tony. But looking at it, I realized it was Tony or something that was a part of him. I can't really explain how I knew this, but something in me started to make sense of what I was seeing.

"Are you okay?" Tony asked. I nodded as I slowly walked towards him, never taking my eyes off this thing that was now hanging on his arm. When I got closer, it hid behind him, only peeking out once or twice, then quickly hiding again. Then when I got about a foot from Tony, the thing popped its head out of his stomach and then jumped back in. Its sudden appearance startled me, and I jumped back again but this time I laughed. Tony was really confused and grabbed my hand and told me he was taking me home. I told him to give me a minute so I could call my mom to let her know I was on my way home. As I began dialing, I noticed from the corner of my eye that Tony's little companion was watching me. It was perched on his shoulder and staring at my cell phone's screen as I dialed. It would look at me and then back at the screen. I was getting too comfortable with this.

Back home, I paused outside my front door for about ten minutes; afraid to see what type of supernatural things would be attached to my family. When I finally got the nerve to open the door, I noticed the house felt different and oppressive. The atmosphere was so toxic, I almost walked my butt right back out of the house. But I decided to keep going towards the kitchen when I heard my mom's voice. I really needed my mom at that point; I just wanted her to hold me in her arms. Maybe her love could help me calm my nerves and make things better.

But after seeing the monstrosity attached to Jason, I knew no amount of hugging would make things better. Jason's entity was death materialized before my eyes. It was rotten, horribly disfigured, and moving like a serpent, slithering in and out of him. Calling it aggressive would be an understatement. It seemed to feast on Jason, biting and gnawing at him. Even though it couldn't physically harm him, it appeared to be devouring pieces of Jason and swallowing them whole. I screamed when it stared at me and grinned, allowing pieces of rotten flesh to fall from its mouth.

I don't know what is going on with my family. I can see ghosts attached to people, Aiden can control and walk through fire, and Jason was a demon sent by someone named Alal to kill us.

Snapping myself back to the present, Tony keeps pressing for answers. I just want him to drop it, but he deserves some explanation.

"Listen, Tony, I really can't talk about this right now. I need time to process everything. I'm sorry."

He looks like he won't let it go. Just like Aiden, dense and persistent. But I can't deal with this now. I need to focus on my family. I got up and walked towards the receptionist's desk. As I pretend to ask the receptionist a question, I see six agents walking towards me. They surround me, ignoring the receptionist. I quickly notice their ghostly entities are hideous and aggressive. I started to conclude that the uglier the attachment, the uglier the person's soul they are attached to. I try to leave, but they block my path.

"Uh, Tony! A little help here?"

Tony tries to intervene, but the agents won't budge. One demands, "Where is Aiden?"

I stare them down, not answering. They threaten to take me into custody, but I stand my ground, defiant. After a few minutes of playing the silent game, my patience was exhausted, and I decided to break the silence.

"Why are you looking for my brother? What are you planning on doing to him?"

"We plan on doing what anyone in our position would do... kill him!" one agent finally says.

"Tony! Get me out of here!" I shout, fighting against the agents. Tony joins the fray, and security gets involved. Just when it seems hopeless, my brother Manny appears with four uniformed men. The agents retreat, and Manny's team chases them down.

I collapsed into Manny's arms, crying. I've been through too much today. Now, all I want is to be with my family and hope we can find a way through this nightmare.

CHAPTER TWENTY-THREE
TIME TO GO

I was awakened by aggressive whispers from familiar voices. I tried opening my eyes, but they felt so heavy and burned from the glaring light above me. I heard a constant beeping sound to my right and quickly realized I was in a very uncomfortable hospital bed. My vision was blurry, but I could make out Sarah, Mom, Tony, and Manny. What was Manny doing here? From their body language, it was clear Mom and Manny were in a heated argument while Sarah and Tony looked on. They were so engrossed in their argument that no one noticed I was awake.

"Mom," I croaked, trying to get their attention.

The sound of my voice brought immediate silence. Everyone just stood there, frozen, trying to process that I had spoken. Then Sarah broke the silence, screaming my name as she ran to me. She threw her arms around me, holding me tightly and kissing my cheek. She had never been this affectionate before, and while it felt a bit weird, I was too weak to protest, and honestly, I didn't want to.

Soon, everyone was hugging me—everyone except Manny. He just stood by the door, staring at me with a stern look on his face. What was his problem? We'd almost been killed by a supernatural entity, and I managed to save us, yet he looked like I had messed up something important. Both Mom and Sarah were crying, and even Tony seemed choked up. It was a touching yet disturbing scene because my big brother seemed so distant that he was no longer part of the family but merely an observer.

"How did I get here?" I asked.

"Tony," Sarah answered. "Tony went into the house while it was burning to pull you out."

"Thank you, dude, I know..."

"Don't even say anything, bro," Tony interrupted. "I would have run in there twenty times if I had to. You're like my brother, and no matter what we go through, I won't give up on you, let alone leave you in a burning house to die."

"Mom, are you okay?"

"Yes, baby, I'm okay, just a few deep cuts and bruises, but I'm going to make it. I'm not supposed to be out of bed, but your brother hasn't been the most graceful visitor, so I had to get up."

"What? What do you mean? Manny? What's going on?"

I was really confused. We had almost been murdered, and Manny had an attitude? What was really going on with him? I would think he would be happy to see us alive, but instead, he seemed almost disappointed.

"How dare you blame me? I wasn't the one that invited and slept with that... that... thing. How could you? You just pissed on my dad's memory by fu—"

"Hey! Wait one minute. I'm still your mother, and you won't talk to me that way!"

165

"You aren't acting like my mother! You know what's out here; you know better than most. Instead of being careful and responsible, you acted like some hormone-crazed teenager and put us all in danger. You knew! You knew how dangerous things are for our family these days, but you still decided to act irresponsibly. So no, I'm not all choked up and relieved."

As I lay in bed, things became confusing. Manny kept saying over and over again how my mom knew. Knew what? How could she know that Jason could possibly be a murderous demon? While I was daydreaming on the bed searching for answers, the argument grew louder, and soon people began to gather outside the door, watching and listening to the heated exchange.

"Stop it, both of you!" I said. "From what I've been told, I was in a coma, and our mom was viciously attacked by something we can't even begin to explain. I'm awake, and we are all alive. Yes, we are hurt, and the house is destroyed, but we have our lives, which is more important than anything else. So right now, we shouldn't be arguing but celebrating our chance to see another day! Plus, you are giving me a headache!"

Everyone just looked at me, mouths open. If I weren't so tired and groggy, I would have looked the same way. Where did all that come from?

"Mom and I need rest, Manny. We've been through a lot, and we'll have all the time to argue when we get out of the hospital in a couple of days."

"A couple of days? Do you think you are spending another minute in this hospital? No, little brother, we are leaving now! It's no longer safe here. Actually, it's no longer safe in this country, period. So, I hope you haven't used up all your energy making that passionate and moving speech because we have a plane to catch... all of us!"

Something was very wrong here, and nothing in my wildest dreams or nightmares could prepare me for what was to come in my life after that night.

Spain, in my humble opinion, was one of the most beautiful countries in Europe. It was full of culture and history and happened to be where my grandparents lived. Even though most of their family lived stateside, my grandparents refused to live permanently in the US. My grandma would say America was only worth a vacation, never a one-way ticket. My grandparents stayed in the town of Marbella, located on the Andalusian coastline known as Costa del Sol. It was a very beautiful and luxurious resort town located in southern Spain. They owned a magnificent beachside estate that was just steps away from the coast. The views from every window of their home were breathtaking. Things in Marbella were elegant yet simple. Life moved at a much slower pace in Marbella, so a vacation there was better enjoyed than some other well-known vacation spots in the world.

You could do a lot in Marbella and the surrounding towns but still get the much-needed rest to justify a vacation. Because what good is a vacation if you come back exhausted? Marbella was a somewhat secluded town, so I guess that's why Manny decided to bring us all here. I was still very weak, and my mom was still healing from her wounds, so everyone let us be for a few days, giving us time to heal and get our heads together. During those few days, I mostly stayed in bed, looking out the window at the beautiful view and trying not to think about all the unanswered questions swirling in my head. During the nights, though, I slept with the lights on, fearing what could be lurking in the darkest corners of my room.

Manny warned me not to get comfortable when we got to Marbella. Not knowing what he meant, I decided not to let it wreck my brain. He was getting on my nerves with all the cloak-and-dagger stuff, but that was Manny, always the soldier. Sometimes I thought he was overreaching and trying to make his role in the armed forces more important than it was, which made his behavior even more annoying. But I guess pride will do that to the best of us. When I was strong enough to move about on my own, my grandfather called me into his study late one night. When I walked into the large study, I noticed Manny standing next to the door's entrance. He seemed to be at full attention, with some luggage sitting at his feet. Both Manny and my grandfather remained silent when I walked into the dimly lit room. Okay, so now Manny has my grandfather in on this James Bond-themed fiasco? This was really getting old.

"What's going on?"

"No time to talk, Grandson. Take this and put it on."

The lack of ample light in the room made it hard to make out what he was handing me, but when my eyes adjusted, I realized it was a black head covering.

"Wait! You want me to cover my head in that? What are you guys—Al-Qaeda? You can't be serious right now. I'm not putting that over my head! Grandpa, what's going on?"

"Listen, we don't have time for this. Either put it on yourself, or I'll make sure you don't need that to black out your vision!" Manny warned.

"Try it! You just try it! I'm not that little boy that followed you around the house. It's not gonna be easy this go-round, I promise you that, Manny. I'm not pu—"

Without warning, I felt a sharp pain in the back of my head, and then darkness.

CHAPTER TWENTY-FOUR
BLOODLINES OF WAR

"Amazing! Simply amazing! How could this be?"

"We were hoping you could tell us."

These were the words I heard after regaining consciousness. My head felt like it would explode from where Manny hit me.

Wait… he did hit me. What the hell? Oh, it's on now!

"Where is Manny?!" I yelled. "His ass is mine!"

An unfamiliar voice answered from behind me.

"Your brother is gone, young man."

His voice sounded old, with a strong English accent, so either I was in the home of a British national in Spain or I wasn't in Spain any longer. My grandfather stood in front of me with a look of worry and amazement in his eyes.

"Who is that?"

"My name is Sir Jaffrey Landers, and I am Baraqu (*Ba-rock*)."

I turned around to face Sir Jaffrey Landers. At this point, I needed answers for everything. Jason, my sudden ability to create and control fire, and Manny knocking me out. The Manny thing had better have a damned good explanation; otherwise, he and I had some unfinished and unpleasant business to attend to.

"Who are you really, and what the hell is a Baraqu?"

The man before me was much older than my grandfather. His hair was completely white, and he had the bluest eyes I had ever seen. They were an ultramarine blue that made the rest of the room fade into the background. He stood over six feet tall and, despite his age, seemed to be in great physical shape. He wore a fitted short-sleeve collared shirt and casual slacks. Strangely, he was barefoot, standing on what appeared to be a very cold concrete floor. The room we were in seemed to be on a lower level of an old structure, well-lit and decorated in an old-world yet elegant decor. There were paintings and maps all over the walls that seemed much older than any I'd seen anywhere, including museums.

He stood grinning at me with a look of admiration that gave me a weird vibe. I was very uncomfortable because my questions weren't being answered. The old man was just standing there, looking me over like I was some kind of new specimen ready to be studied and dissected.

"Okay, is anyone going to answer me? No? Then show me the exit because I'm out of here! Grandpa, I don't know what you and Manny's malfunction is, but I am not amused by how this has all gone down. And tell Manny that he better watch his back because that hit he gave me isn't a freebie; it's on credit right now, and one day I will come to collect with interest."

I started walking towards what I thought was the door, but the old man was standing in my way, still smiling with amusement at my reaction.

"Excuse me! Please let me by."

"Oh, by all means, be my guest," Jaffrey said and stepped aside with his arm extended towards what I believed was the exit.

Now he's trying to be gracious. Prick!

As I walked past him, I noticed what I thought was a door that was actually another painting that was so big it covered the wall from floor to ceiling. Where is the door? I looked around the room, trying to find a way out, but there wasn't a door anywhere. Maybe it was behind one of the paintings. At this point, I was getting very upset and afraid, willing to rip every painting from the walls until I found an exit. I noticed my grandfather and Jaffrey watching me with amusement as I ran around the room, but when they saw my intention of snatching some of the paintings off the walls, they looked at each other and said in unison: "Wait!!"

"Have a seat, Aiden, please," my grandfather pleaded. "There is a lot that you don't understand, and you will need to sit down to hear this. This man, Sir Jaffrey, has all the answers you seek. He can help you with the changes you have been going through."

"Changes? I don't know what you're talking about," I denied.

"Aiden, please, I know exactly what's happening to you, and Jaffrey can make sense of everything, but you have to be willing to listen and learn. He has a lot to show and teach you, but you have to be open to receiving what he has to share with you. I trust him, and if I didn't trust him, I wouldn't have brought you to him. I've known him all my life, and your father also knew him."

"Dad knew him?"

"Yes, he did. He helped your father on several occasions, and he's here to help you, too."

"So, my dad went through this, too?"

"Not exactly, Grandson. Your situation is very unique, and because it's so unique, it's also very dangerous to keep you in the dark any longer. So please calm down and listen to what Jaffrey has to say."

I decided to have a seat for two reasons: one, I had concluded that if I wanted to leave this place, I would need Jaffrey or my grandfather to show me the way out, and fighting them wasn't going to make that exit just appear. The second reason was I needed answers and a lot of them. It seemed like everyone knew something except the person experiencing this phenomenon. My mom, Manny, Grandpa, Grandma, and even my deceased father. This had better be good.

After I took a seat, Jaffrey walked towards me and asked if I wanted something to drink. I declined, even though I was thirsty. I wasn't in the mood for any more delays. I needed answers now.

"Ask me the most important question in your head right now, Aiden."

"What am I?"

"Good, very good question. Well, you are Baraqu, and the light inside you has awakened. You and I are the last of our kind. I am also Baraqu, and before you started going through the awakening, I believed I was the only and perhaps the last of our kind. But you… you surprised us all."

"Hey, Jaffrey, I'm not sure you are aware of this, but that name holds no meaning to me. I don't know what that is or what I am."

"Yes, you are correct; you are not aware because if you were, this room would not be able to hold you, your brother would not have been able to touch you, let alone knock you unconscious, and the man you knew as Jason would not have been able to infiltrate your home and attempt to murder you and your family. To explain what we are, I must start from the beginning."

"What beginning?"

"Creation, Aiden, the beginning of all things in this realm."

"Realm?"

"Yes. You see, some of the smarter people on this planet believe that the universe is filled with life on other planets, and they are partially correct. There is life elsewhere, multitudes of living beings that inhabit countless worlds, but we are all separated by realms. One realm can't cross over into the next without certain keys or invitations. Some realms are uninhabitable by other beings from other realms because the environment is toxic to them. Like a fish out of water, eventually, it will die because its oxygen is found in the water and not in the open air, and vice versa for humans. This separation is crucial to the harmony and continuity of the universe, but it wasn't always so. Eons before man walked the earth, the universe was a dark abyss filled with dark entities of evil. The Creator decided that the time had come for order, so she spoke the most powerful words ever in the history of this universe: 'Let there be light.'"

"God isn't a girl and creation happened in seven days, according to the Bible."

Laughing, Jaffrey shook his head and continued.

"One day in the eyes of the Creator isn't the same as in the eyes of man. Creation wasn't automatic, nor was it a peaceful process. When *she* uttered those words, she commissioned her warriors of light, the Immaru, to go forth throughout the universe and expel the evil that inhabited the darkness. Creation was a process, just like the seasons changing to bring about a year or the day going through its stages before it ends. Everything happens in stages, and creation was no exception.

"The Immaru fought for eons against the demons of the deep, and after each victory, the Creator created a new realm of light and life. Because the Creator loves variety, each form created was never the same, and she created some of the most beautiful forms the Immaru had ever seen. Then the time came to strike at the very heart of the demon realm. Here, in the center of the universe where this planet Earth resides, was the last stronghold of the demon race and their sickening darkness. The Immaru, after so many realms of war and death, had grown weary, and one of their most decorated generals decided he had enough. He despised the Creator for driving the Immaru to such lengths without any reward, so he decided to create dissension among the ranks by lying to them, saying he had been assured by the Creator that when they had conquered this final realm, the Creator would give the Immaru this realm to call their own as a reward for their undying service.

The Creator would create a lasting paradise for them so that they would be allowed to not only rest but also be given the ability to procreate and live in peace. You see, the Immaru were eternal entities, and unless they were killed by another eternal being, they would live forever, but they were never given the gift to continue life from themselves. They were created, not born, and during the 'War of Light,' they found themselves longing for the ability to have children of their own.

They watched as the Creator granted the gift of continuous life to mortal beings and observed the joy it brought to them. But it was here at the final stroke during the war in this realm that the great deception took hold of them, and their desires turned to envy when they discovered that the Creator had not intended to grant them such a reward. But the General knew that this would happen; he intended for the Immaru to turn against their charter of being the protectors of the realms and the keepers of the light. But what the general didn't intend was for the Creator to create a form as unique as man. Not only did she grant them continuous life, she also granted them free will, something that only the Creator possessed.

After observing this, the Immaru were enraged and decided to march against the Creator in battle. Needless to say, the war was swift and brutal as the Creator single-handedly defeated the Immaru. For their betrayal and disobedience, the Immaru were banished and made to remain in this realm to live among the creation they hated the most. The General was punished for his deception by being cast into the dark realm where all the conquered demons were banished. He soon became their king and has vowed vengeance on the Creator and mankind ever since his fall.

With the Immaru banished in this realm, they came to a crossroads in their existence. They lost their immortality and their access to the cosmic power that was theirs to wield at will. They were still superior beings, and some decided to separate themselves from mankind. But some embraced their new existence and began to mingle with humans, helping Mankind advance. Then one day, an unlikely union revealed a most intriguing discovery. The Immaru may have lost their favor with the Creator, but they also gained the one thing they truly desired—to create life from themselves. But this gift wasn't without irony because only through man was this gift given. They could not create life with each other, only with humans could their bloodline continue, but the bloodline would be diluted, and the purity of who they were would be lost forever.

Along with having to rely on mankind to continue the bloodline, the Immaru also discovered that through man lies the key to unlocking their powers. Instead of accessing the cosmic powers of the universe, the Immaru were able to access the power of emotions and the energy that they created. They discovered that the energy emotions created, although not nearly as powerful as the cosmic energy from the universe, was still a formidable power source. Like having a power cable connected to each living creature on this planet and the emotions they felt daily; the Immaru drew their power from the emotional content of humans. At first, there seemed to be no difference in the energy mankind's emotions emitted, until one day twin brothers in a field took up weapons against each other, and by the time the fight was over, one had been murdered.

The emotional energy of murder and pain was broadcast across the realm, and when the Immaru felt this energy, it was unlike anything they had ever experienced. Some became instantly addicted to the power negative energy created; like a drug addict, they needed more and more. Others were repulsed by the feeling and refused to use the negative energy, and this is when the great divide occurred.

Eventually, two factions of the Immaru emerged: the Lalartu, which means shadow or phantom, and the Baraqu, which means lightning. The Lalartu decided to only use negative emotional energy, and the Baraqu decided to only use positive emotional energy. Of course, this divide posed a huge danger to mankind because for the Lalartu to get the energy they yearned for, they would need to create pain and suffering to mankind, and they went about that task with precision and vigor.

The Baraqu became the protectors of mankind and were chartered to keep the Lalartu, or the Shadows, from destroying the world of man. Now both sides, due to their arrogance, did not find it necessary to hide their presence from mankind, and eventually, the antics of the Lalartu caused mankind to take matters into their own hands. That is when the Kashaptu, or Wiccan, came into existence."

"The who?"

"Witches and Warlocks. Humans, when created, were given free will, and with this blessing, were given limitless possibilities to advance themselves, knowledge being the fuel that fed their advancement. Eventually, mankind began to delve into a realm of energy they call the paranormal or spiritual realm. This is a realm created by the Creator, but mankind was not supposed to have access to this realm; however, for reasons unknown to us, even to this day, humans were given access, and the knowledge poured out. Soon the Kashaptu possessed enough knowledge to be able to combat not only the Lalartu but the Baraqu as well. The more knowledge humans can internalize, the more powerful they become. A human's power comes from within, and even in the most hostile environments, mankind can flourish, and that is a power that neither side can touch.

So, the Wiccan began their campaign to rid the world of both sides of the Immaru. Eventually, a pact was reached once the Wiccan discovered that the Baraqu weren't a threat to them, and the Wiccan and Baraqu joined forces to rid the realm of the Shadows. Mankind began calling us Elementals because of our ability to control the elements of the planet. Just when we thought we had the Shadows defeated, a new evil arose, and its name was Alal (*Ah-laal*). Half Shadow, half Warlock, yet all-powerful, he began leading the Shadows, and he seemed to have knowledge unlike anyone, even the Immaru. He taught the Shadows that to control man's emotions, they must control the human mind, and they began to start working in the background. No longer fighting on the battlefield but executing a campaign of greed and deception that would cause mankind to shed any idea of positive thinking.

Humans became self-centered and self-destructive. Each century, humans gave off less and less positive energy, and our ranks became weaker and weaker. Soon the human seed became more dominant than the Baraqu seed, and fewer of us who possess power were being born. Creation will only create what it needs, and because negative energy became the most dominant energy in the realm, nature began to produce more Shadows than Baraqu.

Things seemed hopeless, until Anshargal, which means 'great prince of heaven,' was born. He was a hybrid, having a mother who was a Shadow and a father who was Baraqu. He wasn't Baraqu or Lalartu; he was Immaru, the original form, and he had a direct connection with the Creator and access to the cosmic energy that the Immaru were cut off from. Something that was seen as an impossibility had been made possible, and the universe made it so to restore balance in this realm. Most in this world called him a Messiah, but he was more than a messiah for mankind. He was the reemergence of the 'Warriors of the Light' and forgiveness from the Creator. He was to be the vessel through which all would return to the source and mend the divide between our kind and bring humans into our fold.

But Alal saw him as a threat and convinced a group of Wiccan to assist him in the greatest crime in the history of the universe. A secret meeting was called that was supposed to be a peace treaty between the Baraqu and the Shadows. With the emergence of Anshargal and the humans' acceptance of his powers and lineage, they led the Baraqu to believe they were ready to mend the divide. But the Wiccan cast a spell to bind the Baraqu, which left us powerless to stop the crucifixion and murder of Anshargal. Alal made sure that neither Shadows nor Baraqu touched Anshargal. He left it up to the humans, and he intended to make the Creator so angry with mankind for the murder of Anshargal that he would destroy the planet, leaving only our kind to remain, but what he didn't account for was Anshargal's sacrifice.

It wasn't a sacrifice of the flesh but of his soul. All energy after being used returns to the source, but what Anshargal did was command his soul to remain here, surrounding this planet and protecting mankind from the wrath of the Creator. The Creator couldn't stand to destroy the essence of Anshargal, so her wrath was kindled, but she turned her eyes away from this realm until mankind became what the Creator intended and the Baraqu and Shadows become the Immaru again.

After the murder of Anshargal, no more Baraqu warriors were conceived, and this planet fell into darkness, with the Shadows led by Alal taking complete control over this planet. Their purpose, as it has always been, is to create an environment conducive to their addiction to negative energy. They are the facilitators of chaos, and mankind carries out their orders with perfection."

CHAPTER TWENTY-FIVE
OF SHADOWS AND MEN

I sat there, confused and terrified by everything I was being told. Any other person would chalk this conversation up as the ramblings of a lunatic, but his revelation spoke to me deeper than any poem or song; it touched the very depths of my soul, and at that moment, I knew I was being fed the truth. A truth that billions of people on this planet were not privy to. But there were still some things that didn't add up, like why me? Why now? And what kind of powers did I possess?

"I know you are wondering, Aiden, what all this has to do with you." My grandfather had now taken over the conversation and began to reveal to me that even though no other Baraqu warrior was born after the death of the hybrid, the bloodline never died, and there were people on this planet born with extraordinary abilities. Athletes, musicians, soldiers, etc.—all kinds of people born with an edge that gave them abilities others saw as superhuman, and the ones gifted with the more extreme abilities were recruited to join the fight against Alal and the Shadows. They were everywhere, working in secret, trying to prevent a complete global meltdown of everything good in this world. But they were seriously outgunned and outnumbered, and with the humans siding with the Shadows, things had gotten worse. The Shadows had heads of state, businessmen, and people of influence in their pockets, doing their bidding across the globe. Anything that caused mankind pain and anguish wasn't an accident.

Everything was planned, right down to small details like traffic jams and bad customer service. Anger, pain, murder, injustice, hunger, wars, pollution, racism, religion, disease, and oppression. All these things were assets in the Shadow's general ledger, and from what my grandfather was telling me, business was booming. Manny and my father were part of the resistance, and they carried out dangerous covert missions against the Shadows to weaken their grip on the realm. But they never had a Baraqu Etlu, or warrior, on their side, and this was basically a recruitment meeting for me. They needed my help to fight the good fight, and even though all this sounded noble, I had my reservations, and anyone in my shoes would feel the same.

"Okay, what is so special about a Baraqu warrior exactly?"

"We are wielders of time and space."

"Huh? Jaffrey, you have to break that down for me because I don't follow."

Jaffrey got out of his chair, smiling, and walked towards the far side of the room.

"We can- control time and space, which means that anything that falls under the realm of time and space we can change. For example, the chair you are sitting in is controlled by time and space. Right now, that chair is sitting at that exact location at this exact time, and it's taking up an exact amount of energy and real estate within space and time. Well, if I wanted to, I could remove it from the equation and move it to the other side of the room instantaneously."

"Bullsh—"

Before I could finish my curse word, I was falling to the floor, the chair having disappeared from beneath me, and just when I was bracing myself to feel the hard floor connect with my ass, the chair reappeared underneath me as if it had never moved.

"What the hell was that?!"

"That was me moving time and space and altering reality."

"So, what you are saying is, with all this power, all we can do is move chairs around? Great, call U-Haul and tell them they're saved."

"No, that was on a smaller scale, Aiden. If you possess enough positive energy, you can do things that would seem impossible. You could appear to possess superhuman strength by altering your muscle density. You could soar through the skies, changing the rules of time and space to fit your desire to fly. You could split the earth to swallow an entire city, or you could make the entire planet disappear."

"Wait, are you saying I could pull a 'Kris Angel' on the planet?"

"Yes, if you can harness enough positive energy. Mr. Angel is a Shadow, by the way; so it's not exactly the same thing, but you are grasping the concept. Anything that falls within time and space is at your disposal, but just like a car, if the tank isn't full, the automobile can only go so far. Because there is very little positive energy left in this realm, making the planet disappear is impossible."

"So, if I feel all positive and chipper, I could do whatever I wanted?"

"Exactly! And with my training paired with external positive energy, you can be a very powerful ally for the order of the Baraqu."

"Training?"

"Yes, I have always been a keeper of our history and a teacher to those who possess the powers of the Baraqu."

"How long have you been doing that?"

"Over six thousand years."

"What! You're telling me that you are over six thousand years old? Man, whatever. Now you are playing with me."

"The Baraqu don't age like humans. Yes, we eventually die if not killed in battle, but some of us can live to be tens of thousands of years old before we succumb to old age."

"Do the Shadows know about you still being alive?"

"No, they do not. That is why you needed to be blindfolded..."

"No, I got knocked out," I interjected.

"Yes, knocked out because we can't risk them finding me here."

"So, you don't trust me?"

"Actually, no, I don't, and I won't trust you until you decide to accept the charter of the Baraqu and rid the world of the Shadows and their evil leader, Alal."

"Accept the charter? What do you mean exactly by that?"

"Aiden, it's no secret that we are losing this war, and I am unable to take the battle to the Shadows because of my lack of access to positive energy. You have to understand that this world is producing vast amounts of negative emotional energy, and any positive energy that may be produced is quickly eliminated. One of the best places to draw positive energies, until late, was sporting events. They were a goldmine for me, and I could draw that energy from anywhere in the world. But now the Shadows have moved to eliminate that source as well by allowing games to be rigged, quelling any cause for the fans in the stands to rejoice and give me the energy I need.

"But even if I was to act, I need to do so behind the scenes because if the Shadows found out a Baraqu warrior was still drawing breath in this world, they would stop at nothing to prevent me from seeing another day, and I don't have access to enough positive energy to repel all of them."

"And he is important to this war, Aiden," my grandfather added. "Without him, we would have no inside information as to what we are up against. He has been around for a very long time, and even though he can't join the resistance on the battlefield, he is a great tactician and has led our cause to many victories."

"So let me get this straight. What you are telling me is I am a descendant of cosmic super beings that were banished here on Earth. That I am some kind of half-breed that feeds on human emotions to gain powers, and I have an enemy that is addicted to negative human emotions. That enemy has managed to take hold of the entire world by creating an environment of suffering and pain, making it almost impossible to use my powers, and you want me to join in the fight to stop them? From the way things look, you've already lost. I mean, potentially your most powerful ally is a dead, drained battery that needs recharging, but the enemy controls the energy source, so basically, you are bringing a toothpick to a nuke fight.

I don't know, but it doesn't sound like I could do anything to turn the tide. I am bound under the same laws he is," I pointed out.

"No," Jaffrey said. "Somehow you can produce your own energy source from within. And I can tell you that energy source is very powerful if you were able to destroy a Shadow like Telal (*Thelaal*), the man you knew as Jason. Telal was the right hand of Alal and the second most powerful Shadow in their order. He was also the deadliest assassin this world has ever known. He was a master at getting so close to his targets that they would fall in love with him and wouldn't see their demise coming until it was too late.

Aside from being a very powerful Shadow, he possessed a unique ability; a rare gift that very few in history have had the privilege to possess."

"And what is that?"

"He was a shapeshifter."

"He could change his physical form to look any way he wanted?"

"Not exactly, Aiden. You see, humans see things in the physical form, but the reality is who we really are is embedded in our soul. The unseen denominator that determines what kind of people we are and will become in the future. Our soul is what drives our character and how we interpret the world around us. It is often referred to as your Zini by our kind. It is true the flesh profits nothing; it's only a shell that covers up what matters. Telal could see a physical manifestation of your soul and change his soul to match your own, causing a false sense of security and trust in him. It's something that no one can combat, not even the Baraqu and Telal is responsible for murdering numerous key leaders of our order.

He was a formidable warrior, and he commanded an elite squad of assassins who were insanely dedicated to him. His death will send shivers through the Shadow's ranks, and they will want retribution. I am also certain his death has already gotten the attention of Alal, who rarely gets personally involved in this war. He has minions, both Shadow and human, across the globe doing his bidding with almost perfect efficiency. So, until now, he's had no reason to personally get involved; but seeing that his second-in-command has been killed, I can predict he may look into this matter himself."

"So, is that why you guys whisked us away to the other side of the world and then proceeded to get all cloak-and-dagger with me?"

"Yes, after the events at your house that ended with the death of Telal, your life is in more danger than it was before. So if you are to face this danger head-on, you will need to learn how to harness and use your powers."

"Okay, why would I want to do that? I never asked for this, nor do I want it! All I want to do is be normal, play football, go to the NFL, meet a nice girl, get married, have children of my own, and did I mention being normal?"

"Yes, you did mention that" responded Jaffrey.

I could tell he was getting agitated by my lack of willingness to accept who and what I was.

"How about I just hide out and don't go back to Deerfield? Start over somewhere else where they can't find me."

"Aiden, there is no place in the realm you could hide from the Shadows. They can track you now. If you try to use your powers or have them awakened further by any emotional stimuli, they will find and destroy you. The only reason why they can't find you here is because I have cloaked my energy signature in this place. But make no mistake, you and your family have been marked for death."

"Why them? They aren't Baraqu, are they?"

"Yes and no... you and your siblings carry the bloodline, but you are the only Baraqu warrior. But all of you are gifted, and they will also murder your mother to close the circle. Our experiences with their execution squads are they leave no one alive to carry on the bloodline."

"So, they must have known I was a Baraqu Warrior all along and that's why they sent that murderous monster, Jason!"

"No, they didn't. They couldn't have known because your powers were dormant, so there was no way for them to know this. Your family has a long history, starting centuries ago, of fighting Alal and the Shadows, and some of your ancestors are responsible for some of the greatest defeats the Shadows have faced. So, your family is well known, and we think he was sent there to get close and observe, waiting for your brother Manny to make contact so that they could track him and murder him."

"Manny? Why would they want to kill Manny?"

"Because he and his team are on to something big, and not even me or your grandparents know what they are doing. It must be a serious threat to the Shadows for them to send their best assassin and his followers to come after your family. I think his attack on your family was triggered by something he saw in your sister because, from what she said, he was concentrated on her."

"Do we know what he saw in Sarah?"

"Not at the moment. She's not talking about it, but hopefully, she will, because we need as much information as we can to better train you both in protecting yourselves."

"What about my mom, is she…?"

"No, she's not. The Baraqu bloodline comes from our side of the family. We hope you see the seriousness of the situation you face, Aiden," responded my grandfather.

"I understand to an extent, but I'm still wondering why you would want a teenager to join the resistance. I mean, you guys are worse than an African warlord recruiting child soldiers."

"I wish I could offer you some kind of comfort, Grandson, but I can't, and I am sorry you have been thrown into this war. We all tried to keep you and your sister away from the minefields, but the recent events have forced our hands. You have to stop seeing yourself as a child or teenager. Your childhood was over a few nights ago, and now it's time for you to step up and be a man."

"I'm not ready for all of this, and I don't know how you expect me to be so accepting of becoming some kind of super-soldier. I didn't even want to go to the armed forces when I thought we were all normal, and now you want me to join in a war that's full of supernatural beings that want revenge on me because I accidentally killed their greatest assassin. I'm just not so eager to go out and kill people."

"That's understandable, but you must know that the people you are trying to avoid killing didn't offer your father the same courtesy," Jaffrey responded.

"What are you saying? The Shadows murdered my dad? So he wasn't killed in action in Iraq?"

"No, he was returning from a highly classified mission when his team was ambushed. The rest of his team managed to escape, but he was captured, tortured, and killed," Jaffrey answered.

I felt anger swell inside of me at this new revelation. Everything I thought I knew or believed was all a cloak hiding the real truth, and discovering my father was a victim of the Shadows made things even more complicated.

"If the mission was so secret, how was he ambushed?" I asked while trying to fight back the emotions I felt when I played back that violent vision I had on the night of my birthday. I began to understand what I saw, and realizing my father may have actually gone through that torture almost made me lose my cool.

"I won't lie to you and tell you that every Baraqu can be trusted, and they support the resistance. Some of them would rather not fight and hope that the Shadows will show them mercy. They are rarely correct in their assumption, and once their usefulness is drained, they are disposed of."

"So, he was betrayed by his own people? Nice, and I'm supposed to fight for the same people that gave my dad up? Yeah, that is really giving me incentive to take up the battle for the Baraqu."

"Aiden, the fight isn't for you or those people who made those decisions. It's for the future of this realm and all the other realms that stand to fall if the Shadows succeed. It's only a matter of time before they figure out how to cross over into other realms and cause the same havoc they caused here. Their evil and power will be limitless if that is allowed to happen.

"I still don't see how I can make a difference. They have the same power I have and, according to you, a lot more of it."

"That is incorrect, Aiden. I'm sorry if I led you to believe your powers and theirs are equal. Positive energy is much more powerful and potent than negative energy. Positive energy keeps the sun active; negative energy would cause it to falter and shut down. Some see that as a great and terrible power—to possess the power to shut down the sun. But in reality, the sun would shut down not because the negative energy is so potent, but because the energy that has taken control of it isn't powerful enough to sustain its unrelenting power. One of us could, with a snap of a finger, lay waste to legions of Shadows with the right amount of positive energy at our disposal. But heed my warning: Don't ever underestimate their power. They are still formidable adversaries. But their power has limits and boundaries, which positive energy does not.

"Baraqu controls time and space, which creates reality, and Shadows control that reality," added Jaffrey.

"Wait! You are confusing me, Jaffrey. You just said time and space equals reality, and the Shadows control reality, so that would make us equals, correct?"

"You have much to learn, Aiden. Reality is made up of time and space, so that would mean you control the elements that give Shadows their powers."

I sat there for about a minute, trying to make sense of what Jaffrey was saying, but it still wasn't clicking for me. How could the

Shadows controlling reality make them weaker than those that control time and space?

"I can see you are trying to wrap your head around this concept. Let me make this easy for you. Without time and space, there is no reality. But time and space can exist even if reality doesn't."

It was starting to make a little more sense to me. I still needed more time to think about that concept to fully understand what Jaffrey was trying to teach me. But I was getting there.

"So, you are saying I could just walk into a host of Shadows and just start handing out cans of whoop-ass?"

"Yes and no, but we will get into that more once we start your training."

"Training? I never agreed to join the resistance!"

"No, you didn't, but I will train you all the same. You must learn to protect yourself and your family if you are to survive another week. So enough talking for tonight. Tomorrow, we start training, and during your training, you can think about joining the resistance. But by the end of your training, you must make a decision."

"How long is my training?"

"That's entirely up to you, Aiden. Get some rest. Tomorrow is going to be a very interesting day for both of us."

CHAPTER TWENTY-SIX
MAKING HARD CHOICES

To say I couldn't sleep that night would be an understatement. Actually, I didn't even attempt to fall asleep. My head was a traffic jam of thoughts, emotions, and fears. My entire world had been turned upside down, and everything I thought I knew about reality was just smoke and mirrors. Everything about my dad, the world, my family, and my future was now an unknown variable. I felt completely exposed to this new world I had awakened to. Throughout the night, I found myself praying that all of this was a horrible nightmare and that when the sun rose, everything would go back to normal. The whole ancient battle between two races of superior beings—and me being one of the last warriors—sounded like a really good RPG video game.

If only it was just a game. If anyone had told me any of this before experiencing Jason the other night, I would have laughed in their face. And if they had told me this before coming in contact with Jasmine, I would have suggested they get medicated immediately. But after experiencing those two, it all made sense. As much as I wanted it to be some kind of sick YouTube conspiracy theory, I couldn't ignore what was happening to me. And Jason... I still felt the closeness and love I had for him. He did a serious number on me, and no matter how hard I tried, the remorse of taking his life hung over me like a dark cloud. I knew it had to be done, but I wasn't happy about taking another human being's life. Even though Jason wasn't completely human—he had some extra shit going on inside him—just like I did. Never in my darkest nightmares did I imagine that I would be forced to kill someone, especially someone I thought loved me.

All these thoughts played on my sanity and emotional stability. I knew my grandfather and Jaffrey wanted me to become a man, but I was only seventeen years old, and no matter how you slice it, this was a much bigger piece of cake than I was expecting from life. The more I replayed the scene from my mom's room in my head, the more emotionally unstable I became. What did Jason do to me? Why was I feeling sorrow for the man who was planning to murder all of us? I tried to fight back the sorrow and anguish, but I couldn't. Before I could regroup, I began to cry uncontrollably. The more I fought, the harder I cried. I found myself gripping the covers in anger. My muscles were so tense they began to shake, and soon it was like I was having a seizure. My heart was racing, I began to sweat, and my eyesight became blurry. The room was spinning, and I felt like I was being pushed toward the wall.

What is this? I thought. Am I having a heart attack, or am I being attacked by some unseen force? My symptoms worsened the more I fought my emotions, and before long, I'd fallen off the bed, unable to move. It felt like my body was shutting down, and eventually, I felt my lungs would too. As I lay there unable to move, the only thing I could think of was Sarah and my mom. I felt like they were both in the room with me, begging me to stop fighting and let my emotions flow. But I didn't want to feel the way I felt.

I didn't want to feel sorrow for Jason, and I definitely didn't want to feel the love I had for him. I wanted to hate him with every inch of my body, but no matter how I tried, I couldn't. I loved him, even at the moment when I took his life, I loved him. This was a truth I didn't want to accept, but in that room, feeling my body shut down, I needed to make a decision. Either hate Jason and die, or admit I killed a man I loved as a father and live.

Was this a test? Whatever it was, I was willing to fail before I succumbed to my emotions. My lungs had completely stopped working, and I could feel the burn in my chest as my body fought to survive. I was moments away from blacking out for probably the last time, and I welcomed the darkness. There was no way I would ever admit I loved Jason, so if this was my end, so be it—let the darkness take me. A thin veil of darkness began to cover my eyes, and then...

I heard two thunderous claps and found myself kneeling in a garden. I could feel the sun's heat on the back of my neck and the breeze blowing past my face. When I lifted my eyes, I beheld the most beautiful natural setting I had ever seen. The colors of every tree, flower, and blade of grass seemed enhanced and illuminated in the most beautiful hues. The air tasted sweet and free from the pollutants and odd smells one would encounter in today's world. Was this heaven? I thought as I smiled, looking around and taking in more air and the beauty that surrounded me.

"No, you are not in heaven." The voice came from behind me, and it was none other than Jaffrey. I quickly turned to see him standing there with a worried look on his face.

"What is this?"

"This, Aiden, is the beginning of your training, and you failed your first lesson. You failed it miserably."

"Are you telling me that whole seizure thing I experienced back there was a test?"

"Yes, and you failed."

"Whatever! What was the point of it? To make me admit I love the man who tried to kill me and my family?"

"No, that was just the surface of the test. The purpose was for you to accept your emotions and use them to save your life. But it seemed you'd rather die than let your emotions flow."

"You got that right, Jaffrey! No way will I ever let love and Jason be in the same sentence with me, let alone feel it."

"Then you will never be able to protect your family and become Baraqu."

"Oh damn, there goes my dream! Bummer!"

From the look on Jaffrey's face, I could tell he was not amused by my sarcasm.

"I told you already, I want no part in being a Baraqu. So not passing the test really doesn't ruin my day. Sorry, but I'm just keeping it real with you, Jaffrey."

"Keeping it real? You have no idea what that means. You are lying to yourself, Aiden, and if you don't accept the emotions that flow through you naturally, you will succumb to the unnatural emotions created by man and be ultimately destroyed."

"Man-made emotions? C'mon, Jaffrey. Are you telling me that man created his own emotions?"

"Yes, hatred being the most vile and powerful of them all. When you are born, you have no idea what hatred is. A baby can only love. It is when we fail that a child begins to feel unnatural emotions like hunger, abandonment, and pain. When we fail, we introduce these unnatural emotions that teach a child to ultimately hate. Hatred is taught to a child; it's never a gift from life but a curse from man. So when we fight and ignore the emotions that flow naturally, we again fail and become our worst enemy. Like you, Aiden. You decided you'd rather die than let your natural feelings flow. This way of thinking and feeling has to be unlearned if you are to become a warrior and possess the power necessary to protect your family. Whether you decide to join our cause or not, the Shadows will not stop until your entire family is dead. And your family's safety is entirely up to you because, though your brother Manny is a very skilled soldier, he is not capable of fighting the Shadows head-on.

You are your family's only hope of safety, and if you refuse the training I am giving you, you are condemning your family to death. Either at the hands of one of Jason's students or another assassin; they will die, and you will be the cause of their deaths because you refused to act when action was needed."

"So, I have no choice? Either train with you or everyone I love will die?"

"Yes, that is your dilemma. You are free to refuse, but for every action, the universe reacts or responds. It's truly up to you."

Jaffrey was right. I had to go through with this if I wanted to keep my family safe. I didn't want the responsibility, but life isn't fair—it never is.

"I will give you a warning, Aiden. Unless you accept your true feelings for the Shadow you killed, you will never reach your full potential and again you will be leaving your family vulnerable."

"Okay, now I will agree to train, but I won't feel what you are suggesting, and I would really appreciate it if we changed the subject concerning Jason."

"Very well, Aiden. Shall we begin?"

CHAPTER TWENTY-SEVEN
METAMORPHOSIS

ver what seemed like five hours, all we did was meditate and exercise. For a man who was thousands of years old, Jaffrey was in unbelievable shape. He put me to shame by outperforming me in every physical and mental category. He constantly teased me, calling me out of shape and a young "Thundercat." I guess he thought it was funny and "hip," but it wasn't. It was kind of weird knowing this man, who was thousands of years old, knew about a cartoon from the eighties. I would think a man of his experience would be reading books on strategy and enlightenment, not watching cartoons. But what was even stranger was that, regardless of how long we had been in this forest, the sun never went through its natural progression. It just remained in the same position in the sky. After so many hours, its position should have been towards the west, not still in the east. I tried to ignore it, but after a while, it kept eating at me. I just had to ask.

"Hey, where are we?"

"Keep moving, Aiden!"

"Wait, we've been at this for hours, and the sun hasn't moved one inch—that's not normal. So where are we?"

"I said keep moving!"

At this point, I was getting upset. I hated being ignored, and given my current predicament, withholding information could mean my family's demise.

"Okay, I'm not going to take another step until you tell me where we are!"

Jaffrey stopped running and turned to me with a look of anger in his eyes.

"I said move! I'm not going to repeat myself."

"And if I refuse? What are you going to do? Kill me?"

"The thought crossed my mind!"

"You actually think I'm afraid of you, Jaffrey? Things here don't seem right, even with all the beauty around me. I want answers, and if killing me is an easier task than telling me where the hell we are, then so be it!"

Jaffrey smiled and placed his hand on my shoulder.

What the hell? He thought this was funny?

I quickly snatched away and took a step back to make sure he couldn't touch me again.

"Jaffrey, you may be all-powerful, but I will not hesitate to kick your ass if you try and hurt me."

Jaffrey began to laugh until tears started falling down his face.

"What's so funny?"

"You remind me of myself during my training with my teacher. He always said I was one of the most difficult yet most talented of his students. I never saw myself as being difficult. I, like you, just wanted answers and didn't trust the process in the beginning. Now I understand completely what I put him through, and it's cosmic comedy at its best."

"Jaffrey, look at my face. Do you see a smile or even a giggle coming on?"

"No, Aiden, I do not. I meant no disrespect."

"So why the threats? Why the games?"

"Aiden, this was all a test!"

"Another test?!"

"Yes. In training, you will be tested to find out exactly what kind of Baraqu you will become and the limits of your potential. I have trained many Baraqu in the past, and you are by far the most intuitive of them all. It only took you mere hours to discover and gain the resolve to question your current situation. Normally, it would take days and weeks before they got the nerve to question their trainer. I am not in the business of training 'yes' men and walking-talking 'sheeple'. No, we train those with a mind to think and use it. Regardless of how things may seem, how beautiful they are, if your soul speaks to you and tells you something isn't right, you must have the courage to speak up. Even if it's someone you love or look up to; it shouldn't matter, you must have the resolve to discern what's right and act. This is the foundation of our order. We can't sit idle and let even those we love to behave contrary to what we know is right. This is one of the major problems with mankind today. Fear—fear prevents people from acting and rising up against oppression and tyranny. They wait for others to act, and while they are waiting, someone else is also waiting, and a chain reaction occurs. The entire planet is sitting on their asses waiting for someone else to make things right. As Baraqu, we can't become mentally lazy and complacent."

The more Jaffrey explained, the more I began to understand how much I didn't understand. I thought even as a teenager I was ahead of the curve. Boy, was I wrong. I was clueless.

"So can you tell me where we are?"

"Yes, we are in an alternate reality that I created just for this training exercise."

"What do you mean a different reality? All of this isn't real?"

"Yes, it is…this isn't an illusion. As a master wielder of time and space, I can create an alternate reality to which I can invite whomever I want. I can create all the scenery I want and create my own canvas. But I am unable to create any life forms that require 'Shi' or the breath of life. Only the Creator has that power. But I can create wildlife, plant life, landscapes, etc., but I can only maintain this alternate reality for a limited time. Once I'm done with it, I must dispose of it. It can't be permanent."

"Why not? I mean, that would be a great idea to create the perfect vacation or chill spot! Beaches, oceans, great islands with all the trimmings. C'mon, Jaffrey, why would you not want to keep a place like that for yourself?"

"Because you are altering the order of the universe and keeping that reality permanent could break our current reality. We are creating an unknown and smashing it into the known without the proper process of creation. We are taking personal order and implanting it into universal order. Who's to say making this reality permanent wouldn't cancel out another reality? Who's to say it wouldn't create a supernova that would eradicate all organic life in the universe? We have no idea what it would cause, so we must maintain it for a limited time and then correct the ripple in the fabric of time and space when we created this alternate reality."

Creating these alternate realities is essential to keeping the Shadows' prying eyes in the dark about what we are planning."

"So now that I've passed this test, what's next?"

"We continue to train. You think you've been here for hours, but in reality, you've only been here less than five minutes."

"What!"

"The most I can maintain an alternate reality without it beginning to affect the universe, is about an hour, tops. If you didn't pass the test within that time frame, we would have to stop, and the training would end."

"End?"

"Yes. I would have to stop training you and revealing the secrets of the Baraqu."

"Why?"

"Because you don't possess the mental capacity to handle the power you would wield, and you would become your own worst enemy and potentially become a harbinger of destruction. That is something we cannot allow. Just because you have the power of the Baraqu inside you doesn't mean you will become Baraqu. It's not just enough to have the power; you must also have the wisdom to use it. Our time is up here. It's time to move on to another form of training."

"Which is?"

"Wielding and controlling the elements."

"You can teach me how to control fire, electricity, water, and other elements?"

"Yes, I can, but can you learn?"

"We'll have to see."

The thought of being able to control lightning was just badass to me. I was hoping this training wasn't all smoke and mirrors. I was standing there picturing myself shooting lightning out of my hands and eyes like a superhero. Yeah, it was going to be badass. Well, that's if I could learn because I had the feeling the whole control-time-and-space thing would come into play, and I still hadn't gotten the concept.

"Shall we leave, Aiden?"

"Yeah, let's go."

Then Jaffrey did the most awesome thing I'd ever seen. He calmly walked forward, stretched out his right arm with his hand held open, and then closed his hand like he was crushing a piece of paper. Instantly, everything around us was absorbed inside his hand; like balling up a piece of paper that was on a wall, but instead of paper, it was an entire world.

When I looked around, we were back at his place. It all happened in less than three seconds, and the swift change in the environment and lighting made it hard for my eyes to adjust. Never in my wildest dreams could I have imagined this kind of power being available to anyone. Not even in comic books or movies was this kind of power displayed. It was amazing and unnerving. I started to understand why my mental state was so important. Someone with a really bad attitude with this kind of power at his disposal could be a walking, breathing Armageddon.

"What was that? How did you do that? That was incredible!" I yelled. I couldn't contain my excitement at Jaffrey's display of power.

"This is the power you will wield, and you must be trained to use this power responsibly. You must understand and honor the laws of relativity and govern yourself accordingly. Using this power is no small matter, and that's why the first thing we have to know is if you have a mind capable of thinking for itself and a will to use it. We will train in the art of elemental powers first. Elemental powers are the weapons of the battlefield against the Shadows and any other enemy you may encounter. The power to alter reality is a power that will be learned much later once you've mastered your ability to harness emotions and the wisdom of which emotions to use."

"Can Shadows create alternate realities?"

"In a way. They possess a power called Erset La Tari, which means 'land of no return.' It allows them to place people in a dark, hellish reality where evil spirits occupy a dark abyss. Many have perished while under the Erset La Tari spell."

As he continued to explain Erset La Tari, it dawned on me that was exactly what Jasmine was doing to me. I never gave it much thought until that second, but it appears that Jasmine was also a Shadow. But how could she be a Shadow yet warn Sarah about Jason the night of the attack? I would think she would rejoice in our demise, not warn us. Especially now knowing she was trying to kill me with that dark nightmare she kept putting me in. I was so confused, and I guess my inner turmoil was written all over my face. The look on my face alarmed Jaffrey, and he walked towards me with concern in his eyes.

"Tell me, Aiden, have you experienced this curse before?"

I was hesitant to answer because then I would have to relive my nightmarish visions every time I was around Jasmine, and from what I've just learned maybe a Shadow.

"Yes, I have."

"Where?"

"At school."

"School? At your high school?"

"Yes."

"That is not good. How many children were affected? How many were lost?"

I was really confused.

"What do you mean how many were affected? No one was lost, I was the only one affected."

"Impossible, Aiden, unless you were alone. Where did it happen?"

"In the lunchroom first, then on the football field during tryouts, and also during a game. I wasn't alone. There were hundreds of students and teachers around."

"That is impossible! When a Shadow performs Erset La Tari, it affects an area, not an individual. Entire towns and armies have been lost when a Shadow performs the Erset La Tari."

"Jaffrey, I'm telling you I was the only person affected."

He still had a look of disbelief on his face.

"Maybe you were not made aware of anyone else that may have been affected. Most of the time only Baraqu can escape the Erset La Tari alive. You are very fortunate that you survived being cursed multiple times even though your powers were not awakened. Although your resilience was amazing, it's still very shocking. I need you to tell me everything."

So, I spent the next two hours explaining every detail of my encounters with Jasmine and all the events that led to the night Jason revealed himself. After I was done, Jaffrey sat in his chair, silent, looking at the floor.

"I don't know what to say. Everything you told me doesn't make sense. I know you are telling me the truth. I can feel that from you, but it doesn't add up. Something else is going on here. Firstly, you should not have survived the first time she performed Erset La Tari, but to survive three times and to have the curse only felt by you is even more bizarre. When Shadows use that curse, it takes a vast amount of negative energy to cast, and it's used to take out multiple targets, never a single individual. I have never seen that kind of power wielded by a Shadow, let alone a teenage girl. It would take a great amount of power for a Shadow to concentrate the Erset La Tari on just one individual and prevent anyone around them from being affected. The concentration and mental control of that girl is something we have never encountered before in all our dealings with the Shadows. If what you say is accurate, she would be even more powerful than Jason, who was the second most powerful Shadow in their order. His powers were only exceeded by Alal, who is a Shadow and a warlock. A very powerful and dangerous hybrid.

But that would also mean you possess a power that no other Baraqu has ever possessed. Even while your powers lay dormant, they still protected you. That is the only explanation why you survived Jason's attack and were able to destroy him. Aiden, you must understand that very few people in this realm, Baraqu included, would have been able to defeat him. You possess a power inside you unlike any other. If you apply yourself, you could be the most powerful Baraqu in history.

Only a pure Immaru would be more powerful, and they are the original form of our kind that wielded cosmic energy, not just emotional energy."

"I'm still not impressed, Jaffrey. This whole situation is hard to deal with."

"I understand, and it is unfair to expect you to be able to deal with it, but life isn't fair, and if you wait around for life to play fair, you will die. It's that simple."

"Dying isn't simple, Jaffrey."

Jaffrey laughed at my comment.

"Yes, Aiden, that is correct. Death is complicated."

Jaffrey decided to call it a day after our talk about Jasmine. I knew he was going to try and research more about her and see if maybe there was something he could find. I hope he did because if I was to ever run into her again, I wanted to be prepared. The last thing I needed was for her to get the upper hand on me again. I guess one good thing was that now I knew I wasn't turning into a serial killer. But after everything I've been told, I almost wished I were a serial killer; it would be much simpler to deal with. I almost wished that... almost.

The start of the next day of training didn't consist of any alternate realities or secret tests. Just Jaffrey and me standing in a room he used to train in. There were all kinds of targets on the walls and other contraptions I was unfamiliar with. A lot of them had various blades and weapons attached to them. I got the eerie feeling that today's training was going to hurt... a lot. According to scientists, there are 117 known elements. The truth is, there are close to five thousand different elements in the realm. This does not include the man-made varieties. The Baraqu have always known of the existence of these elements but refused to reveal them to mankind to preserve the little life and sanity that remains in the realm. And Baraqu can control every one of them. We can combine them, create from them, see them, and also use them as weapons with just a thought. This ability gave us the name Elementals by those of mankind who had the privilege of knowing our true identity. Depending on the situation, we will use a certain element or a combination of elements to either neutralize or identify a threat. Whether it's a Shadow, man-made weapons, or viruses. Through this power, we can fight and defeat almost any threat. First, we must identify these elements, and the only way to do that is to harness time and space.

Damn! Things were sounding so good until he said that. I wasn't prepared for this, so I hoped he had some kind of manual.

CHAPTER TWENTY-EIGHT
MOVING MOUNTAINS ONE BOX AT A TIME

"How do I do that, Jaffrey? I'm not gonna play games with you. I'm still finding it hard to comprehend the whole control-time-and-space thing."

Jaffrey smiled and walked over to the far side of the room and clapped his hands. The sound of his hands colliding sent shockwaves through the room, causing my ears to start ringing. I bent down, covering my ears, trying to avoid the shockwaves. Suddenly, the ringing stopped. When I stood up, I noticed I wasn't in the room anymore but in outer space. The shock of being in space caused me to scream without even knowing it was coming out of my mouth. Again, Jaffrey smiled.

"Relax, Aiden, we are safe. I created an invisible air bubble so we will be able to breathe."

"Okay, but can you give me a heads up before you start whisking me to outer-worldly locations? I mean, maybe once I get myself more acquainted with my powers, you won't have to. But right now…I really need a heads up because I almost had a heart attack."

"All right, I can do that."

"So, out of all the places to explain time and space, why are we here?"

"Because to explain what you need to know, you have to see it in action."

"Okay, fair enough."

I began to look around and marvel at the greatness of what was beyond our blue skies. It was miraculous and a moving experience to view space in this manner. It was like looking at the beginning of everything.

"Look around you, Aiden. What do you see?"

"Space—a vast amount of space!"

"Exactly, and everything that occupies it. Time and space are the reasons why our reality exists. Our atoms exist at a particular time in space. This is our reality. In a different realm, different atoms exist at another time in space. We can alter the time and space that anyone or anything occupies in our realm. If you have access to enough power, you could, in theory, move the Earth where Venus is and vice versa. But only by accessing cosmic energy can that be accomplished. Our powers, though great, are on a much smaller scale than that. Time and space are all around us; it is us. So, to harness them, all you need to do is think, believe, and it will be so."

"So, I can do anything I can think of?"

"That depends. Without the confidence and belief in your powers, you cannot. If you believe you are strong enough to relocate a house, it will be so. If you have any doubts and reservations about your ability, it will not, or you could only relocate half of the house and cause more damage than good. That is why the emotional energy we receive from mankind is so important. It's like a battery to our powers. It fuels the powers we possess. We harness the positive energy that mankind gives off from experiences that enrich their lives. The feeling of getting that job they always wanted or the emotions someone may feel from getting that beautiful crush to notice them. When their favorite sports team wins a championship or a crucial game, that first kiss, and love. These emotions, among others, are the fuel that moves the power within us to allow us to do amazing things.

Positive energy is an energy that demands confidence to be wielded. If you are unsure or if you are affected by negative emotions like hate, pain, or fear, that energy source subsides, and your power source becomes weaker. So it's not enough just to be able to harness the emotional energy from mankind; we have to remain on the frequency of the energy we use. Positive thought for positive energy. You can't hate and use the powers of the Baraqu. Your powers will become ineffective, or they will become tainted by negative energy, and soon you will become what you are supposed to fight against."

"So, I must be in a constant chipper mood to use my powers?"

Jaffrey laughed at my question, but I could tell he was expecting it.

"No, it is impossible to feel like butterflies and butterscotch on the field of battle. No man, unless he is inherently evil, can find joy on the battlefield where death and destruction surround him. You will experience emotions that you've never thought you could in those situations, and joy isn't one of them until the battle is won. It is your intentions that drive the positive thoughts that enhance our powers. You are on the field of battle to protect your loved ones, you are protecting those who can't protect themselves, you are a warrior of light fighting evil and preventing the entire planet from falling into darkness—these, among other reasons, are the driving forces that should provoke us to respond to a threat. We never react; always respond. Always keep your head and understand that even though you possess great power, you are a servant and not a master."

"A servant? Now wait a second, Jaffrey, I'm no one's servant."

"And it is that attitude that will break your power source and leave you vulnerable to attacks."

"I don't understand how you can say we are servants when we possess such great power."

"Because we are here to serve, not to be served. These powers were given to us for a purpose greater than ourselves. If you try and use these powers strictly for your own personal gain, you will not only fall to temptation, but you will also lose your power."

"How is that possible?"

"This power we possess is a gift, but not a gift for us. It's for mankind, and we are to use it to protect mankind, not enslave them."

"Isn't that what the Shadows are doing? I mean, looking at the state of the world, it seems like not only do they still possess powers, but they are winning!"

"Yes, it may seem that way, but what you fail to understand is that even though they still possess power, it comes at a cost. That cost is being weaker than intended. The Shadows found a much darker source of power that doesn't have the same rules we are governed by. So they can use their powers for personal gain and to enslave mankind."

"So, they have no rules and we do. Seems kind of unfair, doesn't it, Jaffrey?"

"Maybe to the untrained mind, yes, but without guidelines, there is chaos, and the universe is built on order, not chaos. Of course, the inhabitants of this planet have been led to believe that the universe is filled with chaos, and everything just happens by coincidence. It's a free-for-all universe, and the only reason why this planet exists is because of a Big Bang millions of years ago. Even if a Big Bang did occur, there had to be something that initiated that bang. There can't be a vast universe of nothing, and then one day…BANG!" Jaffrey responded.

"Without a deciding factor. Something greater than us decided to allow that bang to occur, and something greater than us decided to let life flourish in the realm. It is because of this that we serve a cause greater than ourselves. We are the warriors of light and order. Look around you, Aiden. Does the universe look chaotic to you?"

"Actually, no, it doesn't. It seems like everything has a purpose."

"Exactly. You are learning, Aiden. Open your mind to being more than yourself, be Baraqu, a warrior of light, a warrior for life and order."

Listening to Jaffrey explain how all life is connected and our relationship to it made me realize how wise this old man was. Only someone who has been around thousands of years could amass this kind of knowledge and wisdom. He understood his purpose and the purpose of the powers we possessed, and he wanted me to understand them as well. I was getting it, but it still seemed like such a big responsibility. Before, all I wanted was to start as a running back on the school's football team, and now I was being coached and trained to be, for lack of a better reference…a superhero. It was a lot, but I knew I had no other choice but to learn as much as I could, so that I could protect my family—because their protection was now in my hands.

"Now it's time to return to the training room. Do you think you have grasped the time-and-space concept?"

"Honestly, I still don't know, but I do have something up here dancing around now that makes sense."

"That's a start. Let us return." And just like he did before, he began clapping, and shockwaves started to fill the air bubble.

Just as suddenly as he folded the alternate reality the day before, he managed to get us back in the training room, but not without my ears suffering from the transition.

"Jaffrey, can I ask you something before we continue?"

"Sure."

"What is with all the theatrics when using your powers? I mean, that last session actually hurt. Is that something I'm going to have to do to get my powers to work?"

"No, each of us uses what we feel comfortable with to invoke our powers. I love theater, always have. The way men and women create a whole world just from their imagination—no powers or tricks, just great imagination and skills. What do you feel comfortable with or what relaxes you, Aiden?"

I had to think about that question because no one ever asked me that before. I mean, I loved playing video games, football, and driving my new car, but I didn't think that would translate well, and none of these things relaxed me. The only thing I knew that relaxed me was Tai Chi. I practiced Tai Chi every morning before going to school to relax and get my blood flowing. When I did it, I felt like I was swimming in the air. That's it! Tai Chi! When I told this to Jaffrey, he seemed very pleased. He went on to say that using Tai Chi as my expression to invoke my powers would help me to focus and maintain a level head during intense situations and encounters.

He then told me to focus on the far side of the room. There, on a table, was a big cardboard box. It looked like a moving box of sorts. It looked harmless enough, but the only thing was, it hadn't been there before. I wanted to ask, but I decided not to; I didn't want it to appear I was stalling the process of training.

"Now I want you to make that box appear on the other side of the room."

"Don't you mean move it?"

"No, teleporting that box is easy; making it appear without any time lapse isn't. You must learn to use your powers to manipulate time and space and not the power to manipulate reality."

"There you go again, Jaffrey, confusing me."

"Okay, where is that box?"

"Over there."

"What time is it?" I looked at my watch and noticed it was only nine-thirty in the morning, but it seemed like I had been awake for much longer.

"It's nine-thirty."

"So that box is over on that table at nine-thirty in the morning, correct?"

"Yes!"

"So now make that box appear on the other side of the room at nine-thirty in the morning."

After listening to him explain it that way, things started to make sense, and I began to understand the concept of manipulating time and space.

"So that box being over there on that table is the current reality?"

"Yes."

"And when I manipulate time and space, I change the current reality to the box being on the other side of the room at the same time."

"Exactly! Moving the box is only manipulating reality. Shadows can move that box, but they can't make it disappear and appear instantaneously on the other side of the room. You can see reality being manipulated, but you can't see with the naked eye, time and space being manipulated. A Shadow can throw a tank just by thinking about it. A Baraqu can make that tank appear right above an enemy's head without seeing any transition between the original location of the tank and the new location without time ever progressing forward. If it's nine o'clock in the morning and one second when the tank is sitting at its original location, it's still nine o'clock in the morning and one second when it appears above the head of an unsuspecting enemy. When a Shadow moves the tank, time moves forward, and the space it once occupied changes as well."

"So, it's like teleporting things but never losing time?"

"Yes, something like that, but not exactly. But you are getting the idea."

I got myself into a position to attempt the impossible or what I once thought was impossible. I started jumping up and down and swinging my arms like I was loosening up for a big run. Suddenly, Jaffrey began laughing so hard he almost fell over. What is so funny? I thought. Here I was about to relocate this box or control time and space to relocate the box, and he was over there laughing it up. It was starting to piss me off, and I was getting aggravated. But I wasn't going to let him deter me from doing this. I pointed my fingers toward the box and said, "Okay, box, I want you over there," and then I swung around and pointed to the other side of the room. After about four or five tries with nothing happening, Jaffrey was rolling around on the floor, wailing and squealing with laughter. By this time, I was ready to smash his head in with the box.

"Stop laughing at me!" I yelled.

That made him laugh harder, and he started coughing and hacking, trying to breathe in air.

Good, choke on it, I hope you turn blue and faint so that I can concentrate, I thought.

But to my dissatisfaction, he found some oxygen and laughed even harder. I felt my confidence wane, and I began to believe that either I couldn't do it or I was being played for a fool by Jaffrey.

Some extravagant practical joke telling me I had this power when I really didn't.

"Man, whatever, keep laughing then! Enjoy yourself. I'm leaving."

Jaffrey immediately stopped laughing, jumped to his feet, and appeared in front of me out of nowhere. He was just on the other side of the room, and now here he was right in front of me. He'd done to himself what I wanted to do to that box but couldn't.

"So, you're giving up?"

"I can't do this, even after you explained it to me and I thinking I understood. But I couldn't do it. I'm not who you think I am."

"And what made you come to that conclusion?"

"Huh? Did you just see me fail over there?"

"You didn't fail until you stopped trying, and what made you stop trying?"

"I stopped because I couldn't do it."

"How do you know that? At first, you seemed confident enough to attempt it, correct?"

"Yeah, but then nothing happened."

"But what happened between the time you attempted and when you quit?"

Is this man bipolar or something?

"You started laughing at me, that's what happened."

"Because I started laughing meant you couldn't do it? Why did you attempt to do it in the first place?"

"Because you told me to."

"Hmm, so how did you expect to accomplish it if you didn't decide for yourself why you were attempting it? Just because someone is laughing doesn't mean what you are doing is wrong or impossible. How many people laughed at Thomas Edison? Martin

213

Luther King Jr.? The Wright Brothers? Countless; but they continued regardless of ridicule from shallow and limited-minded people. If you had attempted to relocate the box for your own reasons and not just because I told you to, my laughter would not have deterred you. If the great men I just mentioned and other men and women who have done great things that changed the course of history had acted just because someone told them to, they would not be remembered today. You must find your own purpose to tap into the powers inside you. You must find your own inspiration for being Baraqu. I can teach you, but only you can give your life purpose to be greater than the flesh you now reside in. There may come a time when even those who have given you orders may betray you and behave in a manner outside of your perception of them.

Does that mean you stop being who you are just because they set you on the path and now they have forsaken that very same path? No, you must find your own purpose. Guidance is one thing I can give you, but you must find your own reasons to take that guidance and act. Even if I laugh at you, there shouldn't be a reason why you don't have the confidence to complete the task. This way of thinking prevents Baraqu from being corrupted by those they look up to and respect. No one is perfect, so we can't put our will to act in the hands of anyone else. This is what controlling your destiny means. This is one of the main reasons that the Baraqu forbid the practice of religion. Now go back over there and relocate that box and find a reason why you want to move that box and not why I want you to move it."

I knew I was in for a very unique experience training with Jaffrey, but I had no idea it would be like this. Everything was a test, everything I did, every choice I made, and every thought process was analyzed, tested, and graded. It was like I was being made into a whole new Aiden. Transforming me from a cat into a lion. I slowly walked over to the other side of the room again. After getting so angry at his laughter and convincing myself that I didn't have the power to do what he asked, I was reluctant to try this again. But what Jaffrey said made perfect sense. I always complained about people doing things just because someone told them to instead of doing things with a mind of their own to think as they pleased. And here I was suffering from the same mental disadvantage as so many in the world. I didn't want to be this way. I wanted to have my own reasons to learn from Jaffrey, my own purpose.

I stood there, closed my eyes, and began to breathe slowly. Jaffrey was now singing "Livin' la Vida Loca" by Ricky Martin; a song I loathe with all my being.

How did this man know what would get to me?

I continued to breathe and concentrate. Soon he started teleporting himself all over the room, still singing, sometimes even popping up right next to me screaming in my ear, "She will turn you out, living la vida loca!" Man, he was so annoying. I continued to breathe and concentrate, and soon the annoying sound of his singing started to fade until it was only a whisper. I began to reflect on all the things that made me happy or proud to be Aiden Storm.

What inspired me, the driving force to be better, and much to my surprise, the only image that popped into my head was Sarah. At first, her image made me uncomfortable and confused, and Jaffrey's singing temporarily got louder. I couldn't understand why Sarah, "the troll princess from the north," would be the only image that popped into my head. We argued constantly and rarely saw eye to eye. But when I thought about that night in my mom's room with horror and darkness all around us, she was the reason that something awakened inside of me. Protecting her and the love I felt for her were the deciding factors. Yes, I loved my mom more than I could ever express, but Sarah was my little sister, and regardless of how annoying she could be, I loved her, and it was my duty to protect her. I never wanted to see her cry, have her heart broken, or feel pain.

215

I wanted to protect her and would give my life to do so. She was my reason, and it all made sense to me now. I always wanted to impress her, and when she was impressed, it made my day so much better. I wanted to be a great example for her, and because of her high standards, impressing her was truly something to be proud of.

Soon a warm vibration started flowing through my entire body, and I began to feel focused and relaxed. Everything was silent now, even though I was aware Jaffrey was still bouncing around the room, singing that horrible song at the top of his lungs. He and his actions didn't matter; I was completely within myself, and even with my eyes closed, I could feel and sense everything around me. The room, the box, Jaffrey, the area outside the room, and outside of this place. I then realized where I was. Jaffrey's hideout was located underground beneath a Buddhist temple. It was daytime outside, almost noon, and the monks were going about their day, oblivious of what was going on beneath them, unaware of the power that was about to be unleashed right below their feet. There were hundreds of children here as well, training, learning, and doing chores. The temple was beautiful and tranquil. I made a mental note to come to this temple one day and just enjoy the atmosphere. Now I understood why Jaffrey chose this place; it was full of positive energy twenty-four hours a day.

These monks only wanted to live in peace and teach those willing to learn. It was a perfect sanctuary for anyone needing this kind of energy and environment. Then I felt myself being whisked away beyond the temple, beyond China, beyond the seas and mountains, until I came to a place very familiar to me. My grandparents' home in Spain, and there she was; Sarah sitting in her room just staring out at the coastline with tears running down her face. She was afraid, and I could hear her whispering something, and then I heard my name escape her lips. She was repeating the same thing over and over again, "Aiden, where are you?" I've never seen or felt Sarah's emotional energy the way I felt it that day. She was in pain emotionally, and the only person she felt she could relate to and could ease her pain was me. At that moment, I decided to make sure that I would always protect her, and I was willing to move entire galaxies to ensure my baby sister's happiness and safety. That was a life-changing experience for me; while my physical body was standing in that training room, my consciousness was standing next to my inspiration and my reason to fight.

I then realized she was the reason why I burst into a flaming torch and destroyed the threat that was Jason. Her fear in that closet had awakened something in me that led me here. On that day, I began to realize my purpose and what being a big brother really meant, and how it could change or destroy everything depending on the decisions I made. I wasn't a hundred percent clear, but I was beginning to see clearer. And just like that, I was back in the room with Jaffrey still singing that horrible song and the box. At that moment, I began to feel the power surge that made me Baraqu vibrate through my entire body. Every organ, every inch of me was feeling the rush of this strange yet powerful ability. I looked at the box, and soon I saw things I never thought possible. It was like the box was there but wasn't, it was no longer completely solid. I could see everything that made the box a box. All the man-made elements as well as the atoms that made up those elements. It was an amazing yet terrifying image. I refused to look at Jaffrey for fear of seeing him the same way. That would have broken my concentration completely.

Suddenly, the thought of relocating that box wasn't impossible, and just with a thought, the box was gone, leaving an empty space where it once sat. By now, Jaffrey had stopped singing and was staring at me, smiling brightly.

"What? Why are you staring at me?"

"I'm not staring at you; I'm looking behind you. Turn around."

CHAPTER TWENTY-NINE
THERE'S ALWAYS A CAVEAT

I slowly turned to behold the exact box that had disappeared sitting on the opposite side of the room. A feeling of monumental success came over me. I could feel the positive energy flowing through this place. I could also feel the monk's energy as it fueled my powers. It was an indescribable feeling.

"You feel that?" Jaffrey asked.

"Yes, I do, it's wonderful!"

"Now try to imagine that feeling a million times more potent."

"Oh my God! How could that even be possible?"

"It is, and that is the feeling a Shadow gets when they absorb the energy of pain and suffering."

"That is an impossible feeling to even comprehend."

"Yes, it is, and now you have a fraction of an idea of what the Shadows are fighting to maintain and how they could be led to destroy this realm without a second thought of the consequences. It's a feeling and power that should never be allowed to continue. This is what the Baraqu are up against. The addiction of power, power that has been tainted by the pain, death, and suffering of the life we were chartered to protect."

Considering what Jaffrey just told me and the wondrous rush I just got from tapping into the positive energy around me, I started to understand how someone could become enslaved by this power and the feeling it gave. This was my first time, and I was already anxious to feel that rush of power again, and if a Shadow's rush was even more intense than what I just felt, I could fully understand why that would drive anyone to madness.

"But why doesn't the Baraqu become addicted to their power?"

"Who said we aren't?"

"Are you saying that even the Baraqu are addicted to their power source?"

"That is a simple question that has a complicated answer. How do you feel right now?"

"I feel great! I feel like I can do anything. Like nothing can touch me, and I have no worries or burdens tying me down, preventing me from doing anything my mind and heart desire."

"Now tell me, Aiden, when was the last time you felt this way?"

"Never! I've never felt this great in my life!"

"Now tell me, would you like this to be the last time you feel this way?"

"No! Of course not. If I could, I would feel this way all the time."

"Would you be willing to do anything to keep having this feeling?"

The question of what I was willing to do for this power made me pause and think. What would I do? What was I capable of doing for this power and feeling? I couldn't deny my excitement and connection to this energy that flowed through my body and how it affected my physical, mental, and emotional state of being. I was like a boy experiencing sex for the first time; the world seemed different now. Everything seemed enhanced, and I now had something else to pursue that made me feel incredible.

But what was I willing to do to keep this feeling alive? Would I lie, deceive, murder, and betray? The same things people today are willing to do for sex, money, fame, or other carnal desires. I could say no, I wouldn't, but in reality, would I be lying to myself and Jaffrey? The sound of Jaffrey calling my name awoke me from my deep thoughts concerning his last question.

"Relax, Aiden, the fact that the question made you think is a good thing. If this same question was asked of a Shadow, they would respond almost instantaneously that they would be willing to do anything. As Baraqu, we cannot be willing to do anything. We must have a code of honor and ethics. What helps us to reign in our unbridled desires of power and conquest at all costs is the source of our power. Positive energy, whether it's emotional or natural, the source that feeds our powers engulfs us in an aura of peace and positive thought. It keeps us grounded and focused on what's important. It helps us shed selfish intentions and aggressive actions. We want to protect and heal, not destroy. Sometimes to do so, we must become a force of power, but only to protect those who can't protect themselves from forces far more powerful. Are we immune to selfishness and abuse of our powers? No, but we are more suited to fight those desires because of the source of our powers."

"But I just noticed you made a difference between emotional positive energy and natural—what's the difference?"

"Emotional positive energy is the positive output that living things exude when they are experiencing euphoria or guiltless satisfaction."

"Guiltless satisfaction?"

"Yes, you see, even though having sex with a beautiful woman may give you a good feeling, if that beautiful woman is someone else's wife, then that energy cannot be used or harnessed by a Baraqu. We can't use the feelings of satisfaction that derive from an act of negativity. If we could, then that wouldn't make us any different from the Shadows. Natural positive energy is what scientists refer to as the building blocks of creation. The energy that creates the perfect scenario for life to begin. The energy that allows things to grow, the energy that creates tropical paradises and perfect weather. It's the energy of creation itself, and it allows the birds to fly, the seasons to change, and the trees to produce the oxygen we breathe. It is the energy of order."

"So that would make natural negative energy evil?"

"You have to look at it as the other side of the same coin. You can't have a coin without two sides. Natural negative energy causes the change from night to day. It causes the coldness of winter and for the trees to lay dormant. It causes volcanoes to erupt, and it causes the thunderstorms and severe weather we experience every day. Is natural negative energy evil? No, it is not, but how it's used can be. It is an aggressive energy, full of passion and force, and can cause the person who wields this power to mimic its energy. Before the great fall and divide, when the Immaru were whole and complete, they would use cosmic negative energy on the field of battle and use positive energy to heal the wounded and for protection. We were never meant to be divided and to solely use one kind of natural energy."

"But what's so special about natural negative energy? I mean, like you said before, positive energy is more powerful, right?"

"Yes, but when it comes to matters of war, the power of a singularity or a black hole is more useful than sunshine, don't you think?"

"How so? The sun is so hot it can burn entire planets!"

"That is true, but a black hole can consume entire galaxies, including your sun."

"Oh yeah, you got me there. So it's like rock, paper, and scissors, huh?"

"I guess you can say that. You use the energy that best suits the situation, and in war, natural negative energy is perfection."

"So, if the Immaru use both energies, why is what the Shadows are doing so evil?"

"Because they are not using natural negative energy, but negative emotional energy created by the pain and suffering of humans. They are purposefully causing humans and this planet pain so that they can harness the negative emotional energy. It's not natural, nor is it an energy that should have ever been introduced in this realm to be harnessed for power."

"But Jaffrey, people suffer every day. That has been human history from the beginning. Pain and suffering, death and war."

"Yes, as humans, they are one of the most violent species ever created, but only because, like sheep, they've been led to relate pain to reality by men of power who are puppets of the Shadows."

"They? Are we not humans as well?"

"No, Baraqu or those blessed with the bloodline of the Immaru are not human. We are something more."

"But how can we save a race of people we refuse to relate to? We have human blood running through our veins as well, Jaffrey. Don't you think it's kind of arrogant to believe we are more?"

"How is it arrogant to state facts about our lineage? We are not human, nor are we from this realm."

"Are you saying that your goal is to go back to where the Immaru are from?"

"If the Creator wills it…yes! We will attempt to return to our place of origin."

I was very confused because, on the one hand, I was being given the keys to save humanity, but at the same time, I was being torn from it. I felt human; even with all this power within my control, I still felt in essence, human. I could tell Jaffrey was worried about how I was taking everything, so he called it a day and said we could continue training the next day.

Another sleepless night trying to make sense of everything I was taught that day. What was even more amazing to me was that I was able to comprehend all this madness. Most would have been driven crazy by now, and honestly, I could relate because it was definitely an information overload. But the vast amount of information didn't worry me. Not even the fact that I was now able to manipulate time and space. What disturbed me the most was Jaffrey's outlook on the human race. Even though he said we were given the responsibility to protect humans, I could still sense resentment from him. As if he was sworn to protect us but didn't like the idea of serving an inferior species. That is the very thing that causes so much division and death in the world today. Racism being one of the worst by-products of that kind of thinking. My best friend is African American, and I have sat through many angry rants from him concerning how the color of his skin creates fear and resentment in others who have no idea the type of person he is. And here I was in the company of probably one of the oldest and most knowledgeable men on the planet, but he seemed to still have some hang-ups about the charter of the Baraqu bloodline. And to make matters worse, he possessed a power that could lay waste to the entire planet, and he felt like this planet was beneath him.

I already had reservations about joining their cause, and his attitude towards the human race didn't make it any better. His outlook on his responsibility was similar to a police officer from a bad neighborhood who now patrols that very neighborhood. It's his job to "serve and protect," so he does it, but he hates and resents the people and area he's protecting. It's not a good combination, and we're reminded of this in the news about cops abusing their powers. I hope his comments were another test, and he would come clean and say it was to see how I would respond because if he was for real, I feared that if the oldest of the Baraqu felt like this, I could only imagine what was in the minds of those who looked up to him or shared his views.

Even if we were the descendants of a superior alien race, we were still part human, and I kind of doubted that if there were any Immaru left, they would welcome half-breeds like us. But what did I know? I was only seventeen and a few days into my revelation of who and what I was.

Over the next few days, my training with Jaffrey became more intense, and he continuously pushed me beyond my physical, emotional, and mental limits. I went from boxes to relocating an entire battalion of tanks from a military depot in Russia to the Alps and back, all within the same time-and-space bracket. I learned how to teleport myself as well. It didn't matter if the object was alive or inanimate. If it was made up of time and space, I could manipulate it.

My favorite lessons were those using the elements of the periodic table for aggressive combat. From controlling fire to creating a safe made of titanium and then changing that safe's makeup from titanium to water. I also learned how to change landscapes and shatter entire mountain ranges. Most of the time, I was terrified of the power I displayed, and I would either hesitate or hold back, which made Jaffrey pretty angry. I had to keep reminding him that not less than a few weeks ago, I thought I was turning into a serial killer, and today, I was a real live-action figure with powers included. Kung Fu grip sold separately. Sometimes I would do things beyond what Jaffrey would expect or ask. I would ask him, "Isn't that badass?" He would just roll his eyes and warn me to stay focused and humble and continue as he instructed. Before long, I became very comfortable tapping into the positive energy that surrounded me and using my powers. I began to lose the concept of time and had no idea how long I'd been training with Jaffrey. It could have been weeks or months. I had no thoughts of the outside world, my school, friends, or even my family; just training and all the knowledge that Jaffrey was sharing with me about the history of our bloodline.

CHAPTER THIRTY
ACCEPTANCE

After a while, I could feel Jaffrey warming up to me, and our training sessions became more personal. One day, after going through battle training that involved fire and teleportation against conventional weapons, we were sitting down for a meal. As I reflected on the power and skill I displayed during training, I couldn't help but feel a surge of pride. I didn't mean to be boastful, but I was undeniably badass. How could anyone or anything stop me when I could conjure up whatever I imagined? It puzzled me how the Baraqu, who centuries ago numbered in the thousands, allowed the weaker order of the Shadows to take control of this realm.

I hesitated to ask Jaffrey because he could be extremely long-winded. A simple question could turn into a lecture lasting hours. But the question nagged at me, and I decided it was worth the lengthy answer. When I asked, his response sent a chill up my spine and shattered all notions of invincibility.

The story goes that after the great divide and the discovery of negative emotional energy, the Shadows embarked on a campaign to destroy humanity. They obliterated entire civilizations for the quick hit of negative energy produced by pain, suffering, and death. Driven mad with power, they were close to eradicating all human life in this realm. However, a secret order from within the human ranks, the Kashaptu or the Order of the Wiccan—witches and warlocks gifted with the knowledge to fight back—rose up. They used a spell called "binding," which inhibited both Shadows and Baraqu, rendering them powerless.

The Kashaptu didn't differentiate between Baraqu and Shadows and declared war on both factions. Eventually, a truce was reached with the Baraqu when the Kashaptu realized their purpose was to protect mankind. But then came Alal, half Shadow, half Warlock. The legend of his immense power spread, and he created his own order of Kashaptu, waging war against mankind and the Baraqu. Some Wiccan still sided with the Baraqu, combating binding spells cast by the opposing side. Things changed when the hybrid Anshargal was murdered. After several thousand Baraqu were massacred by Shadows while bound by the Kashaptu, the Baraqu decided to wage war against all Kashaptu, regardless of allegiance.

Witches and warlocks were burned at the stake, and tortured into admitting they worshipped the devil. This persecution caused many Wiccan to side with the Shadows, using their binding skills to hunt down every Baraqu on the planet. The Baraqu were powerless to stop the onslaught, leading to the reign of the Shadows. The Dark Ages were not just about the black plague but the Shadows' rise to power. Eventually, the number of Baraqu Warriors born dwindled until none were born at all. With the planet controlled by negative energy, nature's selection produced more Shadows. Men and women with special physical or psychic abilities became the norm for the Baraq, a watered-down version of the Baraqu.

Baraqu and Baraq were forbidden from exposing their powers in front of normal humans. The rule had no leniency, and punishment was banishment from the order. In the old days, the punishment was death, but with dwindling numbers, the punishment scale was revised. Killing off allies when they were so few was no longer an option.

In a nutshell, we were outgunned, outmaneuvered, and outnumbered. This revelation dampened any enthusiasm I had about joining their ranks. Positive energy was a rare commodity, limiting my effectiveness. Suddenly, I felt less omnipotent and more like a kid with potential he couldn't realize. It was a depressing revelation.

With this new information, hand-to-hand combat and weapons training became crucial. Jaffrey wanted me to defend myself against witches and warlocks. I thought I was well-trained in martial arts, but Jaffrey's training revealed something entirely different. He taught me to overcome my adversary in three moves or less, emphasizing speed and precision. Learning every pressure point on the human body was essential.

I also discovered abilities to change the makeup and density of my body. Increased density meant superhuman strength and durability but came at the cost of increased sensitivity to pain. Training to withstand pain was harsh, but Jaffrey's tough love prepared me for what lay ahead.

Shadows were masters of deception, capable of projecting negative energy and creating environments of despair. Their greatest weapons were their ability to manipulate perception and emotions. I needed to master my mind and emotions to prevent them from controlling my thoughts and feelings.

Despite Jaffrey's assurances, I couldn't help but think about my mom and Sarah. I often let my consciousness wander outside Jaffrey's sanctuary to check on my family. I trusted Jaffrey, but not completely. So, I kept my ability to travel outside my body a secret. I didn't want to give away everything.

One night, I decided to check on my family. They were having dinner, laughing, and talking about the good old times. The scene filled me with a yearning to rejoin them. As I watched, I heard a low screech and murmuring from the backyard. My consciousness moved outside, where I saw a cloaked shadowy figure peering into the window. It was a Shadow, and I knew they had found us. I couldn't attack it in my current state, so I rushed back to my body.

I frantically searched for a way out of Jaffrey's place, throwing things in a fit of rage. The thought of my family being mutilated by Shadows enraged me further. I was so enraged that it felt like my skin was on fire. Jaffrey stood behind me, watching my meltdown.

"Aiden! What are you doing?"

"I need to get out of here, now! My family is in danger!"

"How do you know that?"

"I can feel it! The energy inside me is telling me they are in danger!"

"Aiden, our powers don't work that way anymore. Baraqu hasn't been able to foresee the future for thousands of years. You are hallucinating! Relax and stop destroying my home!"

"I can't! Let me out of here, Jaffrey, or I swear I will burst out of here by any means necessary. I'd rather die than sit here knowing my family is in danger and I did nothing to stop it."

"Aiden, it is dangerous to allow you to leave."

"So, I am a prisoner here?"

"No, you are not; it is for your own protection that I keep you here."

"I don't need protection—my family does. Jaffrey, let me out of here, now!"

I was hysterical, tears and sweat blurring my vision.

"Let me out!!!"

"Stop! Stop now, Aiden! I will release you, but you must promise me you will return. Your training is not complete, and I refuse to let you leave without a promise that you will complete your training with me. Again, you must be blindfolded when you return here; I can't risk my location being compromised. The power is awakening inside you, and it is only a matter of time before you figure out where I am. For our kind to continue, I must remain a secret and invisible to the eyes of the Shadows. But this is not the only term of my agreement of releasing you."

"Anything! Jaffrey, just let me go, please!" I begged.

"You must admit to the one thing you refuse to feel."

"What are you talking about?"

"You know exactly what I'm referring to."

As much as I wanted to play dumb, I knew exactly what he meant. Jason: he wanted me to admit, after almost being murdered by him, watching him attack my mother, after the betrayal of loving him to find out he was my worst enemy, after being forced to destroy him; he wanted me to admit that I still felt love in my heart for that man, that I felt remorse about taking his life.

"Jaffrey, you know I can't do that."

"You can't or you won't?"

"I can't. Why would you make me admit that? What kind of game are you playing?"

"This isn't a game; this is life and death. If you go out of this place with that lie stuck in your heart, I fear this will be the last time I see you alive. You can't live a lie, whether it's right in front of you or hidden. Lies will weaken you, distort your perception, and lead you down a path of destruction and failure. Truth and acceptance are the only way to release the last shackle you have on your mind."

I fell to my knees at that moment, tears streaming down my face. I knew Jaffrey was right, and if there was one thing I'd learned here, it was that my belief in myself was my greatest weapon, or the lack thereof could be my worst enemy. Carrying this lie and anger was not going to help me, and I felt that whatever I faced tonight would be formidable, requiring every ounce of faith in myself to defeat it. But what he was asking of me was world-shattering. I didn't want to, but as the tears kept pouring and my heart ached, I had no other choice but to face this emotional tsunami.

He was dead and I still found myself thinking about him—the times we talked, all the games he took me to, the way he made my mother feel, and how his presence made us complete as a family. It was because of him that I was able to focus and win that first game of the season and it was his belief in me that pushed me to want to do better. I wanted to make him proud and deep inside I wanted him to be my real father instead of the man who lay in the ground dead for over a decade.

I admit that I traded in my father for Jason, that I turned my back on his memory for my enemy. I admit and accept that I allowed my enemy to share a bed with my mother and I let my guard down when I should have been more vigilant. I am just as guilty as Jason in this betrayal, and I am just as responsible. I had a father and his memory deserved more than what I gave him. As I knelt in pain at the acceptance of my failure as a son and brother, I admitted that I still loved Jason, and I deeply regretted I had to kill him.

CHAPTER THIRTY-ONE
CHASING SHADOWS

uddenly, I felt a cool breeze across my face, and when I looked up and opened my eyes, I found myself kneeling on the beach behind my grandparents' home. I could see the house from where I was, and all the lights were out except for the glow of multiple vehicle headlights shining from the driveway. The Shadows were already there, waiting for me.

Let's not keep them waiting.

With everything I'd learned from Jaffrey, I was certain they knew I was there. Over the centuries, they'd become masters at hunting the Baraqu, and I was no exception. They knew I was near, so sneaking in would be a waste of time. I decided to walk up to the front door and face them head-on.

I prayed that, since it had been so long since they hunted a fully functional Baraqu, they might have forgotten how and left their pet witches at home. If they hadn't, this could get very interesting. Despite the serious and dangerous situation, I felt uncommonly calm and relaxed as I hurried up the beach toward the house. I was focused and confident in my ability to fight my adversaries. Then it dawned on me: what if I hadn't admitted my guilt and feelings for Jason? The doubt and self-deception would have clouded my mind, leaving me unfocused. As annoying as Jaffrey was, his training had prepared me perfectly. There could be no room for doubt when facing a foe as powerful and skilled as a Shadow.

Was I one hundred percent sure any of us would survive that night? Hell no! But I was certain I would give my all and had the skill and power to increase our chances of survival. They had the upper hand of being there first, but I had the advantage of purpose—protecting my family, especially Sarah. She was my reason for taking this path. Tonight was my coming-out party to the Order of Shadows, and I aimed to misbehave. After tonight, even the thought of touching my family would bring nightmares to my enemies. They had taken my father, made us love a man who planned to mutilate us, and now invaded my grandparents' home. They had miscalculated on all fronts, and I would show them no mercy.

I finally arrived at the front driveway, where at least twenty armed men in full tactical gear stood with their guns aimed at me. One of them stepped forward.

"Identify yourself!"

I remained silent, watching this dark opera unfold. These men wouldn't hesitate to fire on me, regardless of my age. I felt a surge of energy flow through my body as I concentrated on saving my family trapped inside.

"Identify yourself! I won't ask again! If you don't speak, we will open fire! Who are you?"

I decided to oblige him. "Aiden. My name is Aiden Storm."

"Fire!"

His order was obeyed without hesitation. The sonic crack of hundreds of bullets flying through the air was deafening. Any other time, the sudden order and sound would have startled me, but this man was no Shadow—just a mercenary doing their bidding. The Shadows had underestimated me.

First big mistake.

Following Jaffrey's advice, I ended the confrontation in three moves or less.

First move. They opened fire.

Second move. I teleported all twenty men to where I was standing, directly in the path of their bullets, and teleported myself to their original position.

The switch was so fast they had no time to react to their deaths coming at two thousand-three hundred feet per second. I quickly turned and moved towards the front door, not lingering to see them fall.

I heard their bodies drop as I opened the front door and entered the dark house. I had no idea what else my family's captors had in store for me, and watching people die wasn't a must-see experience. I knew I had to take the lives of those here tonight, but I wasn't proud of it.

The darkness in the house was thick and familiar like the night Jason revealed himself. The Shadows were near; I could feel the fear and depression in the air. I wasn't prepared to fight them in the darkness, so I decided to take control of the electricity to see what was around me. I managed to flash the lights on for about ten seconds, long enough to see I was surrounded by six cloaked Shadows and a strange man in the corner—a warlock, likely Haitian or from another Atlantic Island. He was here to bind me so the Shadows could kill me. *Cowards!*

One of the Shadows hissed at me, "You are a fool to face us, Baraqu. *We* are the masters of this realm, and your kind are just a dead species too stupid to know when your time has ended."

Arrogant piece of shit. I should have been terrified, but I felt only determination to save my family. If I was to be bound by the warlock, I would fight with everything I had. A physical confrontation with six Shadows was suicide, but I was determined to take a few with me.

The warlock began chanting in an unknown language: *"Usella Mitutilk kalu Baltuti, Usella Mitutilk kalu Baltuti."* I prepared for the first strike. Jaffrey had explained how it feels to be bound—cold sweat, bones freezing, hindered coordination. But despite the warlock chanting six times, the effects didn't happen. I still felt the surge of my power, and it was increasing.

The first strike came—a glowing claw slashing through the darkness towards my face. I snapped my fingers, and the Shadow that it belonged to instantly burst into flames, screaming in agony. The other Shadows scattered while they screamed at the warlock, "Bind him! Bind him!" and he replied in a heavy Caribbean accent, "I did! I don't know what's going on!"

Their panic was palpable as they cowered away. Their fear fueled my powers, and I pursued them in the darkness. One Shadow tried to escape through the door. I sent an electrical charge to the handle, shocking and throwing him across the room, slamming him into a wall where he exploded into a black mist. The warlock kept chanting, hoping his spell would eventually work. Before he could try further, I manipulated the elements and created a steel safe around him, vacuuming out the air and heating the safe until it turned white-hot. His muffled screams were silenced when I crushed the safe with a clap and made it dissipate like dust.

The other four Shadows met their ends in equally imaginative ways. The last Shadow's demise was my dark opera's finale. I trapped him in a glass bubble and opened a portal to the Mariana

Trench, dropping him into the deepest part of the ocean. Once I closed the portal, I expected the lights to return, but the darkness remained, signaling another Shadow's presence.

Enhancing my eardrums for superhuman hearing, I listened for the remaining Shadow's whereabouts. Moving towards the kitchen, I sensed its violent intent, searching for the best angle to attack. It was too fast to pinpoint in the small kitchen, so I backed into the family room. The Shadow didn't follow. It floated in the kitchen doorway, an aura of hatred and violence emanating from it. This was personal. While distracted by its presence, it attacked violently, sending furniture and anything it could throw at me. Its aim was terrible, and after each miss it screamed in rage, tearing holes in the walls with its claws. Intoxicated with malice, it began spinning faster and faster, creating a miniature tornado, threatening to bring the house down. I had to stop it before the house crumbled.

I stretched out my hands in front of me and began slowing time until everything moved in slow motion. Through the time delay, I pinpointed the Shadow, and sent a lightning bolt into the vortex. Returning time to normal, everything fell, including the Shadow. The lights immediately flickered back on, and I saw the Shadow in the corner, smoke rising from its body.

I approached, ready to deliver the final blow, then noticed the Shadow was now in its human form. It was a child—a boy no older than ten or eleven, lying in the corner with burns covering his body. He cried in pain, trying to stand. His eyes, seared red with hatred, looked up at me. When he spoke, his words chilled me to the bone.

"I hate you. I hate your kind! I wish death on every single one of you!"

"I'm sorry, I didn't know you were a child. I'm so sorry."

"Why are you crying?" he snapped.

I hadn't noticed I was crying until I wiped my face.

236

"You shouldn't be crying; you should be smiling. You defeated your enemy! If I were in your shoes, I would piss on your corpse!"

His hatred shocked me.

"Why do you hate me so much? I've never done anything to you or your people!"

"How could you say that?" he screamed, coughing in pain. "You took everything from me! You killed my father, Telal— Jason. The Baraqu already killed my mother years ago, and my dad was all I had. Now, you've taken him from me! I hate you! Curse you and your family. I hope you all die horrible deaths at the hands of my brothers!"

His words pierced my soul. Here lay the son of the man who tried to kill us. I never considered Jason might have a family. I assumed evil men were incapable of love, incapable of bearing children. But this dying boy was proof of my ignorance. He was angry, hurt, and alone, driven to revenge and murder.

The boy possessed an extreme amount of power for his age, likely inherited from his father, but he lacked proper training. Though he had almost destroyed the house, he acted on rage alone. His eyes, filled with dying rage, revealed a father's love that had turned destructive. Despite my justified actions to protect my family, I felt deep remorse for taking his life. Jaffrey's words echoed in my mind: every action—good or bad—warrants a response from the universe. This boy was my response.

I should have felt anger and hatred towards this boy who had tried to kill my loved ones. I should have taunted him about his father's death, revealing the truth about who Jason really was. I should have gloated over my victory. But to my surprise, I felt only sorrow and remorse for what I had done to this boy. He belonged to his father, and my actions had severed that bond forever.

As he lay there, gasping for air, I placed my hand on his head. His eyes met mine, and I saw the fear of death in them. He was

237

entering the unknown, and the fear of darkness gripped him. In that moment, I understood that no matter how fearless or evil one can be in life, death strips us bare. I wanted to know his name, and how old he really was, but it would have been a waste of the precious time he had left. So, I remained silent and kneeled by his side until the end came.

Death is complicated.

Watching life leave someone's eyes, knowing you caused it, is devastating. Stories of war and conquest glorify vanquishing enemies, but these are lies perpetuated by evil men. Man was not meant to take life but to care for it. Taking Jason's life made me cold; taking the Shadows' lives made me hateful. But taking Jason's son's life made me ashamed. I felt like a young man without protection or favor, a killer of children. There was nothing good that could come from this moment of victory. I had considered joining the order of the Baraqu, but after this battle, I knew I didn't have the stomach for it. This was not just a casualty of war; it was a dead child driven to violence and hatred.

I cursed Jason and the Shadows for creating an environment that led this boy to the arms of death, and I cursed myself for not having the power to change the outcome. We possessed all this power, but what was it good for if we couldn't prevent children from finding themselves in adult situations? At that time, I was still very much a child, thrust into combat, trained to be a killer. I was a weapon of mass destruction with no real purpose or road map for what to do with all this power.

I began to understand how the Shadows became slaves to their addiction to pain and suffering. They caused mayhem for the surge of negative energy that made them feel powerful. I felt a similar surge of energy every time I used my powers. That night, I was in a zone, never thinking twice about my actions. I was acting on pure emotion, and my conscience wasn't an inhibitor. Because of that, I was kneeling next to a dying boy, a boy driven to attempt murder, resulting in his demise. Jaffrey told me it had been centuries since the Shadows faced a worthy adversary that could dispatch multiple Shadows within minutes. That night, they met their match, and instead of a victory lap, I was weeping for my enemy.

There was no way I could carry out these kinds of attacks regularly and maintain my sanity. I vowed that the way of the Baraqu would never be my way. Killing wasn't for me, but I knew I would be forced to make this kind of decision again to protect those I loved. It was a hard reality for a seventeen-year-old to accept. My presence was known, and I felt Jaffrey's hesitation to let me leave was to protect me from this reality. He knew I didn't have the stomach for this yet. He knew that on this night, I would face a greater enemy than any I would ever face from the Shadows…regret.

After several weeks, we were all preparing to return to Deerfield. Our home had been completely repaired, and Manny assured us that the security was now competent. We were assured that we would never know they were there, but someone would always be watching over us. As promised, I returned to Jaffrey's place to continue my training.

I still wasn't comfortable letting him know about my secret ability to travel. He never mentioned it in my training, which led me to believe it wasn't something that Baraqu normally did. I also kept to myself the fact that the warlock was unable to bind me that night. Jaffrey was the best source for explaining these powers, but I still found it hard to trust him completely, so I remained silent.

Again, I needed to be blindfolded, and even though I knew exactly where his place was, I played along. This time, I was aware and awake for the blindfolding and didn't put up a fight—well, besides sucker-punching Manny in the jaw and knocking him clean across the room. It felt good being back in Jaffrey's company, and we concentrated on training. Not once did he bring up that night at my grandparents' house. He knew everything that transpired, including Jason's son, but he knew that bringing it up would hinder my training.

I had one week left, and instead of using it to train, I decided to spend time with my family. This ordeal had brought all of us closer, but none as close as the connection between Sarah and me. Gone were the days of bickering and arguing over stupid things. She depended on me, and I was protective of her. She looked up to me and confided in me about her abilities inherited after fighting with Jasmine. She made me promise not to tell anyone, not even Jaffrey, and I kept that promise. I tried my best to explain to her what she was seeing from what I'd learned from Jaffrey. Those who carried the blood of the Baraqu but not the power to control time and space sometimes possessed special abilities. Most were physical abilities like extraordinary strength, agility, intelligence, and heightened senses.

Then there were abilities beyond the physical. Mind reading, telekinesis, and the ability to see into other realms were some of them. Sarah's ability was extreme—she could see people's true selves or soul signatures. Depending on a person's actions and personality, their soul signature would appear as a beautiful creature or a hideous deformity. These signatures change and mutate with a person's day-to-day actions and thoughts. Sarah could not only see them, but she could also communicate with them. This powerful ability allowed her to control people's actions by controlling their souls.

It went beyond mind control. If Sarah commanded someone's soul to cause the flesh to kill itself, the person would keep trying until they succeeded. Normally, the soul follows the person's actions, suggesting what to do or not do but never stopping them. What Sarah's ability did was remove free will from the equation and allow the soul to take full control. No one, not even a Baraqu, was immune to her powers; if it had a soul, she could control it.

Some of the images she described were frightening, and I felt sorry she had to see them. Sarah no longer looked at people the same because she could see who they really were. Her outgoing personality subsided, and she became more introverted. She rarely smiled and always looked away from people to avoid seeing their soul creatures. I did all I could to make her comfortable with the new Sarah, explaining my abilities and what happened the night I rescued them. We both cried about Jason's son. Jason was a monster, but his son didn't deserve to die that way. No matter what I said, Sarah still felt cheated. She felt the burden of her ability more acutely than I felt mine. She couldn't even watch television because she could see the soul creatures on there as well. It pained me to see my sister go through this, and I wished for the old sarcastic, smart-mouthed, mean, and conceited Sarah. She was happier then, and I wanted her to be happy again.

Manny stopped speaking to me for a while after that sucker punch, but eventually, we started talking more. His team cleaned up after the fight at my grandparents' and discovered disturbing truths. The FBI agents who harassed me weren't FBI agents but Shadows posing as agents. All of them were at my grandparents' house that night and now all of them were dead. Jason, like Manny, commanded his own team of skilled and dangerous Shadow Assassins. When they discovered their commander had been killed, they immediately sought revenge. What remained unexplained was why we were targeted in the first place. Manny had been in this fight for years, according to Jaffrey, and not once did they make an attempt on our lives. So, what was Manny up to that caused things to escalate? I confronted Manny about my concerns, and he told me he didn't know and his team was working on finding out.

For some reason, I didn't believe him. I almost asked Sarah to use her ability to make him tell me the truth, but that would have crossed a line. I didn't want to create more problems for our already troubled family. I was still concerned about returning to Deerfield, but Manny assured us we would be safe with very capable people looking after us. My mom was upset and asked Manny to come home and protect us himself. That argument didn't go well, and by the time the yelling subsided, Manny stormed out and my mother was in tears. Manny found it hard to forgive our mother for dating Jason, a Shadow. He was angry with all of us for falling for Jason and not thinking about our dad. To Manny, Jason's ability to make us fall in love with him was no excuse. To him, our mother shouldn't have talked to Jason romantically in the first place. He blamed her for everything and didn't bite his tongue about it.

CHAPTER THIRTY-TWO
IT'S NOT HOW WE LEFT IT

eerfield, Illinois—home sweet home. Our house was looking better than ever, with everything repaired and remodeled. The kitchen had been completely transformed, and the first floor had an open-concept design that made the house feel much larger. Manny had made a smart move by having the house totally redone with new furnishings, modern finishes, and updated electronics and appliances. My room was amazing, and they had even managed to save my car from the flames. When I stepped into the garage, my beautiful Camaro was still there.

The entire team and cheerleading squad were waiting for us when we returned. Front and center was Tony, my best friend and the one who had pulled me out of the flames. I might have lost my innocence, but I regained my friend. I wasn't sure how much he knew, but if we were to continue being friends, I would have to bring him up to speed—minus Sarah's abilities. I had made a promise, and I intended to keep it.

After all the hugging and smiles, things settled down. Tony and I went upstairs to my room so I could tell him everything that had happened. After I finished, we just sat there, staring at the floor. Neither of us knew what to say, and neither wanted to be the first to say something stupid. I decided to go first because I owed the most.

"Tony, I want to thank you for saving our lives."

"You're welcome, bro. I love you guys, and I wasn't going to let anything happen to any of you. You're like family to me."

"You are family," I responded. "I'm sorry for how I behaved before, in the car. I was afraid and didn't know how to deal with everything that was happening."

"Hey, it's cool, Aiden. I don't think anyone in your situation would have handled it any better. And after all the new stuff you just told me, I think you handled it quite well. How are you dealing with all of this?"

"To be honest, I haven't been able to sleep or relax since that night at my grandparents' house."

"I understand completely, but as your best bud, I have to remind you that had you not killed those guys, they would've killed you and everyone you love."

"I'm aware of that, Tony, but having a valid reason to kill someone doesn't make you feel better about it."

"I guess you have a point there," Tony agreed. "I can't even imagine how it feels to take someone else's life. We all talk a lot of shit about killing people and what we'd do if someone hurt our loved ones, but how many of us actually have the balls to do it when faced with the reality?"

Tony was right. Most people, regardless of offense, would have serious reservations about killing. But then there are people like me who have the mental fortitude to kill without hesitation. I was trained, but it takes something inside a person to utilize that training. This idea about myself wasn't something I felt proud of. I was ashamed and terrified of my capabilities. I knew that, as repulsive as I found taking another's life, I could stomach it again if necessary. But being a super-killer wasn't on my kindergarten "what I want to be when I grow up" presentation.

"Can I say something stupid, dude?" asked Tony.

"Sure, be my guest," I said with a chuckle.

"I wish you were just a serial killer."

Tony placed his hands on his head and let out a deep sigh. He laid back on my bed as if the weight of the world was on his chest. Most would be offended by what Tony said, but I understood his point. A serial killer, as horrible as it sounds, is something that can eventually be handled. But me possessing powers documented only in comic books and action movies? That's different. I couldn't be cured or given some treatment to make this all better. The revelation that I wasn't the only one with such powers and that the world was controlled by a secret order of supervillains addicted to mankind's suffering added another log to the fire. I know some would say I shouldn't have involved Tony in this, but because of how close he was to me and my family, he would eventually become involved or a casualty of ignorance. I couldn't have that on my conscience.

While I was away, Tony made sure all my classwork was done so I wouldn't end up in summer school. We were both juniors, looking forward to graduating together next year. I was grateful for Tony looking out for me, and having him back in my life made the craziness less taxing. I knew he would have my back in any situation, and I would have his.

We had the weekend to try to bring some normalcy back to our lives. Sarah spent a lot of time in my room, talking to me and trying to get as much information about our abilities as possible. I knew she was afraid of being alone, so on Sunday night, I let her sleep in my room while I slept on the floor. If anyone had described this scene to me three months ago, I would have laughed in their face. But here I was, allowing my little sister to sleep in my bed while I lay on the floor.

The next few days at school were full of "glad you're back" and "we're sorry" from teachers and students alike. It was starting to get on my nerves, but I just smiled and said more "thank yous" than ever before. Sarah, on the other hand, had more to deal with. She could see when someone's concern wasn't genuine, and it disturbed and angered her. She ended up in the principal's office more that week than ever before. I knew she needed help dealing with her abilities and feared I wouldn't be enough. She needed someone like her or someone who could relate to her. I wanted to be that person, but I didn't have what it took to get her where she needed to be. I was saddened and angered by this fact, blaming myself for not being the protector and big brother I wanted to be.

The principal decided not to discipline Sarah, considering what she had been through, but warned her that his mercy wouldn't last forever.

On Friday, the coach called me into his office to discuss the team's transitions and to inform me that top college recruiters were interested in me. His office was flooded with letters, emails, and phone calls about scholarships and campus visits during the summer. He advised me to review the colleges, pick my top five, and visit their campuses. I could tell Coach was concerned but also proud. When I started playing football, I imagined this happening, but now it seems overwhelming.

He asked if I planned to play college football or go pro. If he had asked at the beginning of the season, I would have said "going pro" without hesitation. But things had changed so much. The last thing I needed was to parade myself on national television, making it easy for those who wanted me dead to find me. But what were my options? Live in seclusion like Jaffrey, hiding from the world? I understood why Jaffrey did it, but I wasn't him, and I wasn't planning on joining the fight. I felt like a genie in a bottle—great power but limited happiness and accomplishments.

Jaffrey sacrificed everything to stay alive, and I wasn't sure I could do the same. I felt being limited like that was worse than death—a prisoner of my greatness because others were threatened by it. I never asked for this, but it was given to me, and I couldn't give it back. This wasn't a movie where I could fight crime in a costume. I was only seventeen, capable of causing entire cities to burn, but I lacked the mental fortitude and discernment to know when to stop. What happened at my grandparents' house was a direct reflection of that. I had gone too far, resulting in a dead eleven-year-old boy. His death was a constant reminder of why I shouldn't join the fight. I needed to stay out of it because I didn't trust myself.

Evil began with someone with great power and good intentions lacking discipline and restraint. I didn't want to become what I feared and hated most. Coach could tell I was dealing with a lot and told me to take my time thinking about it, even if it took until NFL draft day.

Another thing that caught my attention during my first week back at school was Jasmine's absence. She wasn't anywhere to be found, and trust me, I looked for her. I knew who and what she was, and she wasn't going to get the drop on me again. If she tried that darkness curse on me, I would be ready. As much as I hated to get into another confrontation, I would with her. Whatever she did to Sarah was ruining her life.

It was only April, but everyone was already buzzing about prom—who was going with whom, and what the night would bring. Plans were well underway: limousines, suits, dresses, after-parties, alcohol, and sex were the main topics of conversation among students. But I wasn't interested in any of it. Tony, on the other hand, was thrilled. He was planning to take not one, but two beautiful seniors to prom. When they both asked him, he cheekily agreed on the condition that they "share the wealth"—his exact words—and to my disbelief, they accepted. The whole school was talking about Tony's arrangement. I expected Sarah to be furious, but to my surprise, she seemed indifferent. She was losing herself to her abilities, and there wasn't anything I could do to stop it. But who was I to judge? I was going through the same thing. No matter how hard our mother tried to make things easier, we just weren't the same kids anymore.

Our mom was at a loss. I could see how much our changes were tearing her apart. She tried to convince Sarah to go to prom, but Sarah wouldn't budge. So, she turned her attention to me, determined that I would go, no excuses. She took me shopping for a suit and shoes and even tried to find me a date. That's where I drew the line. If I wanted a date, I could find one myself. I agreed to go, but I was going alone—end of discussion. Maybe next year, at my senior prom, I'd take a date, but not this year. Not during this transition in my life. I just wanted to be alone or be around people who understood who and what I really was. I decided to take Sarah with me. It might have seemed strange to others, but since that night with Jason, we had grown closer. It made sense to us, and we didn't care what others thought. If we were going, we were going together. And we agreed that if anyone even whispered the word "incest," they would regret it for the rest of their lives. Both of us had the power to make that happen.

The months leading up to prom were slow and uneventful. I saw Jasmine a few times, but she made sure our paths didn't cross. She knew that I knew, and she didn't want any trouble. I was fine with that. Picking a fight with her could lead to someone disappearing, and this wasn't Spain; covering up a disappearance in a town recently rocked by murder would be impossible. Besides, if Jasmine was a Shadow, then it stood to reason that her entire family was too. And considering Jaffrey's warnings that Jasmine might be one of the most unique and powerful Shadows he'd ever heard of, I knew I was out of my league. Her family might be more than I could handle alone.

I'm ashamed to admit it, but despite loathing Jasmine and everything she stood for, she was still the most beautiful thing I'd ever seen. Her body had matured even more in my absence, making her all the more tempting. Forbidden fruit always seems irresistible, doesn't it? In another reality, I might have pursued her and only her. But because of who she was and what she did, I couldn't let myself entertain the thought of dating her. I had to stay focused, knowing she would try something eventually, and I wanted to be ready.

And then there was my family to consider. What they couldn't do to me, they could certainly do to those I loved. It was a lot to process for a seventeen-year-old, but I was learning to think first and act later. It wasn't easy—my impulses urged me to rid the school of her presence—but I had too much to lose, so I held back. For now.

Prom night felt more like Halloween to me. People without class dressing up as if they had it, and those with class being made to feel like outsiders. But for one night, Sara and I could pretend to be normal.

On prom night, I wore a black Armani suit with a white dress shirt, no tie, and an open jacket. Sarah looked stunning in a black-and-white Vera Wang print dress, paired with black heels and our mom's diamond necklace. Initially, she had her hair tied up but decided at the last minute to let it flow down her back. For the first time in months, she was smiling and even threw a few classic Sarah-zingers at me about my lack of a tie. At that moment, everything felt normal again—no Baraqu, no Shadows, no special abilities, and no killer boyfriends. Just us, being a family.

We decided to skip the limo and drove to the prom in my Camaro. After all the money our mom had spent on our clothes, it didn't feel right to have her spend even more on a limo. Plus, arriving together in a limo would have felt too much like a date instead of a big brother taking his kid sister to prom. The prom was held at a hotel ballroom in nearby Lincolnshire. Many students had secretly booked rooms upstairs, planning wild after-parties. Tony, of course, had been invited to all of them, but he assured me he had his hands full with the two seniors he was taking. He joked about being "Jack Tripper" for the night—a reference I didn't understand at the time but got later after watching an episode of "Three's Company".

When we arrived, Tony and his dates were waiting outside. His eyes nearly popped out of his head when he saw Sarah step out of the car. I don't think Tony had ever seen Sarah like that, and I didn't like the change in his perspective. I warned him that if he kept looking at my kid sister that way, he'd find himself living on Mars for the rest of his life. His dates laughed, thinking it was a joke, but Tony knew I was serious and quickly looked away. Sarah smiled at his reaction and whispered in my ear, "Don't be so mean to him; he can't help it that I'm beautiful." I smiled back, hoping that tonight would help bring her back.

CHAPTER THIRTY-THREE
THE TREE

s much as I hated to admit it, after arriving at the prom, we began to have a lot of fun. Sarah was by far the most beautiful girl there, and I was getting more attention from the ladies than I had anticipated. The music was great, the food was excellent, and the energy was intoxicating. This prom was well planned, and everyone was having a fantastic time. I made a mental note to request that the same people plan next year's prom.

Just when I thought things were going well, they took a turn for the worse. And by worse, I mean Jasmine. I was standing by the refreshment table, watching Sarah dance with Peter Swartz, the captain of the debate team. Peter wasn't the best dancer, but he made up for his clumsiness with effort and not taking himself too seriously. Sarah found him funny and relaxing to be around. Despite his good nature, I knew Peter wished on some distant star that he and Sarah would become more than friends. But that was never going to happen in this lifetime.

Sarah was laughing with Peter when her entire demeanor changed. Her smile disappeared as she stared at the ballroom entrance. Soon, half the room was staring in the same direction. I turned to see what the commotion was about, but I already knew who it was. I just didn't know how extreme the visual would be. My mouth dropped open as I beheld the most stunning girl I had ever seen. Jasmine was breathtaking. She wore a mid-thigh-length red dress that caressed every curve of her body. It was strapless, exposing her beautiful, tanned shoulders and neck. Her hair was pulled up, exposing an exquisite red ruby necklace. Her hair seemed blacker than usual, contrasting perfectly with her dress. Her long, toned legs were perched atop three-inch high heels that matched her dress perfectly. Her attire was simple yet elegant, and even from across the room, you could tell it wasn't cheap.

Much to my surprise, on her arm, was none other than our starting quarterback, Brian, wearing a black suit with red accents that paired perfectly with Jasmine. He seemed exceedingly proud as he walked into the ballroom with her. Their entrance seemed to suck the air out of the room as all eyes were on them.

I became enraged at the sight of them and the attention they commanded. Who does she think she is? If everyone knew who and what she really was, they wouldn't be so taken by her. And what was Brian doing? Why would he come here with her? I know he didn't have all the details, but he knew Jasmine and I were not on good terms. I couldn't believe this! My anger began to get the best of me, and I started to let my teenage impulses take over. I knew I couldn't start anything here, so I quickly turned and stormed out of the room into the hallway to avoid any eye contact with Jasmine. I was afraid that if she gave me that smirk again, I would go full "Stephen King's Carrie" at this prom, and that wouldn't be good at all. In the hallway, I started pacing back and forth, rubbing my hands together, trying to calm down. But I couldn't. What was wrong with me? Why was I so upset?

Tony walked up behind me, and I should have turned around to face him, but I couldn't.

"Dude? What's up?" Tony asked with concern in his voice. "Did she do that thing again? Dude, talk to me, what's up?"

I couldn't answer or face him because I didn't know what was "up." Tony decided he had enough talking to my back, so he came around to face me.

"Aiden, bro, you got to talk to me, right now. You are standing out here pacing and tweaking out, and I am nervous, very nervous. If you and the dark princess get into it here, a lot of people could get hurt or worse. I thought I was afraid of what could happen when I thought you were turning into a serial killer. But now, I know you're something more. This shit really got me nervous. So, I need for you to talk to me, 'cause this ain't it, chief."

"I know, Tony, I know, but honestly, I don't know what's wrong with me."

Tony stared at me, then his eyes widened as if he had just had an epiphany. From his reaction, I knew it was both amusing and terrifying.

"Dude! You are hating on Brian! You like this girl! Or at the least, you are attracted to her. Oh shit, dude, that's crazy!"

"Huh? Tony, you are tripping right now. I don't want her!"

"Dude, I've known you since the sandbox days, and I know when you are jealous. Like that time my mom got me the PlayStation, and your mom waited a full year before getting you one? Yeah, you were 'jealy,' my friend. You refused to even play with me on that thing until you got yours."

"Dude, whatever, I wasn't jealous. I just didn't feel like playing video games at the time."

"You are a horrible liar; you always have been. You are attracted to Jasmine. It's freaky and dangerous, but I don't blame you. That girl is off-the-charts beautiful, and to see her prance in there with Brian, the little brother of your nemesis, is almost poetic justice."

"Shut up! You don't know what you are talking about, Tony!" I snapped back.

"Dude, you can get angry all you want, but the truth is the truth, and you are attracted to Jasmine. That's crazy, though, because you guys are mortal enemies. Man, I tell you, God has a sick sense of humor. The one girl that gets you all emotional and involved is the one girl you can't have."

"Whatever!"

"Hey, wait! Aiden, you know you can't have her, right? You and her dating would be bad, very bad, especially if she's connected with the assholes that tried to murder you and your family. Have you ever heard the term 'sleeping with the enemy'? Yeah, that would be it if you decided to date that girl. I wouldn't even suggest you let anyone know how you see her because they could definitely use that against you."

"Tony, I'm not even getting involved in their crusade!"

"Dude, wake up. You are already involved. You took out not only one of their top guys but his entire crew too! Oh, trust me, you are involved. You may not want to organize with them, but you are involved. So I would suggest you keep those feelings to yourself."

"Tony, I already told you, I don't want that girl! I'm just upset about what she did to Sar—"

"What? What she did to who?"

I had to catch myself because I was about to spill the beans about Sarah's abilities. You see my point here? Teenage impulses causing you not to think before you speak.

"Aiden, I'm talking to you! What did she do to who?"

"Nobody, Tony."

"Nah, bro, it sounded like you were going to say, 'what she did to Sarah.'"

"What? C'mon, look at my sister. Does she look like she's had something done to her?"

"Uh, yeah? She hasn't been the same since that night."

"Who would be if someone you trusted tried to kill you? That's all, Tony. She's just trying to move on like the rest of us."

"Dude, why are you lying to me? Not cool, Aiden, not cool at all."

"I'm not lying to you!"

"Okay, you know what? I'm going back inside now because I don't want you to keep lying to my face anymore. It's bogus, and it's getting me upset, and I've got two beautiful seniors in there who can't wait to use and abuse me. So I'm going to leave you here, okay? Handle that, though. Get it together, dude. We don't need you and Jasmine's kind of arguments or fights here tonight. Some of us are actually having fun."

Tony then quickly walked past me, but not before bumping into my shoulder. Tony was furious about me not telling him the truth, and I felt bad about it, but I had made a promise to Sarah, and I wasn't going to break it. Sarah was already having trust issues after Jason, and I wasn't going to be someone else close to her who would abuse her trust. But the nerve of Tony to say I was attracted to Jasmine! I didn't know where he pulled that craziness from, but the last thing I wanted to do was kiss her. What I wanted to do was on the other side of the spectrum of affection, and it wasn't romantic or nice. Brian had no idea the type of danger he was in, and as much as I wanted to warn him, I decided to let him experience her evil on his own. I still didn't understand my reaction, but I knew I needed to get Sarah out of there before she relived that night all over again.

I slowly walked back to the ballroom and looked around for Sarah. I didn't see her on the dance floor or at one of the tables. I saw Peter standing by the punch table and walked over to him.

"Hey, Peter, where is Sarah?"

"I don't know. She just ran out of here as soon as Jasmine came in. She seemed really upset, but she wouldn't tell me why."

"Which way did she go?"

Peter pointed towards the hallway I had just come from, and fear began to pulse through my body.

Sarah couldn't have gone out that door because I would have seen her, or she would have walked over to me. We both knew that once Jasmine arrived, it was time for both of us to call it a night. I looked around again and saw Brian standing alone on the far side of the room. I quickly ran over to ask him if he'd seen Sarah.

"Yeah, I saw her," he answered. "She walked out with Jasmine about ten minutes ago."

"With Jasmine? Why?"

"I don't know; they just left me standing here."

"Which way did they go?"

"Out the front entrance, I think. When you see Jasmine, ask her if she wants something to drink—for me?"

"Brian, after tonight, I don't think Jasmine will be needing anything else to drink."

"Huh? What's that supposed to mean?"

"Never mind."

"Hey, wait, Aiden. I know you think I was bogus for asking Jasmine out, but dude, she's fine. I couldn't help it."

"Brian, it's cool. I just need to find my sister. I'll talk to you later."

I ran out the front entrance to look for Sarah and Jasmine. If anything had happened to my sister, Brian would pay dearly, and Jasmine would have crossed my family for the last time. I don't care how many of them there are. I will exterminate each and every one of them if one hair on Sarah's head is out of place. Outside, I asked the valet if he'd seen Sarah and Jasmine, and he pointed me toward the side parking lot next to a small park. I ran towards the parking lot, hoping I wasn't too late and the Shadows hadn't taken my sister hostage or worse. I ran as fast as I could towards the side of the hotel.

I shouldn't have left Sarah alone!

I ran around the parking lot calling out for Sarah, but there was no answer. Then I glanced over towards the park and saw two figures standing face-to-face in the darkness. I could make out Jasmine's silhouette quite easily—I could pick out that insane hourglass figure with my eyes closed, I thought. I ran towards them to see Jasmine placing her hand on Sarah's forehead. Sarah seemed to be in some kind of trance and wasn't moving at all. She was just standing there with her eyes closed.

"Don't you touch her! Get away from her!"

Jasmine turned to me, exposing "the smirk," and then darkness began to surround me. I knew she was casting the darkness curse on me. The first time Jasmine cast this curse, I was unaware and unprepared, but tonight I was ready. Just like Jaffrey did, balling up the alternate reality like a piece of paper, I did the same to the dark reality surrounding me. My quick response to Jasmine's curse caught her off guard and wiped that smirk completely off her face as she took a step back with a look of surprise and fear.

She tried to cast the curse again, and I crumpled it up and ran towards her as fast as I could. She kept casting the curse, and as I ran, I quickly balled up the darkness and threw it to the side like balls of paper. I then made a car from the parking lot appear right above her head. Jasmine looked up at the car just before it came crashing down. But before it could crush her, she smiled and took control of it, throwing it in my direction.

Her quick response surprised me, and I wasn't expecting to see the same car hurling towards me. I teleported myself out of its path and appeared right behind Jasmine just before it came thundering down into the ground, sending a cloud of dirt and grass into the air. I grabbed her hair from behind and slammed her onto her back. She yelled out as the force of the ground sent shockwaves of pain through her body. I then changed the density of the skin and bones in my arm and fist, similar to hardened steel, and prepared to punch a hole straight through Jasmine's chest as she lay on the ground grimacing in pain.

Her eyes widened as she saw my fist cutting through the air towards her chest. She quickly shifted away from my oncoming blow, knocking me off my feet. The ground was not kind to me when my body fell, and the impact forced the wind out of my lungs.

As much as I wanted to lie there, I couldn't because I knew Jasmine would try to attack while I was down. My assumptions were correct. The same car she had hurled at me was now hovering over me and would come down on top of me in a fraction of a second. Any normal person would have just chalked this one up in the loss column, but not me. I wasn't normal, and Jasmine wasn't aware of what I was capable of. I quickly teleported Jasmine inside the car, and much to my delight and her surprise, she wasn't expecting that. I then sent the car zooming upwards into the sky and, when I thought it was high enough, sent it speeding down towards the earth. I could hear her screaming and fighting to get the car doors open, which I conveniently sealed tight. She then tried to break the glass as a last resort. Too bad I made them unbreakable as well. She was trapped, and before she could figure it out, the car and the ground reunited.

The impact of the car hitting the ground caused several car alarms in the parking lot to go off. The sound of the impact was like a bomb detonating, and I could hear screams coming from inside the hotel. I walked over to the car to gloat in my victory, smiling to myself at what I had accomplished. No one would ever hurt Sarah, not while I drew breath. No matter how beautiful or sexy the assailant might be, they would face a brutal demise if they decided to go after Sarah to get to me. But my victory was short-lived because, to my surprise and disappointment, the car was empty.

"Very clever, Aiden," I heard Jasmine say behind me. "I wasn't expecting that at all. You've been trained very well to control your abilities. But so have I, and I'm not easily beaten."

I turned around to face her, but she wasn't there.

"Just like you, I am different. I am not like other Shadows."

This time her voice was coming from above me, as if she was flying, but when I looked up, no one was there. During my training with Jaffrey, he warned me about the Shadows' ability to be in multiple places at once. He said it was a cheap trick to get their prey to concentrate on the sound of their voice and not the sound of their movements. I closed my eyes and listened. Her voice was everywhere now, surrounding me like a tornado spinning faster and faster. I kept listening for movement and tuned out the sound of her voice. Then I heard her move by a tree no more than three feet behind me. I quickly harnessed electricity and sent a bolt of electrical energy in her direction. I heard her scream as the electricity struck her body, throwing her to the ground. I opened my eyes and saw her lying on the ground, smoke coming off her body as she moaned in pain, trying to get up.

She was different. The other Shadows I'd faced were easily killed by such a shock of electricity, but not Jasmine. I could tell she was in a lot of pain, but she wasn't dead. The only thing that was physically damaged was her dress. I thought the smoke was coming off her skin, but it was coming off her burning dress. Before she could get up, I used telekinesis to lift her body from the ground and forcefully slammed her against the tree behind her. I made sure she couldn't move by using my powers to keep her bonded to the tree. She struggled, but eventually, she discovered she wasn't going anywhere—well, maybe to hell, but she wasn't going anywhere until I sent her there. I slowly walked over to the tree, but not before glancing over my shoulder to see where Sarah was. She was now on her knees, weeping with her hands covering her face. Seeing Sarah like that only multiplied my murderous rage towards Jasmine, and I quickened my pace towards her to end this once and for all.

"Before I end you, tell me—what did you do to my sister?"

Jasmine was in terrible pain, and I could tell it was hard for her to speak clearly, but she cleared her throat.

"I saved her life, that's what I did."

Jasmine's response infuriated me even more.

"What!? Are you insane? Look at my sister! How is that saving her life?"

"Listen, Aiden, I know you have no reason to trust me because of what I am. But I am telling you the truth."

"Or you could be trying to save your ass!"

"No, Aiden, I knew who Jason really was, and I wanted to warn your family. But the only way I could was to awaken Sarah's abilities. Your family was marked for execution by the council, and I couldn't just let them murder all of you. Had I not awakened her abilities, she would have never been able to see Jason for what he really was, and he would have killed all of you in your sleep. I tried to warn her, but she wouldn't listen, so my only option was to awaken her ability."

"Oh, so now I'm supposed to believe that a Shadow wants to help a family of Baraqu, right?"

"Believe what you want, but it's the truth."

"So what were you doing now? Saving us again? Look at her—she's a wreck."

"No, Aiden, those are not tears of pain but tears of joy. I gave her more control over her abilities and more confidence. I didn't have time to complete the awakening with her because I heard someone coming when we fought at the school, and I couldn't risk it being another Shadow. Do you know what would have happened to me and my family if they found out I was trying to help your family?"

"Hmm, let me guess. What I'm about to do to your lying ass right now?"

Precisely, Aiden."

"So I guess the darkness curse you were putting on me was a life-saving technique?"

"No, Aiden, I was protecting myself."

"How is that?"

"You are Baraqu, and I didn't know you weren't aware of your abilities. I misread you. Your aura is very powerful, and it appeared you were a threat, and I wasn't sure what you were going to do to me! You were staring at me pretty hard!"

"It wasn't because of that! I was clueless about all of this!"

"So why were you staring then? Oh, okay, I see." Jasmine chuckled. "Boys!" she said, rolling her eyes. Her revelation about why I was staring at her made me blush, and I turned away for a split second.

"Listen, Baraqu stud…you won, and I can see that you are a killer and ready to end my life, so let's get it over with because this tree bark against my back is pretty uncomfortable."

"For someone about to die, you are pretty coy about it."

"Everyone and everything dies, Aiden. We can't escape it, and if I am to die here telling you the truth, then so be it. But I'm not going to beg you."

Her arrogance was astonishing; even in the face of death, she was still defiant.

"Well, have it your way, Jasmine."

I readied myself to send a bolt of lightning through her body. Jasmine looked towards the sky, waiting for the final blow, and then I felt someone reach for my arm and pull me away from the tree. It was Sarah, and when I looked into her eyes, I saw compassion. Compassion for this evil I was about to destroy.

"No, Aiden, this is wrong. She is telling you the truth. She did help me, and she helped us."

What? I quickly turned to Jasmine and demanded to know what kind of mind control she had over my sister.

"Aiden, stop! Stop it now! I am not under any mind control; my abilities make that impossible. She just completed the awakening in me. When she initially did it, she wasn't done, so I wasn't completely awakened, and my abilities were uncontrollable and inconsistent. Now that it's completed, I can turn it on and off anytime. Let her go!"

"I can't, Sarah. I just can't. I'm sorry, but this is for your own safety. I can't bring myself to trust a Shadow. Not after what Jason did to us."

"No, Aiden, you won't. You won't even try."

I walked over to the tree and looked Jasmine in the eyes.

"Whatever you did to my sister, it doesn't work on me."

Jasmine began crying and wouldn't look at me.

"Just do it, please. You are making this harder for me."

"Harder for you? I thought you were ready to die."

"No, I said everything, and everyone dies, and I wasn't going to beg you."

"So why are you crying?"

"None of your business, Aiden. You don't believe a word I'm saying anyway. Remember, I'm evil. I'm a Shadow," Jasmine mocked.

I could hear Sarah pleading with me not to kill Jasmine. I couldn't bring myself to listen to her. She was young and naive; she had no idea what these things were capable of. She didn't see what I saw in Jason, she didn't see what I saw in Spain.

"I'm tired of talking. It's time for you to die now."

"Death is complicated," Jasmine whispered.

Jasmine looked at me with eyes filled with tears. I was expecting them to be tears of anger or sadness because her time had come, but they were tears of regret. Not the type of regret from bad things we do in life but regret from something unrealized. Something she wanted so much that was being taken from her on this night by my hands. I placed my hands around her wrists so that she wouldn't try to get away while I sent thousands of kilowatts of electricity through my body into hers. I wasn't taking any chances. Jasmine was right; she was different, and Jaffrey warned me that she was uncannily powerful. Sarah began screaming behind me, pleading for me not to do it, but I wasn't listening. I looked into Jasmine's eyes one last time. This time she looked directly into mine, and what I saw in her eyes wasn't regret, sorrow, or anger. It was something completely different, and then she did something that changed our lives forever.

She kissed me.

CHAPTER THIRTY-FOUR
CRAZY, STUPID, LOVE

I felt an electrical charge run through my body from my toes to my hair follicles. It was warm and felt like I was walking on air. This wasn't the electricity I was planning on using to kill Jasmine. This was something else. I was in a trance, and it felt like time was standing still. Then I realized what was happening. Jasmine had kissed me, and I was kissing her back. When I opened my eyes, I discovered that Jasmine and I were floating about fifteen feet above the ground. I looked down at Sarah, and she had the biggest smile on her tear-drenched face. I looked at Jasmine, and she was also smiling and crying. I didn't understand what was happening to me. Jasmine was my enemy. Her kind had taken my father from me, sent a man to our home who shared our mother's bed, and used his powers against us so that he could kill us. Jasmine was a Shadow and my enemy, but floating above the earth on prom night, I'd just discovered that I was madly in love with her, and she felt the same.

Yes, I called it madly in love because we both had to be out of our freaking minds to even let something like this occur. The dangers and ramifications of our love could rock the very foundations of the realm. This wasn't supposed to be. This was impossible, but sometimes the only logical answer is the impossible. Jasmine smiled at me, seeing the confusion on my face. I looked at her, and she nodded in agreement with me. Yes, she too thought this was crazy, but there we were.

Back on the ground, I sat down on the grass in complete confusion. What just happened? Jasmine sat next to me, held my hand, and placed it on her chest over her heart.

With my hands that close to her...you know...I damn near fainted.

"This is what drives my actions, Aiden. Not my heritage or what I am. After our first contact in the lunchroom, I realized there was something different about you and I felt myself being drawn to you. But you are Baraqu and as powerful as I am, I am still a teenage girl. A teenage girl who likes a boy who couldn't possibly like her back. So, I tried to force myself to hurt you, but every time I had the opportunity to kill you, I stopped. Yes, it was mean, and I am very sorry, but I've wanted to kiss you since that day in the lunchroom when we both were trying to grab the same apple. I figured that since you weren't aware, maybe you could love me too. But when I saw Jason with your family at the games, I knew that sooner or later, you would be aware and would hate me. But to experience what we just did tonight, almost killing each other, and then this; even though we both are aware of what we are and the history behind who we are, is a miracle."

I was at a loss for words.

Then I realized Tony was right. I was jealous of seeing Brian with Jasmine, but my hate clouded my mind to the point where I was willingly lying to myself about how I felt about Jasmine. It all started to make sense now. I dreamed about this girl and showed up in her house uninvited on several occasions, looking at her while she slept. But the bloodline of the Baraqu and the hatred for Shadows it carried confused me and my intentions toward Jasmine. Just like her, I now realized that I loved her. I had been so consumed by hate that I hadn't realized it. But Jasmine knew how she felt all along, and to hold on to that love, even though there wasn't a chance in hell that we would find ourselves in this moment, was incredible. Jaffrey was right—there wasn't a Shadow like her.

"Aiden, I know you have a lot of questions, and I will answer all of them, but right now we need to clean this mess up, and you are the only one who can do it."

So, after cleaning up our lover's quarrel, we all went back inside to try to enjoy the rest of the night. Life was going to be very interesting going forward, but at the same time, I was optimistic because, for the first time in my life, I was in love, and she loved me back. I just wished it wasn't so complicated. But when I thought back on all the so-called loves I had in my younger years before Jasmine, none hurt more than when I was twelve years old and had a serious bug for an eighth-grade cheerleader named Asia Radcliff.

At the time, she was the most beautiful thing I had ever laid eyes upon. Half Asian and half African American, she was the top track star in her class and the captain of the cheerleading squad. She also happened to be on the fast track to the gold-digger hall of fame. At the time, I didn't quite understand the concept, and I thought she walked on gold-plated butterfly wings. I couldn't get enough of Asia, and every chance I got, I made myself known to her. At first, I was ignored until she found out through some of her fellow gold-digging acquaintances that my family was "balling." Immediately after that, I was her main concern. She let me carry her books, and we sat together at lunch. I even got her phone number, and to all the guys in my age group, I was "that dude."

But soon I started getting requests from her of a financial nature. I was spending all the money I could get my hands on for that girl. Taking her to the mall and getting her whatever she wanted, but when I didn't have the funds, she would ignore me for weeks. Every time that happened, I got this aching feeling in my stomach, and it felt like I couldn't breathe. My classmates would clown me every time she would ignore me when I called her name. They all knew what she was doing, but no one—and I mean no one—had the character or the balls to tell me to my face that she was using me. During that time, Tony was overseas going to school, so I didn't have him watching my back. But he came home earlier than expected, and the very first day he saw her, he told me exactly what she was doing to me. It was hard, and it broke my heart.

She was my first kiss, and I was hoping I would lose my virginity to her as well. I don't think I cried as much as I did back then, trying to cope with the betrayal and pain of loving someone and finding out they never loved me back. She told me she did all the time, and my dumb ass believed her, too. Now here I was again in a very complicated situation, but the currency this time was life. My life and the lives of those I cared for.

I know on the surface it seemed irresponsible and I hadn't learned my lesson after dealing with Jason's treachery. Yet there I was, accepting the love of someone I just wanted to kill and giving my heart back to her instantaneously. It was fast, I know, too fast, but even with all the anger and hatred I felt, something deep inside was telling me that this was the love I should be investing in. This is the girl I should be with. So, I trusted my gut and went with it; also the way she looked in that red dress helped a lot too.

What? Shame on me? No, shame on you for thinking otherwise. I was seventeen years old and had an unlimited amount of hormones flowing through my body, and Jasmine was a hormone-magnet. Just looking at her inspired fantasies of me and her doing things that would make even Tony blush. And then to find out she actually had a heart was just icing on the cake. I was so excited about this new love, and I didn't hide my disdain toward Brian when I saw him again. I heard him whisper that I was "playa-hating," but I didn't care. I was looking everywhere for Tony, but I couldn't find him. Finally, someone told me he had gone upstairs with his dynamic duo, and they even gave me the room number. I had to tell Tony about what just happened outside. I was too excited not to. I had temporarily forgotten about wanting to kill her and everything I had experienced before this night. I was just filled with so much joy, and it felt like a huge weight had been lifted off my chest. I was knocking on the door for about five minutes before I heard Tony yelling,

"Who is it?"

"It's Aiden. I need to talk to you. It's important!"

"Aww, dude, come on! I'm in the middle of something," he yelled from behind the door. "Literally in the middle of something."

"Tony, seriously, you know I wouldn't come here if it wasn't important!"

"True," he said. "Okay, one sec."

Tony flung open the door wearing a pointy happy birthday hat, boxers, and a smiley face made of whipped cream on his bare chest.

"Dude, what the hell?!" I yelled at the sight of him in the doorway.

Tony just stood there with a mischievous grin on his face in a Superman pose. I guess he figured if I had the nerve to interrupt his hotel room romp, I had the nerve to see him in this unnerving manner. I didn't even want to go there with him.

"You know what, never mind. I hope you are having a great time. Listen, something incredible happened to me outside tonight."

Tony leaned forward to get a closer look at me, then sniffed me like he was trying to smell something unique. Then his eyes widened, and he started jumping up and down like an idiot. His whipped cream smiley face started to come apart and slide down his chest. I quickly took a step back just in case he tried to hug me and ruin my suit.

"Wait? You got you some? Like some real good some? OHHH, my boy Aiden is a man now...I told you, boy, when you get the good stuff, you want to tell the world, but you can't because she won't give it to you anymore...I remember I did that, and I still regret it to this day...did I tell you about that...maaan..."

"Tony, Tony, no, it's not that," I interrupted.

Tony would have ranted on and on, and I needed to tell him so that he could get his silly-looking ass back in the room before someone called animal control because something just wasn't right inside that hotel room.

"Me and Jasmine are a couple now!"

"Wait, what the hell did you just say to me?" Tony asked.

The tone of his voice sounded like I had just called him a racial slur.

"I said, me and Jasmine are a couple now."

"A couple, huh? Yeah, I agree, a couple of freaking idiots! Man, what is wrong with you? First, you wanted to kill the evil bitch, right? I mean earlier tonight, you looked like you were ready to get all buckets of blood on her ass, and now you're telling me you two are dating?"

"Yes!"

"So first you wanted to take her out, and now you want to take her out, but this time on a date, under the moon and stars, riding unicorns and eating honey-covered wafer snacks, right? Aiden, get your mind right so your ass can follow! What is going on in that head of yours, dude? Let me guess what happened: you two had to have a confrontation outside for you to get that close for her to tell you she loves you, right?"

"Yeah…"

"Right, so then you whipped her ass, and right before you were about to deal the final blow, she professed her undying love for you; am I on point?"

Damn, he's good.

"Yes, you are."

"Dude, listen to yourself. She played you, man!"

"Tony, your whipped-cream smiley face is melting," I jokingly interrupted.

"Don't worry about my whipped cream! Worry about your ass! She didn't want to get her bag tipped, so she preyed on your weakest desires. Which are love and lust because it's clear you are attracted to that evil bitch."

"Hey, watch your mouth, Tony."

"Oh, so now she's a laaaady? After almost killing you in the lunchroom and almost ruining your chances of getting on the football team, now she's a lady and demands respect? I guess she had a viable explanation for that too, right?"

"It wasn't viable, but it made sense," I responded.

"It made sense? Aiden, does any of this shit make sense to you? Dude, the last Shadow you got close to tried to kill you and your entire family. Wipe all of you off the map. Remember that? I do because I was pulling your unconscious ass out of a burning house with emblems of fire attached to my ass. So now you are willing to jeopardize the lives of your mom and sister? For her? For love? I don't know what she did to Sarah, but I know she did something, and what you are telling me right now is insanity."

"I know it sounds crazy, but we love each other!"

"Ya'll have a crazy way of showing your love. I guess if you guys get married, the ceremony will consist of a selection from the choir and a battle to the death at the altar. You know what, Aiden, I'm going to go back inside this hotel room and try to forget what you just told me. But tomorrow, you and I are going to get into this. Right now, I'm going to get into this," Tony said, pointing inside his hotel room.

And then tomorrow, bright and early, me and you will get into all of this you're talking about right now. But I'm going to tell you one thing—if anything happens to Sarah…I swear to God I'm breaking both ya'll necks. Powers be damned, I'm breaking 'em." Tony then looked at me, shook his head, chuckled, and slammed the door in my face.

Tony was such a downer, but after walking towards the elevator, some of the things he said started to make sense. Did she play me? Was Jasmine another Asia Radcliff all over again? If so, that would really suck because I was really buying into the whole "love conquers all" display we just had in the park. How could it not be real? I had never felt like this before—ever. Not even for Asia, and I thought I was on cloud nine. Right now, this would be cloud one hundred and nine. If she did play me, I knew she wouldn't let herself become vulnerable again, and our next encounter might be a lot more dynamic. But I knew one thing— that if she played with my heart like that, there would be nothing and no one that would stop me from snatching her heart out of her chest. Wow, was I a violent kid back then or what?

Just like all things, the party was over, and Sarah and I headed home. I looked for Jasmine, but I was told she left with Brian before I came back downstairs from Tony's room. I instantly got jealous and started to worry about what Brian was planning on doing to my girl or if Jasmine was actually my girl. Would she use Brian to send the message on a more personal level? Halfway home, I got a text message from Jasmine saying how much she loved me and how tonight changed her life, and she couldn't wait to get to know me and I to get to know her. If there ever was a message that anyone needed to ease the storm of insecurity in his heart, that was the message. I immediately relaxed and leaned back in the driver's seat after reading the message. Sarah smiled and asked me if that was from Jasmine. I nodded and asked Sarah how she was feeling.

"I feel much better now. More focused and confident in myself. I can now shut this ability off whenever I want and turn it back on when I need it. Jasmine told me that she could teach me how to master my ability and enhance it."

"Enhance it?"

"Yes, she walked up to me in the ballroom and whispered that in my ear. I was so desperate, Aiden. I needed stability back in my life. I was losing my mind, and I felt that even if Jasmine meant to do me harm, death was better than the life I was living."

"Don't say that, Sarah," I snapped.

"I'm just being honest, Aiden. You have no idea how horrible it is to know everyone's darkest secrets. It's not a peaceful existence, especially when those secrets can threaten you."

"So, you actually can talk to their souls?"

"Now I can, but before my awakening was completed, no. It was a one-way street, and some people's souls are dark and evil, and the things they say should never be heard out loud."

"Wow, that's insane."

"Yes, it is, and to be honest, I would have been happier if I saw dead people walking around. I've found out just how very few good-natured people there are in this world. Now I can relax and keep people's secrets just the way they were meant to be…secrets. So when Jasmine told me that, I was compelled to follow her outside. I'm sorry, Aiden. I should have thought about how you would feel about me leaving alone with a Shadow, but I could see her soul, and even though she is a Shadow, she is a good person."

"What else can you tell me about her?"

"That's all I'm giving you, Aiden. Everything else you need to learn for yourself. But I do know that you have doubts about her feelings, and I can tell you that I have never seen anyone engulfed in so much love for another person before. She really loves you, and I can tell you love her too. But you also hate her for what she is. But that is something both of you suffer from because of our bloodlines. Just don't give up on her, Aiden. You won't find anyone that involved in you in this life. It's very rare for anyone to have that. On the one hand, I am jealous, but on the other hand, I am happy for both of you. You two have a lot of obstacles you are going to have to overcome because no one, and I mean no one, is going to understand your love."

I couldn't sleep that night. All I could think about was Jasmine—her smile, her tears of joy, and the way she looked at me, but most of all, the way she kissed me. It was intoxicating.

The sun seemed to take forever to rise, but once it did, I was up and getting ready to leave and go spend the day with my girlfriend. Girlfriend—that sounded strange, but it felt right. Jasmine was my girlfriend. I wanted to leave before Tony came over, but in Tony's fashion, he was there bright and early. He was still upset with me but eager to understand my insanity. After explaining everything to him, besides the part about Sarah's abilities, he just stared at me. I wanted to tell him that it was okay;

Sarah could see into her soul, and she knew Jasmine's feelings were real, but I couldn't. I made a promise, and some promises, no matter how painful, can never be broken. He still thought I was crazy and made it clear that he would never trust Jasmine, but we both agreed to give this a chance.

"I'll always have your back, dude," Tony said. "I had your back when we both thought you were a serial killer, and I will have your back now, even though I think you are a serial idiot."

Tony could tell I was anxious and asked me why I was so eager. I told him that I was going to go see Jasmine and maybe take her to the movies or something.

"Wait a minute, you are going to her house?"

"Yeah, why not?"

"Oh man, I need whatever drugs you are on because you are blissfully stupid. Dude, it's hard to believe she's in love with you, but let's say she is—do you think the rest of her Shadow family feels the same way? Do you actually think they are at their house right now cooking a 'nice welcome to the family' breakfast for you? You are a Baraqu—wait, you are not just Baraqu; you are a Baraqu warrior, and from what you've told me, most Shadows aren't too fond of your company."

"Dude, I'm sure she's told her family about us."

"Really? If so, you do not need to go to her house because all of them would be here by now taking turns whipping both your asses. So are you going to tell your mom and Manny?"

"My mom maybe, but not Manny. He might try to kill her."

"Yeah, I don't blame him."

"Wait a minute!"

"Hey, Aiden, I'm just keeping it real with you, bro. Manny has been fighting and killing Shadows for years, and I don't think he has any reservations about toe-tagging another one, especially if she's claiming to be your girlfriend."

"Yeah, you got a point. But still, it's my life, and I should be able to love whomever I want."

Tony just gave me a blank stare and shook his head.

"Hey, Aiden, the next time you go to the drug man for that liquid idiot he has, please order me a couple of vials as well."

"Whatever, dude, you'll learn to trust her someday."

"I think I should learn how to be with one girl first before I learn that lesson. Anyway, don't let me hold you from making a fool of yourself at 'Chateau de Shadows.' I'll talk to you later, bro. Have fun."

I was on my way out the door when Sarah stopped me.

"Aiden, where are you headed?"

"To Jasmine's house."

"Really? Does she know you're coming?"

"No, I want to surprise her."

"I wouldn't advise that, Aiden. Text her first because you two still have a lot to discuss."

I didn't want to text her first; I wanted to show up at her door with roses in hand and an invitation to dinner and a movie. But after what Sarah told me about her abilities last night, I decided to trust her insight on this relationship, so I sent Jasmine a good morning text. She responded immediately with "Good morning, my love." Just reading that sent chills through my body. Man, this girl had me wide open. I responded concerning my plans, and she texted me back saying how sweet I was but she wanted to talk to me at our spot.

Our spot?

Yes, the tree where you wanted to kill me but kissed me instead.

She really knew how to put me on the spot; somehow, I felt that I would never live down that confrontation at the tree…ever. Tony came downstairs and saw me sitting on the couch and asked me why I wasn't gone. After telling him what she said, he laughed and said,

"I have to give it to her; she is a smartass."

CHAPTER THIRTY-FIVE
THE SIDE DUDE DILEMMA

asmine wanted to meet at the park around eleven in the morning. It was eight. I had to wait three whole hours before I could see her again. But unless I wanted to come off as weird and a stalker, I decided to wait and not text her until I got to the park. It was hard, but I needed to contain myself before I messed everything up by being overbearing and clingy.

I got to the tree around 10:45, and much to my surprise and delight, she was already there. She wore a yellow sundress and matching slippers with a sunflower on the top of each slipper. Her hair was down, and she sat on the grass under the tree, smiling at me as I walked towards her. When I got to the tree, she jumped up and leaped into my arms, wrapping her legs around my waist and kissed me.

"I missed you," she said.

"I missed you too," I responded. "So, you wanted to talk?"

"Yes," and then the happiness began to leave her eyes. I knew she had bad news, but I was not prepared for what she was going to say to me.

"Aiden, listen, as much as I would love to walk around this world in your arms, the reality is we can't. It's not safe for us or our families, and no one we love will understand how we feel about each other, nor will they support it. We have taken a road very few have traveled, and those roads have always ended in disaster because they all felt that their love could conquer all. The fact is, love can't conquer all. I wish it could, but the reality is it can't. We are mortal enemies that have found a reason to love each other, and it's dangerous. I don't want anything to happen to you, and I'm sure you don't want anything to happen to me."

"So, are you saying we have to be a secret?"

Jasmine hesitated and then nodded. That yes tore through my heart, and I started to feel alone even though she was right there with me.

"Why? I can protect you; I can protect everyone."

"Yes, Aiden, I believe you can, but my family won't want your protection, and if they found out about us, they would send me away from you."

"I would find you."

"You probably would, but we are both teenagers. We are not adults, and we should be learning how to be adults, not thrust into a fight like the one we would face if we made our love known to everyone."

The more she explained, the more sense it made, but it still hurt like hell to hear her say it. I didn't agree with her, even though it made practical sense. I felt like it would all be a lie if we hid how we felt about each other from the world. This kind of rare love was to be shared, not silenced.

"I promise you, Aiden, we are a couple, and we can go out on dates, to the movies, and anywhere else. We just can't do it around people we know, and even when we are out, we have to be careful not to be seen by anyone we know."

Tony's words of "she's played you" kept echoing in my head as she spoke about the terms and conditions of our so-called relationship.

"So that's it?"

"No, there's more. My parents think that I am dating Brian, and in order for me to get out to see you, we have to keep it that way...for now."

"Aww, hell no," I yelled and jumped up. The anger and jealousy I felt were boiling my blood.

"So not only do I have to keep this a secret, but I have to play along with you and Brian? What kind of fool do you take me for, Jasmine?"

"I don't think you are a fool, Aiden. Look at me."

I couldn't look at her because even though I was protesting, I already knew in my heart that I was willing to go along with this charade, but I was going to show her that I didn't like it. How could I fall in love with someone so deeply that I was willing to play along in this manner? I mean, this seemed like I was the "side guy" and Brian was the main squeeze. How was I supposed to deal with him holding her? Kissing her? Bragging about their dates and going to her house for dinner with the folks? All I would have were memories of secret rendezvous that I couldn't share with anyone, especially those who believed Brian was the luckiest boy on campus.

"So that means you will be dating two people?"

"Yes and no. I promise you that I will not let Brian get past the dugout, let alone first base. I promise you this, Aiden. On my life, I promise this to you. But my father isn't a progressive man, and he likes Brian, so if I say I'm going out with him, it's fine by him, but I don't think he would understand us. It's breaking my heart to tell you this, Aiden, because I can feel you pulling away from me. I'm not trying to play with your heart or take advantage of you. I love you more than you know, and I am willing to go through whatever to be with you. But right now, if we want to spend time with each other, this is the only way. Please sit next to me, please."

I hesitated but eventually sat next to her. It was still hard to look at her after hearing everything she had to say. She reached over and held my face in her hands and kissed me on the lips. I looked at her, and she told me she was sorry and then started to cry, saying how unfair the world was. We just held each other under our tree, angry and saddened by the reality we currently faced.

Over the next few weeks, my love life was like the best and worst roller coaster ride ever. The times we spent together were like magic. We talked and had fun, but we were always looking over our shoulders, never quite feeling comfortable unless we were at our tree. How dysfunctional was this relationship? We related this tree, which was the spot of violence and hatred, with our love. But it was the place where we discovered how we felt, and it felt like the world couldn't touch us while we sat under this tree. We were invisible to the outside world, and no matter how crowded the hotel or the park got, we felt like no one could see us there. At school and around Deerfield, things were a lot different. Brian constantly boasted about his relationship with the most beautiful girl in school and how much her parents loved him. He always made it a priority to make sure I was around when he did it.

The jealousy consumed me so much at times that I felt like I was having a heart attack or stroke. He would hug her in the hallways or sneak up behind her and tap her on her booty. I would get furious and sometimes catch myself slamming my locker door shut. Jasmine would try to keep the peace by sneaking away with me under the bleachers to kiss, but after she left, I felt alone again. I wasn't sure how she was dealing with it all, but I knew she didn't have any competition from other girls, so I had to believe this arrangement was much easier for her than it was for me.

Tony, being Tony, always reminded me how stupid I was to put up with the bullshit. He even went as far as to say that no matter what we were, we shouldn't have to carry on that way, and it's going to bite us in the ass one day soon. I was basically a weekend boyfriend while Brian had her five days a week, and sometimes he would infringe on my weekends as well. It was becoming too much, and I was starting to lose hope in Jasmine and any future we could have together.

To make matters worse, there were times when we argued and sometimes got into physical confrontations with our powers. It was a dangerous game we played, and sometimes things almost went too far. It was like no matter how much we wanted to love each other, the hatred that flowed through our veins from what we were would win out, and we would forget about our love. It was dangerous and dysfunctional, but it takes time for mortal enemies, bound by thousands of years of war and hatred, to find enough peace within themselves and each other to love one another unconditionally. Our arguments would be over the top, and we constantly screamed "I hate you!" But then afterward, we would be in each other's arms, in tears, kissing and professing our undying love for one another. We could apologize to each other all the time, but it wouldn't change who and what we were. We just tried our best not to kill each other while we figured this thing out.

I know that it would have been easier to love another woman. A woman not of our bloodline or another Baraqu. But the universe had spoken and decided we should be together, and who are we to argue with the universe? Then one day, Brian crossed the line, and everything changed after that. We were winding down the school year towards the summer and graduation for the seniors. I was preparing to do my summer college tour, and Brian was doing the same. We were in the lunchroom when Brian walked up to me while Jasmine was walking by and said to Tony and me,

"Fellas, I'm going to be tapping that ass all summer long."

I let that one slide.

"Yeah right, you wish Casanova," teased Tony.

Tony knew the real deal about Brian and Jasmine, but Brian kept going.

"Dude, I've been tapping that already. It's just that she's going with me on my college tour, so we will have all the time in the world. I might make her my Kim Kardashian and videotape her."

Sorry, but I couldn't let that one slide, and I knocked him flat on his ass with a left hook. As he lay there on the floor, I got up from the table and stood over him. At first, he looked up at me like he was going to get up and do something. But when he saw the look in my eyes, he decided against it and stayed on the floor. I knew that if he had gotten up off the floor, I would have seriously injured or killed him. My training with Jaffrey had taken complete control over how I approached physical confrontations, and I would have ended it swiftly and violently without mercy. Jasmine immediately ran over to us, looking at me like I'd lost my mind. She helped Brian off the floor, and then a long, silent, and awkward moment followed as the three of us just stood there looking at each other.

The time had come for a revelation between the three of us, and I couldn't take loving in the shadows anymore. I couldn't take holding back my emotions because of what others would think or do. Jaffrey trained me to open the floodgates of my emotional rivers, and loving Jasmine in secrecy was damming that up. I couldn't take it anymore. I felt suffocated and strained. I was waiting for Brian to say something else—anything. Even a sorry would get him knocked back down on his ass. I didn't want to hear his voice at all. Jasmine walked over to Brian and told him it was over between them. Of course, he protested and lied about what he said or meant by it, but Jasmine was already on to him. She quietly told him goodbye, then grabbed my hand and led me out of the lunchroom.

CHAPTER THIRTY-SIX
COMING OUT

As soon as we stepped into the hallway, Jasmine held me tightly and whispered, "Take me away from here." Without a second thought, I teleported us to the only place where we felt safe—our tree. We found ourselves under its sheltering branches, holding each other close.

"I heard exactly what he said, Aiden. Thank you for defending me. I just want you to know that I never..." Jasmine started.

"You don't have to explain yourself to me. I know you didn't. But I've had enough; I couldn't take him being with you anymore. I understand the dangers our love can create, but even in secret, our love is dangerous. We fight and argue all the time because our love isn't allowed to grow. It's stagnant because we are afraid of what others think. I don't care what anyone else thinks. I will face whatever consequences being in love with you brings. I'd rather have five minutes of freedom with you than a lifetime of secrecy."

To some, it might seem like a bunch of crap, but after training with Jaffrey and seeing how he had to live in secret and seclusion, I understood that it was better to be free for a little while and die than to be a prisoner for several lifetimes.

Jasmine began to cry, apologizing for her decision to keep our love a secret.

"I know now that I have to love you all the way or not at all. I love you, Aiden, and I'm going to tell my parents about us today. I can't live like this anymore."

"Neither can I."

There we were, under our tree, holding each other and ready to face a world that was unprepared and unforgiving towards what we felt for each other. It was a gamble, but we were all in at this point.

However, there were so many unanswered questions about Jasmine and the Shadows that I needed answered. And having a Shadow by my side, presented the perfect opportunity to get some clarity.

"Tell me about your family," I asked.

"Well, I have four brothers and three sisters. I am the middle child, and the oldest is my brother Nezar. We come from northern Egypt…"

"Wait, I thought you were Iraqi?" I interjected.

Jasmine laughed. "No, that's what some people think about all Middle Easterners since 9/11. We are Egyptians, and our family can trace our lineage back to before the pharaohs and the great pyramids."

"I had no idea."

"Because we are Egyptian, my family was tied to the rule of Alal, and my ancestors fought alongside him for centuries. But back in the 1600s, an entire generation of my family decided to break away and stop fighting this war."

285

"Why?"

"No one really knows exactly, but they did."

"Okay, you are a very powerful Shadow. Are all of your family members as powerful as you?"

"No, actually, my ancestors who broke away from Alal are the reason for that."

"How?"

"Have you ever heard of the Rabum Igisum?"

"No, what is that?"

"Every Shadow or Baraqu, at the time of their death, has the choice to give their powers to someone of their direct bloodline, either living in the present or the future."

"So, our powers don't die with us?"

"Someone wasn't paying attention in science class. No, energy doesn't die; it is transferred or transformed. Most decide to allow our powers to go back to the source, but my ancestors decided to grant me their powers."

"All of them?"

"Yes, an entire generation gave me their powers."

"So how much power is that?"

"Enough to contend with someone like you, but Baraqu warriors are a force no one can reckon with. That's why the Shadows worked so hard to keep your kind from being born."

"Why did they give you all their powers?"

"I don't know. I guess they foresaw a great purpose for me and believed I needed all their powers to contend with what I am to face."

"They foresaw?"

"Yes, back in the old times, both Baraqu and Shadows had the gift of foresight, but the Baraqu saw this gift as evil and forbade any Baraqu from using this gift. The Shadows, on the other hand, embraced this gift and have never stopped using it."

"So Baraqu can't see into the future anymore?"

"Well, you know that saying, 'if you don't use it, you lose it'? That's what happened to the Baraqu's gift of foresight. They stopped using it, so the universe saw no need to keep gifting them this ability. As generations grew, they were born without that gift."

"That kind of sucks for us."

"Yeah, Aiden, it does."

"Can you see into the future?"

"Not now, I'm too young. But once we reach a certain maturity with our powers, we develop the gift. I guess you could call it a bonus."

"Your ancestors saw something in your future, and they gifted you their powers? Wow, that had to be great to have all that power as soon as you were born."

"Not really."

"Why not?"

"I was conceived aware."

"I don't understand what you're saying."

"When I was growing in my mother's womb, I was aware as if I was an adult. It was torture knowing and being aware as you grew. When I was born, I could understand everything everyone was saying, but I was unable to speak because my body wasn't developed enough.

It sure is developed now. I thought while looking over her body hungrily.

"I couldn't walk because my legs weren't ready. It's like being an adult trapped in a baby's body."

"Oh yeah, that can't be fun."

"No, it wasn't, but by the time I was ten months old, I was walking and speaking full sentences. When my parents discovered my awareness, they made sure that I didn't overexpose my abilities."

"I see, but you know you are still kind of immature."

"I have the awareness, Aiden, not the wisdom. That comes with experience."

"After your family broke away, no one else decided to fight again?"

"Nope. All my ancestors after that, down to my grandparents and parents, have sworn against fighting in this hellish war. We have our own reasons, though. We see what is happening to this world, and it isn't right. We've learned to tap into the negative energy, but we use it for good. The source may be one thing, but what you do with it is something entirely different. That's how we live our lives, and as long as we don't get involved, the order doesn't bother us or call upon us to do anything. When I was born, my father was afraid Alal would not keep his end of the bargain, but so far we have been left alone. My brothers all want to join the fight, but not with Alal."

"With the Baraqu?"

"Oh no, they still see your kind as the enemy. There is a revolution happening among the Wiccan. They want to break away from the Shadows, and my brothers want to join them, but my father forbids it. If one of us gets involved in this fight, our agreement with Alal is over, and they will come for me."

"Why you?"

"Because I am the most powerful Shadow there is, next to Alal himself."

"How is that possible? I thought Jason was."

Jasmine giggled and shook her head.

"Aiden, don't you know that women are more powerful wielders of this power than men? What we possess is all about emotional content, and who harnesses emotions better than women? Certainly not men. The more emotional content one can harness, the more powerful one can become. Jason against me wouldn't even be a fair fight. It's just the male ego that placed him above me. I don't trip, though. It's not important to me who's got the bigger stick at the playground because I don't wish to play in it. I am content with living a normal human life and being here with you. Nothing else seems important. I live and act human, but I'm not confused into believing I am human."

"But we are human."

"No, Aiden, that is the wrong way of thinking. We are more than human. Yes, we have human blood flowing through our veins, but we are far from human. Are we above them? No, but we aren't human. Most Shadows and Baraqu fancy themselves superior, and that's just stupid because all witches are human, and they can bind us whenever they want. After we can't use our powers, we are easy to kill. The order of the witches has killed more of our kind than any of us have. So, we have a truce with the witches, but that truce is coming to an end. The witches are tired of being the lapdogs of the Shadows and hunted by the Baraqu. They hate both our sides equally, and these new breeds of witches aren't rolling over any longer.

They see what our kind has done to this planet. Shadows have infiltrated every fiber of human existence, corrupting governments and corporations to perpetuate pain and suffering on this planet so they can get their fix of power. The problem is something else is going on, and the Shadows are too blind with drug-like power to notice. Alal is up to something, and the witches aren't telling what it is, but they feel like it's time for them to lock this thing down and fight for mankind's existence."

"So how can your family just sit by and stay out of this fight if they know what's going on?"

Jasmine's face saddened as she answered, "Because of me. They love me too much to have me serve Alal; so as much as they want to help, they stay out of it. My brothers sometimes despise me because of it, but I know they love me. They just wish they could do something that mattered, that could turn the tide. Because the Baraqu are too weak to actually make any real change. Well, until now, because a warrior is here, and you are strong enough to fight. But I take it you are not willing either."

I explained to her about my experiences in Spain but conveniently kept Jaffrey out of the picture.

"I heard about that. Every Shadow has heard about that fight in Spain. 'The Baraqu warrior that can't be bound by the witches.' The witches also have taken notice of you, and they are watching you closely. They fear you because you can't be controlled. I don't even know how that is possible. Do you?"

"No, I don't, but I hope one day I can find out. They have nothing to fear. I am not joining the fight; I just want to be left alone."

"I understand, my love, but it's never that simple these days."

CHAPTER THIRTY-SEVEN
WHAT'S NEXT?

We stayed under the tree talking for hours. We talked about my dad and how much I missed him, and she told me stories about him. My dad was a legend, deep in the fight against the Shadows, and his ability to lead and inspire people was a unique gift that proved to be a powerful tool in battle. Most of the time, the difference between victory and defeat is the belief in victory. My father's Baraqu ability was that he could inspire people to believe in themselves and victory. It caused people to fight harder and smarter, and he never lost a battle—until he found himself face-to-face with an even more powerful adversary. His body was never found, but under this tree, Jasmine gave me all the details about him and the events that led up to his death. She said that they knew he was coming and suggested he was betrayed by one of his own. I made a mental note that if I ever met the person responsible for his betrayal, I would make sure they didn't see another sunrise again. She also revealed who actually killed the ref and Steve. Jason had murdered both of them and with his six followers posing as federal agents, their goal was to make me feel like I was responsible and drive me crazy with guilt. They wanted to destroy our family through the media and me being accused of murder. Eventually, after I'd reached the pinnacle of success during my high school football career, they were going to release evidence suggesting I was the serial killer in Deerfield. They were hoping the news coverage would make Manny come out of hiding, and then they would murder him. With Manny out of the picture and me behind bars or worse, they could finish my mom and Sarah off easily, completely wiping our family off the face of the earth. It was a diabolical scheme that would've destroyed us if Jasmine hadn't risked her life by awakening Sarah's ability to expose Jason and give us a fighting chance. Jasmine risked her life for us, and until that day, I hadn't realized how much she sacrificed.

We sat under the tree so long that we forgot to check our cell phones. When I did, I had over seven missed calls and messages— all from my mom, pleading with me to come home as soon as possible. I teleported us back to the school parking lot and drove Jasmine home. I wanted to come in with her, but she advised I wait until she told them everything, and then they would meet me. It made sense, so I decided to go home and spill the beans as well. I was tired of hiding my love for this girl. I just wanted to feel free to love her anywhere. We pulled in front of her house and sat there for a few moments in silence. I didn't want her to leave, and I could tell she didn't want to leave either. Smiling, she climbed over the seat, sat in my lap while facing me, and kissed me passionately. Exhaling slowly, she hugged me. Her embrace felt like a sanctuary from all of the madness I'd faced since that day in the lunchroom. Her sitting in my lap, me holding her in my arms, felt like more than love…it felt like destiny.

After a few minutes, she opened my door and seductively walked into her house without ever looking back at me. I smiled while reminiscing about the time I got shot at trying to escape their house the night of my birthday party. Soon, I hoped I would be invited inside without being run out at gunpoint. It was a far-fetched dream, but I was willing to believe in it. Jasmine was worth it.

Driving home, I reflected on everything that led me to this point in my life and wondered how things would be going forward. From a regular introvert to a suspected serial killer to a Baraqu warrior and now the boyfriend of the second-most powerful Shadow on this planet. All in less than a year. Amazing how life can change and how drastic that change can be. But what is more incredible is how we can adapt and manage to survive, finding happiness in the worst places. Finding love where there once was hate. Finding peace in a time of war. I found love right when I was about to take a girl's life on prom night. If I could find love in such a dark place, then others could do a lot better.

When I got home, there were more cars out front than usual. I wondered who was there, but I knew there wasn't much danger because Sarah would have handled it. Jasmine had been helping her strengthen her ability, and she'd gotten very powerful. Sarah could handle herself now, and I had all the confidence in her that any threat that came to our door she could neutralize. I opened the front door to a living room full of people. Some I recognized from the night at the hospital and some I had never seen before. It seemed Manny and his team were here, but why?

Manny came out from the kitchen, drinking a cup of coffee accompanied by a very beautiful woman dressed in an all-black special forces suit.

"Hey, Manny, what are you doing here?"

"Have a seat, Aiden, we have something to discuss."

At that moment, I became afraid that they had found out about Jasmine and were there to question me about her. I was planning on coming home to tell my mom about Jasmine, but I wasn't going to do it now in a room full of strangers. I didn't know what they would do or think. Plus, having a kid brother in love with a Shadow would seriously compromise his team's confidence in Manny, and after hearing about my dad being betrayed, I didn't want to take any chances with Manny's life. He was already a hothead, and I didn't want to make matters worse. I slowly sat down, looking around the room at everyone. My mom and Sarah were there with worried looks on their faces.

Oh no, they must know about Jasmine.

I wanted to get my side of the story out before anything else happened, so I began to talk, but Manny cut me off mid-sentence.

"Aiden, listen, I don't know what you're trying to say, but whatever personal bullshit you have going on doesn't concern me right now. What concerns me is what we need from you."

"What is that?"

"My team and I are going on an important mission to the Middle East, and we need your help."

"Why would I go to the Middle East? I made it clear before that I don't want any part of this war you guys are fighting."

"Yeah, I heard about that, but you are going to want to go on this mission."

"Why is that? What could possibly change my mind that I would be willing to go to the most war-torn part of the planet with you to fight a war I want no part of?"

"Because it's not just about this war. This is about family."

"Family? You mean the same family that knew what we were and kept it a secret? The same family that knew one day your enemies would come looking for revenge for all of the Shadows you've killed. Or maybe the family that felt comfortable leaving us vulnerable in Spain? I mean, I am losing track of which family we're talking about."

Manny shook his head and looked up at the ceiling while mumbling something under his breath.

"Speak up big bro! I'm all ears!

Manny took a sip from his cup and strolled over to me. He stood over me, looking down at me while slowly sipping his coffee. He didn't say a word. He just kept staring at me. I want to believe he thought this was an intimidation tactic, but if he only knew the places, I was thinking about teleporting him to, he would have taken a few steps back. After a long uncomfortable stare down between him and I, I decided to stand up and face him. We stared into each other's eyes without blinking. Neither one of us was willing to give in or flinch.

"Sir, we don't have time for this!" the beautiful woman dressed in black said.

Breaking away his stare, Manny turned and faced her.

"You're right, we don't. But apparently, our superiors believe we can't complete our mission without him."

"I told you already, I am not joining the fi…

"Aiden, we found Dad. He's in the Middle East, he's alive and you're going to help us bring him home."